A
Polar Bear
Called
Forth

A P Pullan

ACKNOWLEDGMENTS

Many thanks to the following people who gave their time and knowledge to help me with this project –

Katie Malone – Homelink Team, South Ayrshire Council

Jenni McKean – Dementia Advisor (South Ayrshire), Alzheimer Scotland

Karen Richardson – Children s Panel, South Ayrshire

Rachel Williams - Senior Animal Keeper, Highland Wildlife Park, Kincraig

Young Carers Group, South Ayrshire

To the following proof-readers for being so generous to look over the text in all its stages and make me out to be a better writer than I am –

Beckfoot Heaton Primary, Bradford; Echline Primary School, South Queensferry; Allan Ferrier; Olga Kolgan; Timothy McArthur; Antonia Micallef-Eynaud; Peel Primary, Livingston; Wellington School, Ayr; Julie Wallace; Natasha White; Stuart White.

To the gorgeous artwork supplied by the following –

Cover – Cliona Riach (Queen Margaret's Academy, Ayr)

Cover Design – Author (from an idea by Maja Merko)

Rachel Duffy, Cecilia Grant, Grace Grant – (Queen Margaret's Academy, Ayr)

DEDICATION

i.m. Eileen Mhairi Ferrier
— a lover of all people and a lover of all animals

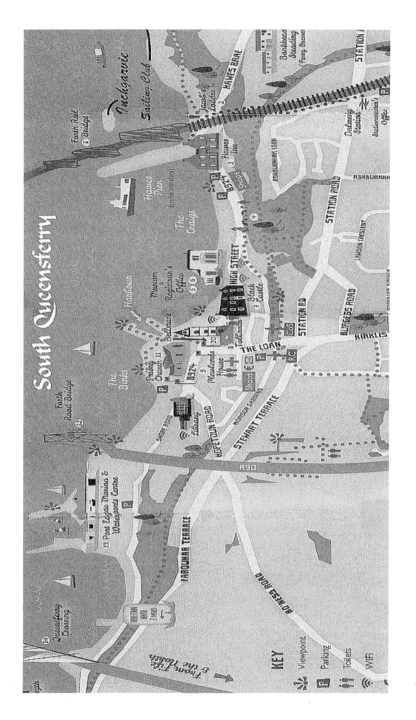

-1-

One December day, a polar bear cub found itself floating down a river. No one noticed the young bear drifting in the Firth of Forth, its current gently carrying it along.

From the Queensferry Crossing road bridge, no one spotted the bear. And even if they did, they would think it was just a piece of rubbish, a piece of white flotsam making its way downstream. Certainly not a polar bear cub, a polar bear cub in Scotland.

Close to the riverbank, a black Labrador was wagging its tail, waiting patiently for the order to jump in and retrieve the bear. Instead, its owner, unknowing of the dog's intent, whistled it back to its lead. The jogger, headphones on and checking her fitness watch, didn't realise that she was running right alongside the bear. The old lady, heading towards a crowd of ducks with a shopping trolley full of loaves, didn't see the cub bobbing and turning in the swirling currents of the wide river.

So nobody saw the young polar bear.

The heavy river, full of the last two days of rain, swept the cub on and on.

A gull made an inquisitive peck at the bear's fur. Unsatisfied, it flew off.

At Port Edgar, it nudged into a moored boat. The bear then slipped under a jetty, staring up at the grey sky between its wooden slats.

Where would the cub go? Would it end up being washed out into the North Sea? And if so, then what? Fate was guiding the young bear, held by the cradling hands of the river.

The cub eddied and rocked as it met swift currents pushing their way around the foot of the rail bridge.

On a large green marker-buoy, two grey seals watched its steady progress with no more than an unconcerned glance.

A backwater steadied its progress and pushed the cub closer to a sandy bank. Here a partly submerged willow tree stuck out its spindly fingers which snagged the bear's fur.

And that's when the cub's journey ended. For now.

Would the tide rise and so free it to be once again at the mercy of the river? Or would it be kept right there? Alone. Waiting. Waiting for chance. Waiting for hope.

-2-

Caitlin McGill shut the door behind her, swung her kit bag over her shoulder and walked downhill into a drab and damp Boxing Day. South Queensferry was quiet apart from a solitary car that rattled over the cobbled high street of the town. Ahead, standing in the dark Firth of Forth, like some red skeleton of a great beast from times long past, loomed the rail bridge.

Another Christmas was over, and Caitlin felt that tinge of disappointment she felt every year; all that waiting and excitement for just one day. That thrill of waking up to find her stocking filled, then running into the living room where her gran would be sitting next to her parcels, all laid out over the sofa. Yet, as always, the day passed all too quickly.

This Christmas though, ten-year-old Caitlin noticed a slight change to the traditional routine. For one thing, Mora, their neighbour, had gone to get the presents rather than her gran. And this year Caitlin seemed to find herself in the kitchen a lot more. She did most of the cooking, all the washing up, not to mention making all the cups of tea for her grandparent. Not that she minded. She liked being ten and feeling so grown up. It was just that last year she got so much more time with her gifts.

One good thing about this Christmas though was the young girl's choice of gift for her gran. As ever it had been something of a challenge. She was determined to get something a bit different, something she didn't have. Her elderly relative's drawers were full of scarves, hats and thick socks that she kept receiving. And for what? Gran hadn't been out of their flat for a good few months. It was Caitlin who went shopping or who went into the town. Not so long ago it would have been both of them.

Just by chance, Caitlin had popped into the local charity shop. She wasn't looking for anything in particular. Yet when she saw it, Caitlin knew straight away that it would be the perfect gift for her grandmother. Picking it up, she blew the dust off and bought it for a few pence.

So, on Christmas Day, the granddaughter's smile lit up her face as she watched her gran struggle to tear off the tape and ribbon.

'It didn't cost much,' said Caitlin, as the old lady finally got through the wrapping.

There was no reply. Gran stared at it: a framed black and white photograph of the old ferry crossing the Forth. Her eyes became watery.

'Och, Caitlin, that's lovely. Thank you, darling,' and she placed a kiss on the girl's cheek. 'And it's not the price of something that matters, it's its worth.' She was still staring at it as she spoke. 'I wonder if your Papa's bringing the ferry in?'

'Maybe. It looks like it's from a time when he was working on her,' replied her granddaughter.

For Caitlin, this was the highlight of her Christmas Day. Yes, she had got the mobile phone she wanted (she tipped off Mora) and she'd got a good deal of clothes (again, giving Mora suggestions) which she was happy about. It was her Gran's face though as she stared at the picture that had made her day.

The colourful lights that adorned many of the windows

and streets of South Queensferry helped brighten the drab day. Turning off Newhalls Road, Caitlin looked out at the Forth. Its dark chocolate colour was flecked with the odd cream splash of a wave from the breeze. Caitlin felt for it on her face and noted the direction it touched her cheeks and her ears.

She was heading towards the local sailing club, not because there was a meeting on, which there wasn't. That nobody would be there was the very reason she was going.

Since the summer Caitlin had been a member of the club. She'd only gone along to a free invitation event out of curiosity. Yet the young girl had proved to be "a natural," as the club Commodore, Alan Brown had said. Her debut race had seen her take first place. Although the racing was exciting, there was another side to sailing that she liked: the freedom it gave her.

When she was out in the middle of the Forth, her thoughts were on the wind rippling the river, the sail filling with a gust or the waves slapping the boat's hull. Here, she was in her element, doing what she did best and for once, doing something for herself. On the water, she felt freer than at any other time in her young life.

She was about to walk along the pier to the clubhouse when she spotted something near the shore. It was white and still, save for the odd wave that gently rocked it. Was it an animal? And if it was, was it alive? Caitlin couldn't tell. Maybe it was just rubbish, caught in the branches of a fallen tree by the looks of it. She walked on.

Minutes later and changed into her wetsuit, Caitlin fastened up her buoyancy-aid and pulled Midge, a club dinghy she had made her own, into the water. Soon the wake was stirring behind her and each rush of air had her stretching out over the side, her back nearly touching the waves. Apart from a moored tanker, Caitlin was alone on the river. She smiled and briefly shut her eyes. The wind, the first drops of rain, the smell; she let it all wash over her as she breathed it all in. Then tonight, cosy in her bed, she'd breathe it all out again, recalling this very feeling; the freedom, the place and the sounds. Being out on the Firth of Forth was a present no money could buy. Caitlin opened her eyes.

As she tacked the dinghy around, all three bridges came

into view. In the far distance the busy Queensferry Crossing then the older road bridge looking quite forlorn as hardly any vehicles passed over it now. The iconic red shape of the Forth Rail Bridge was nearest to her and just about tucked underneath it was the tiny island of Inchgarvie. Its old, empty buildings gave its shape while the rocky shore was marked with white flocks of birds.

She could now see the whole of South Queensferry. Behind the windows of many of those houses, children would be playing with their new toys or possibly opening more presents. Families of all sizes would be gathering There'd be big tables adorned with remnants of food and pulled crackers with laughter filling the rooms as the festivities continued.

Caitlin had her gran. And she had Midge. And that was all she needed. Wasn't it?

*

Walking home, Caitlin noticed the white object again.

What was it? Was it a swan that had got tangled up? No, they weren't feathers. It was fur. Was it a dog then? *A drowned dog more than likely, poor thing,* Caitlin thought, and she shivered slightly.

Wait. Had it just rolled over? Or was it the waves pushing against it? And did it just struggle against the branch of the tree? Or was that the wind trying to push it downstream?

Putting her bag down, Caitlin rolled up her jeans as far as they would go and paddled into the biting Forth. As she got nearer, she still couldn't work out what it was. The water was now thigh-deep as she stretched over and grabbed hold of one of its legs. Caitlin pulled gently and firmly but its other leg was stuck against a branch. She snapped the thin wood and whatever it was freed itself. And whatever it was, was quite heavy with waterlogged fur, the young girl needing both hands to lift it out.

Forgetting the numbing cold, Caitlin stared at the animal. Staring back at her was a polar bear, a young one. She hurried back to the bank where an old man with a small dog stood watching. He smiled as Caitlin lay the dripping bear on her bag.

'Och, he's a long way from home is he no' ?' he said. 'Mind, he'll like our weather, eh?' and he laughed. Caitlin just nodded.

'Taking him to the zoo then?' he continued. 'Ha, maybe the best place for him.'

'My gran says, "finders keepers",' said Caitlin. 'So maybe I'll just look after him the now.'

'Aye, well watch it doesnae bite. He's quite big and he'll keep growing. It'll take some feeding, so it will.'

'Well maybe I'll just look after him until he's big enough, eh?' replied Caitlin.

'Right you are lassie. He's a boy then?'

'I think so.' She opened her bag full of her sailing kit to try and put the cub in, but it would only zip-up so far. The bears head and front legs could still be seen.

'Going to give him a name?'

Caitlin pulled her wet jeans back down and looked to

where she'd found the cub. 'Forth.'

'Aye? Very good. Well, take care of him then. Right Sammy, let's get your ball,' and with that, the old man walked away.

'Forth pal, you just stay put, OK?' said Caitlin as she gently picked up her now quite heavy bag. The cub lay there, quiet and still, staring out at nothing in particular. She walked quickly, anxious to get him back safe and sound and without attracting too much attention.

In the flat, Gran was sat on her armchair watching one of her old movies. Caitlin noticed the picture she'd got her sat across her lap.

'Hi, Gran.'

'Hi, you. Where have you been?'

'I told you, I was away for a sail. It was great!'

'Oh, aye. A bit cold though eh? Did you fall in?' and she pointed at her wet jeans.

'I'll change. Have you eaten your breakfast I left you?'

'Aye.'

'What about your pills?'

'Och! I forgot.'

'Gran!' Caitlin placed her bag down and went through to the kitchen. She rummaged about in a cupboard and came out with gran's tablets.

'There was a movie on,' replied Gran. 'I must have forgotten or something. Good job I've got you, eh?'

Caitlin just shook her head. She picked up Forth, still wet, out of her bag. 'Gran, this is Forth.'

'We can't have a wee dug in the flat, darling.'

'He's no' a dog, Gran. He's a polar bear, a young one. A cub I think they call them.'

'That's as maybe, but they'll put us out, so they will.'

'Gran, I'll keep him safe. I'll keep him in my bedroom.'

'Aye? And how are you going to feed the wee thing and exercise it and all that? You'll have to clean its mess up as well.

And what if it starts barking?'

'Like the picture, Gran?' and Caitlin pointed at the photo. She needed a distraction.

'What picture? Oh aye, that one. I was having another look, to see if I could spot anyone.'

'And?'

'Och, no. Afraid not. It's a fair while ago, mind.'

'Cup of tea, Gran?'

'Aye, that'll be nice, angel. And a shortbread if you don't mind? Kettle's no' long boiled.'

Caitlin felt the kettle. It was cold and on lifting it, empty.

-3-

Caitlin left Gran with her tea and biscuits and brought Forth into her bedroom. Changed, she then placed him, still damp, on the windowsill.

'Well Forth, this is going to be your new home for a wee while. And that out there is Queensferry or South Queensferry to be precise. What do you think, pal?'

They both looked out of the window. This was her town, her place. Familiar and safe. And now, if she had thought this Christmas wasn't quite the same, felt that for whatever reason, she was recently more alone here in this flat, she now had a friend in the shape of a young polar bear. A young polar bear in Scotland.

Rain was falling steadily on the rooftops. The Firth of Forth was slipping under the rail bridge and disappearing into a grey horizon. Corners of backstreets were curtained in shadows as the dank and gloom allowed the evening to seep uninvitedly into the afternoon.

There was the distant sound of a ship's horn sounding out as it left Queensferry. A police siren made its way through the town. The muffled sound of Christmas music came from next door. Above, someone's chair scratched along the floor. Then a pause. A small moment of silence.

Caitlin looked at Forth; young, vulnerable and needing to find his way in this world, needing to find where he belonged.

'Queensferry?' said Forth.

Caitlin smiled. 'Och, not much of a place I know. You'll be safe here mind, until… well, until we find you a home and, who knows, maybe other polar bears.'

'Where's all the white?' asked Forth.

'Well, it has been known to snow here pal, and usually this time of year. So who knows, maybe this year we'll get some.'

Caitlin looked into the distance where the heavy

looking Firth of Forth joined the slate grey sky.

'I miss my mum,' said Forth.

'Well, that's something we've got in common, wee one,' said Caitlin.

'It is?'

'Aye. Mind, my gran's a good mum, if you know what I mean. Like, she's not my actual mum but she's just like one. I do hear from my proper mum. Christmas money. Cards for my birthday, sometimes a day or two late. I've not seen her since I was three. I can't even remember her that well. I've just this photo of me with her which my gran took. I must have been a toddler.'

Caitlin picked up the picture from her bedside cabinet and showed it to Forth.

'So, you never went and looked for her?' asked Forth.

'No. Maybe I will when I'm older. But then she's not come looking for me either.'

'That's sad.'

'There's no need to be sad, wee man. I'm happy enough. I've got my gran. I've got a place to stay. This is all I need. If my mum doesn't want to see me, well... fine. Anyway, I'm Caitlin or you can call me Cat if you want. Most of my pals do. Except Gran.'

Forth didn't say anything and instead he continued to look out of the window.

'Right, pal,' said Caitlin, 'here you are, without a mum. So, you've got me to look after you now. I'll do my best, to be sort of like a mum, making sure you're fed, watered and looked after. Then we'll see about getting you back to where you belong. How does that sound?'

Forth was still quiet, still looking out of the window. Caitlin wondered what he was thinking, what memories he had, where he'd been.

'I'm a long way from home, aren't I?' said the cub.

'This is your new home for now Forth, but yes, I'm guessing your old home is some way away. Who knows, you might like it around here. And I'm sure you'll make loads of friends like all of my pals. You're just so cute.'

'Cute?'

'Of course, wee man. Cute is sort of like... well, it makes you want to do this,' and Caitlin rubbed her nose on Forth's furry head. 'Yuck! You're still soaking, and you smell!'

Forth noticed his reflection in the window. 'Cute.'

'Right, come on, let's get you washed.'

In the bathroom, Caitlin lay Forth down in the bath and used the shower on him. Dirty water snaked down the plughole. She had put it on warm, then realising it was for a polar bear she turned it to cold.

'I liked that water before. It tickled,' said Forth.

'That's good because my hands are freezing. It's called warm water, by the way.'

'Warm water? Mmm... I like warm water.'

Caitlin carried a drier and whiter Forth back into the bedroom and placed him on her bed. From her bedside, she grabbed her laptop computer and lay alongside the young bear.

'See this is a computer and I can find out loads of things

from it,' and Caitlin began searching for "polar bear facts," on the Internet. 'Right, let's find out what you can eat.'

'I find everything out from my mother,' said Forth.

'This can tell me more facts than a mum ever could. Besides, mothers aren't just for learning from. Like, computers are a bit rubbish at this...' and she gave Forth a big squeeze. 'There, a bear hug for a bear.'

'Bear hugs? I like those,' said the young bear.

'Look, there's a picture of seals, pal.'

'That's a seals?'

'No one seal is a... och, never mind. Anyway, they're your main source of food, so they are.'

Caitlin searched for as many facts as she could about polar bears. There were details about their life cycle and their diet. She scrolled through colourful detailed maps that showed where they lived in the world. Another site showed a picture of some polar bears nosing through a rubbish dump.

'It says here,' said Caitlin, 'that you can eat pretty much

anything edible. Seemingly, you've learnt to scavenge when times are hard. So, when food is scarce it looks like you stray into towns and eat human leftovers. Yuck! How gross is that?'

'Well if you're hungry, you're hungry I suppose,' said Forth.

'Right enough. It also says here that because of global warming you're finding it hard to hunt for seals, "due to the reducing amount of drift ice."'

'So, if I can't get food where there's not much ice, can I get any here?'

'Nae problem, pal. It also says that cubs eat solid food at about three to four months old. And look! Oh wow!' said Caitlin. 'This cub is nearly as cute as you!'

A video showed a young female polar bear in a zoo, being cared for from birth. At times it was playing with a cuddly toy or was being fed by a bottle or lay in its keeper's hands whilst she slept. As the video went on, the bear was getting slightly bigger, with its age in days, displayed at the bottom of the screen. Caitlin paused the video.

'There, look, I'd say she's about your size when she's ninety-four days old,' said Caitlin. 'So, let's see, that's about… three months old.'

'That's not very old then?'

'No. Not really.'

'Old enough to eat seals though?'

'Think I'll struggle to get that at the Scotmid shop.' She clicked onto another page. 'Wow!'

'What is it? How to catch a seal?'

'No. Better. Much better.'

'How to catch lots of seals?'

'No, you numpty, look!'

'Look at what?'

'This! It says here, that a female polar bear, in the Scottish Highland Safari Park, may well be pregnant. This was just back in November!'

'Another polar bear cub in Scotland?'

'Well maybe. It says, "no one can go see the mother as she has been put in a birthing den but there is no test that can prove she is pregnant. Staff are excited due to the mother, Agnes', weight increase. The den will ensure that she is left undisturbed for the next few months, as it could raise the chances of a cub being born. It will also ensure that any newborn cub grows and develops naturally." I don't know why I didn't see this on the news. Must have been Gran and all her films.'

'So, I must have been in a den for weeks as well? I can't remember all that time and what I did.'

'Well, you were just wee. Very wee.'

'I do remember the first time I stepped outside though.'

'Really? What was that like?'

'It was cold, I remember that.'

'But you're a polar bear, you doughnut!'

'And I remember how white it was. I miss that. The quiet on the days without blizzards, the days without driving snow. Sometimes it was just clear blue skies and dazzling sun.'

'Sounds nice.'

'It was. It was my home.'

'Well looking at this, a new home may be closer than you think.'

'A home close by?'

'Aye.'

Caitlin then noticed something on another web page. It was titled, "Discovery of Polar Bear Remains in the Highlands." She quickly looked at the pictures then began to read the article.

'What are you looking at now?' asked Forth.

'Oh, nothing,' and Caitlin quickly went onto something else. 'Look, it says on this page that you leave your mum after about two years or so.'

'I do? Just two years old? That's not very long?'

'Yip, then you're on your own, pal. Maybe that's OK in polar bear years. Your mum gives you all the skills you need then it's up to you as an "ad-ol-es-cent" bear.'

'Ad-ol-es-cent?'

'Yeah, I think it's a bit like being a teenager. Sort of moody and stuff,' Caitlin said, smiling.

'Moody?'

'Yeah, like being angry which for you would mean growling.'

'What? Like this, GRRRR!'

'Ha! Yeah but maybe a bit louder.'

'OK like this then...'

'Who you got in there, Caitlin?' came Gran's voice.

'Erm..., nobody. Just me!' she said and looking at Forth, she pressed a finger against his mouth.

'Oh, must be coming from next door then,' said Gran. 'I'll get tea started, eh?'

'OK, just coming. Right Forth, I'll be back with something for you to eat. Now just stay here and haud your wheesht, OK?'

'Hold my what?'

'Keep quiet!' and Caitlin left Forth in the dim of the bedroom.

In the kitchen, Gran was busy trying to light one of the rings on the gas cooker.

'Wrong one, Gran. Plus you need water in for the tatties! And are we not peeling them first?'

'Och, I'm getting sillier every day, so I am.' Caitlin was tempted to agree with her. It seemed that just recently her gran was forgetting the simplest of things.

'Old age, eh? It's a curse, so it is,' Gran tutted.

'Right, I'll see to it, OK? Now, away and back to your films.'

'You're a wee angel, so you are. What would I do without you?'

'Gran, I was thinking about going through to Edinburgh tomorrow. Not on the bus for once but the train. With Forth.'

'Forth?'

'My wee furry friend.'

'The dug? Och, that place will be busy this time of year. People getting ready for Hogmanay.'

'What about you coming too? A wee wander around the shops then a cup of tea and a bun?'

'No thank you, my wee angel, you're fine. I mean, what if I fall? What then? How will you get on with me in the hospital and all? It's not like we have a family to pop round and help us out. No, I'm better in here. My own cups of tea and my own telly.'

Caitlin sighed. It seemed quite some time since they'd gone anywhere together.

'I'd hold your hand, Gran?'

'And what about the dug?'

'He's not a dog. And don't worry about that, I'll sort it.'

'No, you're fine, so you are. Nice of you to ask, though.

No, I'm afraid my days around Auld Reekie are behind me,' and she shuffled off into the other room.

Caitlin got on with the tea: mince for her gran and a tin of mashed tuna for Forth.

-4-

The next morning, before Caitlin was able to go out, there were two breakfasts to get ready, then the washing of their dishes. She made her gran another cup of tea before making herself, and her grandparent, a lunchtime sandwich as well as preparing a snack for a young bear. She then placed Gran's tablets in an envelope labelled, "Take These With Your Lunch," next to her armchair. Eventually, Caitlin was ready.

'Right,' said Caitlin, 'that's me. And what do you think, by the way?'

Gran turned from her movie to see Caitlin, coat on and a rucksack filled with Forth. From the cut-out bottom corners, dangled the young bear's back legs. He looked straight ahead as if he knew he was going somewhere.

'A dug in a bag? What's wrong with a lead? And does he not need a wee jacket on?'

'It's not a dug, Gran! And anyway, he wouldn't like a

lead. He's no' a circus bear! And I think polar bears are used to it being a bit colder than this.' Caitlin passed Gran her purse.

'Aye, well, take care of yourself now. How much are you wanting?'

'I've made my lunch and I'll be back for tea, Gran, so twenty's fine.'

'Right you are, and here you go then,' and she gave Caitlin a ten-pound note, then went and sat back in her armchair.

'Another ten-pound note maybe?' frowned Caitlin.

'Och, take the card, darling. Just lift what you need and maybe some for messages for tomorrow.'

'I've only just been shopping Gran,' sighed Caitlin.

'Really? Och, well just get what you need, there's a good girl.'

At the train station, there were only a couple of other people waiting. Yet, so as not to draw attention, Caitlin whispered to Forth what a train was and where they were going. She had something quite special to show him, something that she had seen yesterday on the Internet. Forth didn't answer, but looked around, as Caitlin, rucksack on her back, paced up and down the platform until their train came into view.

Seated, and with no one opposite her, Caitlin placed her bag on the small table so the white cub could look out of the window.

'Wow!' said the young bear. 'This is like walking, but faster! And easier! It really knows where it's going, doesn't it? How does it stop?'

'The man driving it makes it stop, and aye, I hope he does know where he's going,' smiled Caitlin.

'Tickets, please,' said a uniformed man. He looked curiously at the contents of the rucksack.

'Two halves to Edinburgh Waverley please,' said Caitlin, as she opened her purse.

'Are you twelve, miss?'

'Erm, er...' The ten-year-old Caitlin hadn't thought

about this. She'd walked the streets of her town alone, walked to school alone even sailed alone.

'Maybe bring someone who's sixteen or older next time, eh?'

Caitlin nodded.

'I won't charge for your pal here though, how about that?'

'OK, thanks.'

'Nae bother. Besides, it's Christmas,' and he winked at Caitlin while giving her the change.

Waverley Station was thronging with people. The sound of suitcases zipping along the floor was matched only by the continuous drone of the tannoy announcements. Crowds of people walked hastily this way and that.

'Where are they all going?' asked Forth.

'Everywhere.'

'Everywhere?' said Forth.

'Well, sort of, yes.'

'Do any of them go "everywhere" to hunt?'

'No, we've no need. See that over there, and that one over there? Well, that's where we keep all our hunted food.'

'Really? So, no walking for miles and miles while you're hungry?'

'No, but you need to have tokens called money to get the food. Look, if you're nervous you could just duck down and hide.'

'I'm not scared. If anyone comes to get me, I'll just growl really loud like…'

'Shhh!' Caitlin smiled. 'Besides, you've got me to protect you.'

Out in the cold air, Forth looked ahead and watched the hustle and bustle of a large number of people, as well as the steady stream of traffic. There was also a strange noise.

'Bagpipes, Forth,' said Caitlin as if she knew what he was going to ask. 'He's playing something called music, which we listen to. Well, some folks do. Sometimes we have lots of bagpipes playing all at once.'

'Is it a sound to get you all to come together? Like a roar, like this...'

'Woah! Look, quiet or you'll have folk talking.' Caitlin noticed someone looking at her, so she started singing. 'Folk talking and folk walking, yes just walking and a talking, la-di-da-dum...'

As they walked, Forth asked all sorts of questions. Caitlin tried to answer them whilst also looking at the directions on her mobile phone. Eventually, she stopped.

'Right, pal,' said Caitlin, 'this is where that special thing is, in here: The National Museum of Scotland.'

'What's a museum?'

'It's a place full of...well, interesting stuff. Some of it is very, very old. Including animals.'

'Oh, so it's full of old animals?'

'Mmm, not quite. It also has all kinds of things like old

computers and coins and that. And it has got some animals, mind they're...sort of...dead.'

'Sort of dead?' said Forth.

'Well, aye. I mean, we can learn from them. That's why they're dead. We can look at them closely. Read about them and, who knows, maybe become interested in them.'

'Interested in dead animals? Who could be interested in a dead animal unless it's food? I've got an empty feeling in me so if I could just...'

'No, pal. They're all stuffed.'

'Dead and stuffed? What is stuffed?'

Caitlin blew out her cheeks. 'Look, let's just go in, shall we?'

At the desk, a lady passed a leaflet to Caitlin that showed the plan of all the exhibitions.

'Who's your friend?' she asked.

'This is Forth. We're here to see polar bears. Especially,' and she whispered, 'the one from the Highlands?'

'Ah, now that one's not on show I'm afraid, but I could show you it on the computer?'

Caitlin sighed. She was disappointed.

'Right, and here's the photo,' said the lady and she turned the screen round to show them. '"Polar Bear remains. Found at Inchnadamph, Sutherland, the Scottish Highlands." Is that what you were after?'

'That's it! It's a skull isn't it?' said Caitlin.

'Sure is. Probably dates from eleven thousand years ago. Not only were brown bears living here in Scotland, but polar bears were as well.'

'Look at that, Forth! See, there were once polar bears living in Scotland, thousands of years ago.'

Forth was silent.

'Then where did they go?' asked Caitlin.

'Well,' said the lady, 'they were about during the Ice Age. Then the climate grew warmer and that influenced the polar bears' diet and the way they bred. Presumably, they just went further north, following the retreating ice.'

Caitlin was still staring at the picture. She leant over as far as possible, so Forth could see the screen from the rucksack.

'See, pal, Scotland is your old home, well, some of your ancestors' anyway.'

'I don't think Forth's that impressed,' said the lady smiling. 'Looking at bones of a distant relative is maybe a bit too much for him do you think?'

'Aye, maybe. Thank you, anyway,' and Caitlin went and showed Forth around the rest of the museum. Forth didn't seem particularly interested in the dead animals so she made it a short tour.

It was cold but dry outside, as Caitlin looked at the overcast sky.

'Right, wee man. That's my tummy rumbling now. How about we go and have a picnic in the park?'

'A picnic?'

'It's like eating hunted food but without the hunting

bit, although we do eat it outside.'

'A picnic? I think I might like eating picnic,' said Forth.

'You don't eat a picnic! Och, never mind.'

As they walked, a small group of teenage girls walked towards them. One pointed at Caitlin's rucksack.

'Hannah, look. That's so cute!'

'Oh! Soooo gorgeous! Hey there, wee man!'

The girls surrounded Caitlin and all at the same time began pointing their mobile phones at Forth.

'Don't come any closer or I'll roar!' said Forth. The girls just laughed.

'Oh Faye, get me and Beth in. Got to Snap-a-Gram this.'

'What's he called?' asked the girl called Faye.

'Forth,' Caitlin replied.

'Like first, second, third…?'

'No like, the river. The Firth of Forth?'

'Oh, how cute! Can I stroke him?'

'OK, but mind, he's a wild animal. I'd be careful.'

Faye laughed. 'He's maybe wild, but he's just so cute.' She reached over to stroke him. 'Ouch, wow! Yeah, he just nipped me!'

The other girls stood laughing.

'So long, Forth, you cute thing!' said one of the girls.

'Laters!' said Faye, waving at Forth.

'Jeez oh!' said Caitlin, a little further on, 'you'd think they'd never seen a polar bear cub before.'

'Why did she say I bit her?'

'Haven't a scoobies, maybe she thought it would be funny.'

'Strange. Then they said I'm cute.'

Caitlin ignored him. 'Look, there's the sign, Princes Street Gardens. Not far now.'

'Are we going to eat soon?' asked Forth.

'Just about, pal.'

Once they were there, Caitlin sat on the first bench she came to. She took Forth out of his bag as well as the sandwiches she had made.

A man, with long, scraggly hair wearing a long dark coat, came and sat at the far end of the bench. His trousers were tucked into his socks and his shoes had no laces. From the inside of his jacket, he took out a newspaper.

Forth was staring at him.

'Don't say anything Forth,' whispered Caitlin. 'I think he's a jakey.'

'A jakey?' whispered Forth.

'It's like a tramp.'

'A jakey that's like a tramp? So, not a man then?'

'Yes, a man who is… or became a jakey.'

'Do they hunt?'

'Well sort of. And thinking of it, he may have to build

a den, to sleep in that is.'

'Really? A jakey is quite wild then?'

'Wild? Raging actually,' the man interrupted, and he folded his newspaper back up. 'Now, can a man not get a bit of peace around here without a young lady and her friend a-whispering and a-twittering.'

'Are you a jakey then?' asked Forth.

'Sorry, that was my polar bear cub. He's called Forth.'

'Oh right. Well, isn't he a nosey wee thing? No sir, I am not a jakey and I take such comments as an offence to me and my reputation. I sir, am a vagabond. And a good one at that,' and he winked at Caitlin.

'Oh. Sorry,' said Forth.

'No offence taken, young man.'

'Would you like a sandwich?' asked Caitlin.

'Why that's very kind of you, young lady. I think I will. Thank you very much. What, no mustard?' and he winked.

Caitlin smiled.

'Ah well, it will suffice. And in return I might have something for your man there,' and he pulled out a small tin from inside his jacket. 'Sardines. Now, I only found these last week, so they'll be good to go.'

'Thank you very much,' said Forth. 'Did you hunt for them then?'

'Ha! I did that, sir.'

'And then you go and build a den to sleep in?' asked Forth.

'He means a house,' added Caitlin.

'Oh no. None of that business for me. See over there? The toilets? That's where I sleep. For now, that is. They lock me in if I'm quiet enough, ha! Then I can get a wash. Warm water and all that. Then on the floor, I visit the Land of Nod. Nice and dry and cosy.'

'Smelly though?' asked Caitlin.

'Ha! Well, come to think of it, you might have a point

there. Now, I'm to have myself a drop of the good stuff. To wash your sandwich down. And a toast, to the two of you.' And with that, he produced a small bottle of amber liquid from inside his jacket. He raised the bottle, took a sip, wiped his lips on the back of his mucky sleeve and gave a satisfactory sigh.

'See, if everyone out there was as kind as both of you,' he said, 'well, what a place that would be.'

'So, you're quite free then?' asked Caitlin. 'I mean you don't work and that?'

'No. Not since I lost everything. Everything I loved that is. Now there's a story. I'm free I suppose. Michael comes and goes as he pleases.' He took another sip from the bottle then continued. 'Do you think I don't get told to move on? That I don't have the looks of those who think they're that superior to me? Sure, I'm free from what I was, what I once was. It's some sort of freedom I suppose. Then again, I ask you, who is free? Anyway, I'm rambling. I should get going.'

He stood up. 'Right, that'll be Michael saying goodbye to you two and all the best.' He shook Caitlin's hand and gave Forth a gentle stroke on the head.

'You take care of yourself,' said Caitlin.

Michael smiled politely at the young girl. She couldn't help but think there was a kind of sadness in his smile. In silence, she sat with her young bear friend, the cold nipping at her nose and fingertips. She thought about Michael and who he might once have been and who he was now.

Forth broke the quiet. 'I liked him.'

'So did I, pal.'

-5-

On New Year's Eve, after doing the shopping, Caitlin walked home with a polar bear cub peering over her shoulder. During the last few days, she had got used to taking Forth with her wherever she went. Those who knew her would say hello then they would go on to ask how her polar bear friend was doing. Others would smile as they gazed at her, the ten-year-old girl with a white bear cub at her back.

Once in the flat, she found their neighbour, Mora, sitting with her twins. As soon as the young boys saw Caitlin, they jumped up.

'Hi Mrs Menzies, Ben, Callum.'

'Cat, who's in your bag?' asked Ben.

'Did you get it for Christmas?' queried Callum.

'No way! A wee polar bear!' said Mora. 'Mind he's cute.'

'Aye. I'm, erm... looking after him,' said Caitlin.

'Looks like a wee dug to me,' Gran chipped in.

'Can we look after him too?' asked Ben.

'Aye, of course, but make sure I'm about. He's a wee bit tired, so I'm just going to lay him on my bed, OK?'

'Then will you play with us, Cat?' asked Callum.

'Aye, why not?'

'Caitlin, honey,' said Mora, 'could you do us a big favour and watch the twins with your gran tonight? It's just the pub's got more bookings. With it being Hogmanay, the place will be going like a fair! It's double pay. I'd be daft to turn it down. I'll pay you, mind.'

'Aye, nae bother.'

'It'll be late though. They'll have to sleep over again.'

'OK, no problem.'

'I tell you, Mora, she's a wee angel, so she is,' said Gran. 'I've put the oven on, Caitlin. The tatties and veg are ready.

There should be enough for all of us.'

Mora kissed the twins goodbye as Caitlin went into the kitchen. There, the potatoes, as well as a tin of peas, were untouched on the worktop. Three pans, all empty, sat on the oven's hobs.

Caitlin sighed. The twins appeared at the kitchen door. 'Right, you chooks,' she said. 'Toys? Drawing? I've to make us our tea first, OK?' Ben and Callum smiled and ran out of the kitchen, knowing exactly where the toy box and paper were kept.

*

Later that night, Caitlin tucked the twins up into her bed. The boys were both taking it in turns to stroke Forth, who was lying between them on the quilt.

'Where did he come from Cat?' asked Ben.

'Yeah, and where are his Mum and Dad? Are they in

Queensferry too?' Callum wondered.

'No, pal,' said Caitlin and she rubbed Callum's head.

'So where are they then?' the twins demanded.

'Well...look, seeing as how Forth is nearly asleep, how about I tell you how he got here?'

'Yes, yes, yes,' the twins sat upright in the bed.

'Ah, no way, pal! You both snuggle down or there'll be no stories, got it?'

'Alright,' said Ben, and they both slid down under the covers.

'Right, you ready?'

The twins nodded.

'Promise to listen to the very end?'

The twins nodded again.

'OK, this is the story of Forth and how he got here. One day...'

'Shouldn't it be, "once upon a time?"' asked Ben.

'I thought with you being four and all, you'd be past all that fairy-Mary stuff?' said Caitlin. The twins laughed. 'Right, now quiet or no story. One day...'

'He likes it here, does he no', Cat?' interrupted Callum, staring at Forth.

'I think so. I mean, he shouldn't really be here,' said Caitlin.

'He'd prefer it where there was snow, wouldn't he?' asked Ben.

'I guess. Although he's fine without snow as well. Think of all those polar bears in zoos. They don't all have snow,' and she tucked the quilt in tighter around the boys.

'Now Forth is from the Arctic Circle,' continued Caitlin. 'So...,'

'Is the Arctic Circle like a ball?'

'No, Ben, it's not. It's just where it's really cold.'

'Colder than Queensferry?'

'Yes, Callum, even colder than here, now shh, you two

monkeys or no story, OK?' and she paused for quiet.

'Right then,' and she began to stroke Forth while she spoke. 'One night Forth fell asleep against his mother. Then during the night, a great blizzard started. Big flakes of snow came from the north, south, east and west. The wind howled but the cub's mother lay sleeping...'

-6-

Forth felt his mother's breath, warm and heavy against his face. He squeezed against his mother's thick pelt as best he could. Like one big ball of white fur, the pair of them soon became covered in snow, Forth's mother taking the brunt of it as she lay side on to the wind.

At first light the gale hadn't eased; flakes of snow still spiralled in eddies. Yawning, the mother opened an eye, stood and shook herself. Looking around, her eyelids flickered against a wind coloured white. Her stomach felt hollow. She nosed at her sleeping cub. She still had some of her milk within her, but Forth needed more than that now. They had, very likely, more days of walking, searching for their first meal out of the den.

The parent sniffed hopefully; the air right now couldn't be trusted. In its changing direction, scents were getting lost or were carried from who knows where. She'd have to be extra vigilant for adolescent polar bears or hungry mature males.

So, as soon as Forth found his feet, they set off, the cub walking as fast as he could behind his mother's large hind legs. The going, like yesterday, was slow. Forth would find himself struggling in the deep drifts, whilst his mother occasionally paused to make sure he was still close.

She knew they were still far from the coast and its ice floes, home to fat-rich seals. So, on and on they went, the wind and snow relentlessly pushing at them, briefly calming only to come back stronger, angrier. At one point they climbed through steep and heavy snow. Even Forth's mother began to pant hard. Their reward was in the descent. The female bear slid on her stomach, enjoying the feeling the fresh snow gave her fur and skin. Forth copied, at one point spinning full circle before stopping near his guardian, who licked his snow-covered face.

With no time to pause and rest they kept moving, the blizzard and the snow their only company. Forth snapped at *a large snowflake that dizzily spun around his head.*

His mother stopped. So Forth stopped too, silent only for his breathing and his mother tasting the air with her nose.

She lifted her head higher and sniffed hard to try catch as much of its promise in the moving air. Forth hid between the adult's legs, enjoying their scant shelter.

His mother started walking again, this time changing direction and picking up pace. Forth tried his best to stay with her but a gap remained between them.

Gradually, she slowed and Forth looked to where her head was pointing, her nose and mouth inhaling hard.

There, up ahead, and only visible when the wind eased momentarily, were three bears, and due to their size, adolescent. They lay around a tattered carcass, the snow around it tinged crimson. Arctic foxes, including a pup, barked or howled whilst keeping their distance, constantly watching the trio, who were tearing or chewing.

Forth's mother remained stationary. Three polar

bears, adolescent or not, were too much trouble if she were to approach further. The odds were against her. She would keep Forth safe and remain where she was, although her belly felt emptier as she observed the threesome continuing to feast.

Forth sat by her side. Hunger knocked within his own stomach. He licked his lips as he studied how the bears would hold bones firm with a paw whilst stripping it of flesh with their teeth. He could do that. Forth mewed gently at his mother who looked at him, then back at the other bears. They'd have to wait. Forth made a short, impatient growl. One of the three bears turned to look briefly at where the noise was coming from. Unconcerned, it returned to feed.

Forth's mother was not impressed. She turned and gave her son a low growl. He lay down apologetically. Yet a meal was there, right in front of him. Surely the other bears would ignore a small cub. What harm would it do to go over and join them?

Hunger getting the better of him, Forth trotted up to the group, their grunts and crunching coming and going on the wind. He copied how the other bears were eating and began himself, starting on some scraps that lay at his feet.

Alarmed, his mother called out to him, but her harsh cry was lost. The cub put his whole head into the skeleton. One of the other bears now noticed Forth and, from where it lay, took a swipe at him. Its huge paw managed to only clip Forth's ear, his head protected by the rib cage of the dead animal. The larger bear, now angered, growled fiercely, opening his mouth wide to display his large, blood-stained teeth.

Forth, rooted to the spot, stared anxiously at the larger bear. There was nowhere to go. The big growling mass was between him and the relative safety of his parent.

Out of the gloom she came and struck the aggressive bear's head, flashing her wide, open mouth. Surprised, the bear retaliated, nipping into the mother's neck. She shook him off easily and pawed him to the ground. Another bear approached, growling as fiercely as the first. She lashed out and connected. It shook himself and took off. The third, who for the most part had contented itself on the animal remains, now saw another meal right in front of its nose. Forth heard it sniff from behind his back and he broke out from its grasping claws.

He headed towards his parent, but the noise and commotion of her fending off the taunts and snarls of the other bear confused him. The third bear was again drawing nearer to the cub slowly, stealthily.

Forth didn't know what to do. Where would he go? Where could he hide? His mother, looking like she was now succeeding in keeping the other bear at bay, roared with a sound that was as threatening as it was heartfelt towards the cub. He wasn't sure how to respond. His parent let out the same cry again.

Inching toward him, low and with eyes that pinned the young bear to the spot was the third bear. Forth now realised exactly what he had to do.

-7-

'Right, you two should be asleep,' said Caitlin.

'That was scary,' said Ben.

'Not too scary I hope, pal?' replied Caitlin.

'No. Not scary like with monsters,' Ben said.

'What happened?' asked Callum. 'You can't stop a story like that. And what about his mum?' he sniffed. 'Is she going to be OK?'

'Sorry, pal, but bears fighting is just nature I suppose,' answered Caitlin. 'Sad but true. Anyway, we'll see. Forth's story is long but see if you have a good sleep and don't get up in the night...'

'What about the toilet?' asked Callum.

'You know what I mean,' replied Caitlin. 'Then I'll give you more of the story when you next come over, OK?'

'Aww!' the twins cried out.

'Tell you what, how about in the morning you two draw me some pictures to go with the story?'

The two boys grinned and nodded.

'Right, night, and I'll leave the light on in the bathroom.' She picked Forth up. 'And you come with me pal, these two will never let you sleep.'

'Night, Cat. Night, Forth,' said Ben and Callum.

'Night you two,' and she switched off the light.

Caitlin, with Forth by her side, settled down into her sleeping bag she'd laid out on the sofa.

The distant sound of cars crossing the bridge, perhaps quieter than most other nights, was interrupted by laughter out on the streets somewhere. Upstairs a television was on. Then a door slammed followed by someone whistling. The room was dark, apart from the amber glow of a streetlamp, peering in through the blind.

'Night, Forth,' said Caitlin but no answer came, and

she too fell asleep.

*

She didn't think she'd been asleep that long when the bang and crackle of fireworks disturbed her. Carrying Forth, she made her way to the window and pulled up the blind.

'Happy New Year, pal,' said Caitlin, and she pointed at the colourful explosions: great rainbows spilling across the night sky, then raining down in front of the rail bridge.

The twins quietly joined her at the window.

'Look, the stars are bursting!' said Forth, and the boys looked at each other and giggled.

-8-

Later that week, the twins were once again back round at Caitlin's flat, noisily playing on the living room carpet as Gran watched a movie with the subtitles on. Caitlin lay on her bed, Forth settled on her legs, staring at the laptop.

A website allowed her to track the movements of a female polar bear and a cub out in the wilds of Canada.

'Now that's a lot of miles,' said Caitlin as she pointed to the screen.

'It is,' said Forth, 'but when you're hungry...'

A knock at the door had the twins running excitedly and shouting, "Mummy," towards the figure behind the glass.

'Hi there. Is Catherine McGill in?' said a lady when the door was opened.

The twins looked at each other.

'Who is it, boys?' shouted Caitlin.

'Hi, it's Aileen Young, your new social worker,' the lady said, calling into the flat. 'I'm looking for Catherine McGill?'

'Gran, it's for you,' Caitlin replied.

'Och! Come in, come in,' said Gran from her chair and she turned the television off. Ben and Callum returned to their toys.

'Hi, you must be Catherine? I'm Aileen. I've taken over from Bernadette.'

'Oh, right, very good,' said Gran. 'Here, sit yourself down.'

'I'd tried your phone but there was no answer, so I thought I'd pop by, see how you and your granddaughter, Caitlin, are doing.'

'Caitlin, there's a lady from the social to see you. Eileen somebody.'

'Aileen, Aileen Young.'

'Sorry, darling. It's Aileen. Are you coming through?'

Caitlin sighed and shut the laptop firmly and got off her bed. 'Social work, Forth, so not a peep, OK, pal?'

'Here she is,' said Gran.

'Hi, Caitlin, or...' said Aileen, and she read some papers she was now holding, 'do you prefer Cat?'

Caitlin shrugged as she sat on the arm of her gran's chair.

'Right, in a few weeks it's your annual review, Cat. So, I'm just checking in to make sure you're all OK. I just want a wee talk to your gran first, then I'll get a quick chat with you if that's alright?'

'I'll go get dinner ready, Gran' said Caitlin. Her gran nodded and the young girl went into the kitchen. She heard Aileen asking questions with her grandparent answering back with either an 'aye' or a 'no.' As Caitlin continued to prepare the food, she was sure the word 'school' was mentioned. She shook her head.

'Right, angel,' called out Gran.

Her granddaughter wiped her hands and came through.

'I won't keep you, Caitlin' said Aileen, the twins running toys near her feet. 'You're obviously busy.'

'Ben and Callum, over there with your toys, please,' instructed the ten-year-old and the boys moved to the other side of the carpet.

'Whose are the twins, by the way?' asked Aileen.

'Our neighbour's,' said Caitlin. Aileen fetched a pen from inside her jacket and jotted something down on her papers.

'Are they round often?'

'Now and again.'

'And is that you making dinner for everyone?' said Aileen.

'Och, I'll go and put the veg on,' said Gran, and she got up awkwardly from her chair.

'Right, Caitlin, how are things?'

'OK.'

'Good. Well, you look OK. New clothes for Christmas?'

'Erm… just socks and things.'

'Good. Right, I phoned your headteacher before the holidays, Mrs Reid. We had a wee chat and she mentioned she was worried about your attendance. It's not normally been a problem, has it? It was quite poor before Christmas, and in fact, from September onwards. That's not like you. Can you explain this, Caitlin?'

'It was Gran. She was ill. So, I just looked after her, sort of making her lunch and tea and that. She was in her bed most of the time.'

'So, what about getting her to the toilet? You did that as well?'

Caitlin nodded. 'It's not a bother. She just had a heavy cold. She was poorly. Twice. She was in bed for weeks."

'So why didn't you get a doctor? A cold can become serious when someone is as old as your gran.'

'I did.'

'And?'

'He just gave her some tablets. Antibiotics.'

'So, you didn't go to school because you were looking after your gran?'

'Aye.'

'Caitlin, school is important. I know your gran is important to you, but there are services out there that will assist your gran, given you're the only family she's got. You do understand that?'

Caitlin didn't reply.

Aileen sighed. 'Look, I know you have a computer, so for the sake of the review how about instead of me quizzing you, you answer these questions by email?' and she passed Caitlin a piece of paper. 'The email address is at the top. Myself and others will discuss your answers at the meeting, OK?'

Caitlin nodded.

Aileen became distracted. She sniffed, 'What's that

smell? Is that gas?'

Caitlin hurried through to the kitchen, followed by Aileen.

'Gran!' said Caitlin as she heard two of the hobs quietly hissing.

Aileen opened the small window.

'Och, I just forgot,' said Gran. 'I'm busy peeling the tatties.'

'Gran the tatties were already done,' said Caitlin. 'You just needed to put them into the pan.' She looked into a pot with potatoes but no water.

'Does this happen often?' asked Aileen.

Caitlin sighed.

'Caitlin?'

'Now and again. Not the gas though. Other stuff. She just forgets, when she's busy that is.'

'That could have been dangerous, very dangerous.

What about if you weren't here?'

Caitlin didn't answer but instead filled the pan from a tap.

'You know I'll have to write this up.'

The young girl continued with the preparations for cooking as if Aileen hadn't spoken.

'Listen, you're only ten. You really are special, you know? For someone so young you're doing a great job. But you're also still a child, with a childhood to have like every other girl and boy. And I know maybe you don't see it, but I am here to help.'

The ten-year-old began to fill the kettle.

'Caitlin, look at me please.'

She stopped what she was doing and looked at Aileen.

'Your computer and your sailing kit, social services helped fund these things, didn't they?'

Caitlin nodded.

'So we're not here to just give you a row and tell you off, are we? We're here to keep you safe and let you and your Gran get on as best you can.'

She nodded again.

'Schools are back on Monday, Caitlin,' said Aileen.

'Och, I'll make sure she's at her school,' said Gran. 'She needs her schooling, so she does.'

'And if you can, email me by next week, OK? I'll see myself out.'

Social Care and Health – Children and Families

Aileen Young

Tel: 0131 511101

Email: Aileen.Young@schcf.gov.org

Annual Review – Child's Views

Name: Caitlin McGill   **Age:** 10

Address: Flat 1A, 7 The Loan, South Queensferry

Date of Annual review Meeting: Jan 15th 2:30 pm
Venue: TBA

<u>**So your Social Worker can get to know you and be updated on your current circumstances, please fill out the following questions to the best of your ability and in the spaces provided.**</u>

1. <u>Your name and something about yourself.</u>

My name is Caitlin McGill, but friends call me Cat. I live in South Queensferry with my gran. I have no dad, but I have a mum, only she lives in Manchester and not with us. My dad left us just before I was born, and my mum went to live in England when I was three and a half. I haven't seen my mum since then.

I have no photos of dad. I do have a photo of my mum. I think I was three. I remember my mum saying she was wanting to go on holiday just by herself. I must have asked my gran about a hundred times when she was coming back until I just didn't ask anymore. I think she had that depression stuff. My gran is my family. One day when I'm older, I am going to see my mum and ask her like a million questions. Then we'll go shopping and that.

2. <u>What are your hobbies and interests?</u>

Since August I have been going to a sailing club. I sail a dinghy called Midge. She is a topper dinghy. That is a boat with one sail. I have won competitions. The club Commodore Alan says that I am a natural. I guess that means I am quite good.

I like being on my computer finding out about things. At the moment I am finding out all about polar bears. I think polar bears are gorgeous. I have a friend who likes polar bears very much. He knows lots about polar bears. He's my best friend. One day we are going to find polar bears out in the wild and study them. Polar bears are alone most of the time. Except for females with a cub of course. But maybe that's like human beings - that you only live with a family when you're young. And then when you grow up, you're sort of all on your own, making your own decisions, making your own choices. My friend is here with me right now and he agrees (he doesn't stay with us though as that's not allowed.)

3. <u>Talk about your school. Mention what you like and dislike.</u>

Sometimes I like school. Grace is my BFF (best friend forever). And there's a couple of others. I like my class teacher Miss Bell and the Headteacher, Mrs Reid who is quite strict. Some of the lessons are OK as well. Science is my favourite and art. I like drawing but I'm not very good at painting.

Sometimes I don't like school. Letters home always have, 'Dear Parent of...' such and such. Then there are the 'Parent Assemblies,' or 'Parents Evenings,' or 'make sure your parents sign your homework diaries.' And I'm thinking, but I don't have a parent, at least not one that lives with me. So sometimes I feel I'm different, not normal, which I suppose I am, in a way. And in some ways, I'm not. It's hard to explain.

Not every kid in my class has a mum and a dad. Nicky McEwan doesn't, or Brandon Harris. But they do have a parent, their own mum or dad. Brandon even spends weekends with his dad.

I know my mum loves me. I guess it's just pretty hard to be a mum when you have a wee one to look after. There's the poop covered nappies, the crying, the feeding. Maybe she got sad because of all that.

If I became a mum, I would love my baby and never be away from its side. And when it cried, I'd read a story or draw a picture for it. And I'd walk my child to the school gate. And at three o'clock, I'd be there, and I'd wave and have a sweetie ready.

-10-

Hey Cat x Gud Xmas? 🎄

Kwl thks Grace. U?

Kwl 😎 Got a bike! And other stuff... & u?

Just stuff...oh and a pal... he's called Forth... 😉

Forth??!!

 C U Monday 🙁

-11-

Caitlin felt it had already been a long morning as she headed up the hill towards her school. Gran was fine. Her lunch was made. Her tablets were by her chair and she had her films to watch. Caitlin had also placed a packet of biscuits by her, just in case she got, "the munchies." She would ring her at lunchtime to see how she was doing. The school uniform had been ironed. The living room had been hoovered and she'd made her packed lunch and remembered a snack for breaktime. And a certain polar bear cub was packed into her rucksack, head gazing over the ten-year old's shoulder as the school came into sight.

She tried to explain what a school was but Forth still didn't understand.

'But how can you learn inside and without a mother?' he asked. 'I think you and your friends would be better doing your learning outside.'

'You're right, pal,' said Caitlin, 'but try and explain that to the teachers, the ones who act a bit like a mother. They'd say we couldn't do our sums right or it would be too much trouble and we might get run over by a steamroller or something daft.'

Grace's mum waved at Caitlin, who immediately started to sing. 'Something daft, daft, daft, something daft...bum-di-bum-bum.'

Walking into the school entrance with the school bell ringing, the headteacher came out of her office.

'Well, good morning, Caitlin McGill. How are we?'

'Hi, Mrs Reid. Fine, thanks.'

'And who's this?' and the headteacher leant down to look at the young bear.

'Forth. He's a wee polar bear cub.'

'Well he's cute, I'll give you that. We don't normally have things like that in school. So he'll need to be good in class. And quiet. Like everyone else, Caitlin, OK?'

'Yes, Mrs Reid. I'll make sure he behaves, so I will.'

'Right. Well, let's see if the New Year means a new start, Caitlin? Let's see if we can get your attendance up. We have a meeting next week.'

'I know. It was just Gran. She had a cold. Then it went to her chest. She just stayed in her bed, so I needed to help her to the loo, and...'

'Och, well, I don't need to know every detail, Caitlin. Anyway, I heard the social worker has spoken to you, so I think you know what's expected. Off you go now and have a good day both of you.'

As Caitlin went into her class, Grace saw her first. 'Cat!'

Other classmates looked up and smiled, the majority pointing at the contents of her rucksack.

'Good morning, Caitlin. Lovely to see you again,' said her teacher.

'Morning, Miss Bell, and thank you.' Caitlin went to her desk next to her friend.

'Hi, Caitlin. Happy New Year!' said Grace and she hugged her.

'Happy New Year, pal, I think.'

'How do you mean?'

'Well, being here. Anyway, we'll see. Right, wee man, let's get you out,' and Caitlin took Forth out of the rucksack.

'Wow! Is this Forth?' asked her friend.

'Yip.'

'Is he a bear?'

'Aye. A polar bear. A cub.'

'He's so cute! Can I hold him?'

'Sure,' and she placed Forth into Grace's hands.

'And who's this?' asked Miss Bell.

'Forth,' said Grace, 'he's Caitlin's.'

'OK, well, we're about to start maths, so how about you put Forth by your table, so he doesn't distract you.'

'He's a bit sleepy, Miss, so he should be OK, said Caitlin.' The class laughed.

'OK, OK. Let's get started. Well, I'm trusting you to look after him and keep him from disturbing the class. You OK with that?'

'Yes, Miss.'

Once into the lesson, Caitlin felt as if she had never been away. There were pages of sums to do. Then she had to sit and listen for what seemed such a long time, and then there was the marking of her work when she lined up at the teacher's desk. Lined up next to Sophie Wallace, that was.

'Hi. I like your pal. Is that what you got for your Christmas? Just a wild animal for a pet?' said Sophie. A couple of children laughed. Caitlin didn't say anything. She got her jotter marked and went back to her desk. *Nothing changes,* she thought.

'OK P6B,' said Miss Bell, 'let's see now, it's not quite break-time and we've done all our maths. Well done. So, anyone got anything they want to share with us that happened over the Christmas holidays?'

A few children put their hands up. Caitlin looked at Forth just to check that he was OK.

'Maybe there's a certain person who would like to tell us a bit more about their polar bear cub?' said Miss Bell.

'Go on, Cat,' whispered Grace.

'OK,' said Caitlin and she made her way to the front of the class.

'Are you not bringing Forth with you?' asked Miss Bell.

'He's still sleeping, Miss.' The class giggled.

'Wake him up!' shouted someone.

'Er, thank you, Brandon,' said Miss Bell. 'He's very wee, so like when you were a baby, he probably does a lot of sleeping, isn't that right, Caitlin?'

'I guess. I think he's bored though.'

'Maths?' said Miss Bell, smiling.

'Maybe.'

'Right, Caitlin, all yours,' and Miss Bell went to stand

at the back of the class.

'This is Forth. He's a three-month-old polar bear cub. I found him in the Firth of Forth, so that's how he got his name. I am looking after him. I'm going to try and get him to be with a polar bear family as he has no mum.'

The class gave a sympathetic, 'Aww!' Except for Sophie Wallace, who nudged her friend, then whispered something into her ear.

'He's my best friend,' continued Caitlin, 'and I take him everywhere with me. So far he's been shopping in Queensferry and I even took him to Edinburgh.'

'What? To the zoo?' interrupted Brandon Harris and the class laughed.

'Why would I take him to a zoo to be locked up and stared at by a doughnut like you.'

'Er, thank you, Caitlin, and thank you, Brandon,' said Miss Bell, 'hand up next time. Emma?'

'What does he eat?'

'Well, he usually just eats tuna or what I'm having.'

'Fish and chips?' interrupted Brandon again.

'Brandon, last warning,' said Miss Bell.

'In the wild, he'd eat what his mother would show him to eat, like seal blubber or even gull's eggs. Times are difficult nowadays for polar bears. Global warming means less ice which makes it hard for them to hunt for seals. They have to roam over larger areas. When there is a lack of food, they sometimes eat from landfill sites. That's when humans become scared and try and hunt the polar bears or capture them to take them somewhere safe. When polar bears are hungry, they will attack humans.'

'Really?' said Brandon.

'Really. But it's rare.'

'Right,' said Miss Bell, 'one more question. Grace?'

'Why hasn't Forth got any parents? And where did he come from?'

Caitlin paused.

'Yeah, he must have come from a country that has polar bears?' said Brandon.

'Well there's a story to that,' said Caitlin who looked at Miss Bell.

'Well, we've still got a few minutes till break,' said Miss Bell, 'shall we listen to Caitlin's story?'

Most of the class nodded their heads.

'Well,' began Caitlin, 'Forth's story started with his mother being attacked by other polar bears and then she tried to defend Forth.'

'Why was she being attacked by other polar bears, Cat?' asked Grace.

'Adult polar bears or even adolescent ones can sometimes try and kill young cubs.'

'So, what happened?' asked Brandon.

'Well,' Caitlin began, 'so Forth was alone and ...'

-12-

Forth was lost. He had run as fast as he could through the thick snow. Run, with the wind pressing at him to stop. Yet he kept running. The cub hoped that soon his mother would find him, find his scent, find him waiting for her return. So he had to find somewhere to shelter, but where?

Exhausted, he crouched low, panting hard. If he stayed exactly where he was his mother would have more of a chance of picking up his scent. He tried hard not to fall asleep, but the running, the fear, and the loneliness took their toll. Forth fought but lost as his eyes closed and he sank into a deep sleep.

When Forth woke all was quiet. The wind was now just a gentle stroke on his face. The brightness of the day made him blink. His head, still close to the ground, meant his ears picked up a slight rhythmic sound: footsteps, light and quick. What was it? He raised his head to look. An arctic fox was coming his way. Forth wasn't too alarmed as the fox couldn't be much bigger than himself. Yet it was running directly towards him. Was the fox after him? Did it want to fight?

Thoughts of being found by his mother ebbed away as his fear, once again, began to increase. Forth impulsively ran. Fresh snow made the going tough. The fox's light and nimble movements meant it gained on the cub. It wasn't long before he could hear the fox's presence behind him. It was no use, he would have to face it; fight, not flight. The young bear turned towards the oncoming fate and he gave the fox one of his immature growls. Yet as he did so, the fox swerved out of his way and just carried on running.

Forth, relieved, now became curious. Where was the fox going to? What was it doing? Now it was the cub who gave chase.

It wasn't long until in the clear sharp air Forth caught a scent much like before: the scent of flesh and blood.

And there, as the fox slowed down, was a hole in the ice, where dark water creased with the breeze. Beside it the remains of not one animal, but perhaps two or three. There was one large carcass and nearby, two smaller ones. The fox began eating as Forth sniffed where bloodied debris lay strewn in the clean snow. Among the relics were pieces of white fur. A small piece floated up into the air and drifted away. There were pieces of white hair amongst all three of the remains. He sniffed at one of the bones when he noticed the fox turn and stare, ears flicked forward. It gave a small bark and fled. Forth looked to where it had been looking.

For a moment all he could see were black dots coming towards him. Was that a scarlet smudge? For a slight moment, he couldn't be sure what he was looking at and he tilted his head. The black dots became larger as did the bloodied stain. The eyes, noses and one fresh wound: three polar bears, lumbering closer and closer. The cub held his stance for an instant. Was his mother one of them? One of the bears began to speed up and let out a threatening growl. Forth recognised it. The other two also picked up the pace, spotting food as well as a small defenceless cub.

Forth turned to run once more. As he did so, he trod on something hard: part of a limb, heavy boned and still heavier with ice-laden fat. It landed on him, its weight and its sharp ragged ends capturing and snaring him. He couldn't get a grip on the soft, white ground. He scrambled with all his might, but he could only get up so far before being flattened to the ground again. Forth let out a sad cry. The other bears were only a few feet away now. Forth twisted and kicked out for all he was worth. It was no use. He was trapped.

-13-

It was as if the bell brought the class out of some sort of daydream.

'Well, you're quite a storyteller, Caitlin McGill,' said Miss Bell.

'Is that it? What happens next?' asked Brandon.

'Well, how about we do it for our literacy task tomorrow?' said the class teacher. 'If that's OK with you, Caitlin?'

She nodded and went back to her desk.

'That was superb!' continued Miss Bell. 'I hope we get to hear more of Forth's story, don't you agree class?'

Everyone, apart from Sophie Wallace, agreed.

'Caitlin,' said Miss Bell, 'our class did a presentation project just before Christmas. Free choice. You do the presentation on the computer and a talk to go with it. Maybe you'd like to do one on polar bears?'

She smiled and nodded.

'OK, P6B, that's where we'll have to finish it. It's break time now.'

Out in the playground, it wasn't long before a huddle of children gathered around Caitlin. Some managed to stroke Forth who was sat on Grace's knee.

'Are you going to tell us more of your story tomorrow, Cat?' asked Nicky McEwan.

'Maybe.'

'Good to be back?' asked Grace.

'So far so good. Well, up until now maybe,' replied Caitlin.

Sophie Wallace and a couple of her friends pointed and laughed at Forth.

'Get anything else for Christmas, Caitlin? Or was that it?' said Sophie and her friends laughed.

'He wasn't a Christmas present. And aye, I got other things. Santa good to you, Sophie?'

'Yes, thanks. And we had family over. My grandparents. They came over special. Nice to have them around now and again, that is.' Sophie's friends laughed again.

Caitlin stared at Sophie. She knew she wasn't going to finish there.

'I was just thinking actually,' she continued, 'that if my parents died suddenly, I could always go and live with my grandparents, or my uncles and aunties. I know I would be sad and that, but at least I'd have a family to go to. I just wondered what happened if your parents, oh hang on, sorry, your gran were to die, who would you go and live with? I mean, what family have you got? And what would you do at Christmas?'

Caitlin took Forth from Grace and placed him back into her rucksack, carefully threading his legs through the holes she'd made.

'Why do you ask stuff like that, Sophie?' said Grace.

Sophie just shrugged and smiled, 'I was just wondering,

that's all.'

'She's a numpty, that's why,' said Caitlin, putting the rucksack over her shoulders.

'Excuse me?'

'Are your ears painted on as well, Sophie Wallace? Oh, and by the way, this is a parcel from my gran,' and Caitlin kicked her in the shins. With the sound of Sophie's crying filling one side of the playground, Caitlin ran past the car park and out of the school gates. And she didn't stop running until she was back at her flat.

-14-

Caitlin unlocked the door with her key attached to a shoelace around her neck.

'Oh, hello my wee angel,' said her gran, surprised by Caitlin's abrupt appearance. 'Good day?'

'Fine,' she said from her bedroom, 'just fine.'

'Good. Are you no' having a cup of tea?'

'Sorry Gran. I cannae. I've erm…, forgotten something,' and she reappeared holding her sailing holdall.

'Och, your gym kit?'

'Aye, Gran, my PE stuff. Are you not getting out of your pyjamas and dressing gown?'

'Och, not just now. I like this film. Besides, my goonie keeps me warm.'

'OK, see you later,' and she kissed her grandparent and

dashed back out.

Caitlin was muttering crossly under her breath as she made her way up the High Street.

'I would have bitten that Sophie if you'd let me out of my bag,' said Forth.

'She's some piece of work that one,' replied Caitlin. 'She's so nasty. Who does she think she is? Must be nice being Sophie-I've-got-everything-because-I'm-a-wee-spoilt-brat-Wallace. A good swift kick should teach her, pal.'

'Having everything doesn't seem to make her nice or happy, does it?' asked Forth.

'No, maybe not nice, but she should be happy if she realised just what she has.'

'If she's happy, why does she want to say horrible things about you then?'

'I don't know, pal. I really don't know.'

'Where are we going?' asked Forth. 'Is that school finished then?'

'Sailing, pal, and yeah that's school very much finished.'

At the clubhouse, Caitlin got changed and put Forth, still in his rucksack, inside Midge.

'OK wee man, this is sailing. This beats school easy. No one can say bad things about you when you're right out in the middle of the Firth of Forth.'

'I guess not. Why don't we swim though?'

'Because I've nae fur and this is quicker. Right, stop your yap and watch.' Caitlin pushed Midge into the water, and when it was up to her knees, she climbed aboard. The dinghy stalled a bit before the sail was opened. It quickly picked up speed. A slight gust had her heeling, so to keep her level, Caitlin moved to the side and leaned out. The water and spray hit her face and body.

'Yaay! This is sailing, wee man! What you think?'

'Wow! Is this faster than swimming?' said Forth, his head looking out to where they were heading.

'You bet! Now see that green buoy, on our bow?'

'Bow? What's a bow?'

'Right in front, pal. See it?'

'Oh yes. It's over there.'

'No, you say, dead ahead Captain!'

'I do? OK, dead ahead Captain.'

At the green buoy, two grey objects lay on its small platform.

'Seals!' said Forth.

'Aye, to look at. So, don't get any funny ideas,' said Caitlin as she rounded the buoy and headed further out into the dark-grey water.

When she got to where she wanted to be, Caitlin rolled in the sail and Midge slowed to a stop. She lay out in the boat, arms behind her head. Nothing here would distract her. She could just think. If she could just get to do this every day for the rest of her life. And school? Well, it would have to do without her.

Lying there, Sophie Wallace's words came back to her.

Why had she said what she said? And was there an element of truth in it? What would happen if her gran was to die? Where would she go? Who would look after her? One of those foster families she had heard about. Not a real family. Not a real mum and dad but the next best thing. A sort of pretend mum and dad. And did Sophie-stuck-up-smarty-pants-Wallace know just how lucky she was? Or did she, like so many others, take it all for granted? And that sometimes, like right now, you can feel so alone in this town, this country, this big, big world.

Caitlin sat up, took Forth out of the rucksack then lay back down again, the bear wrapped up in her arms.

'You're not going to leave me, pal, are you?' she asked.

'No. I don't think I will as I'd have to be ad-ol-es-cent.'

Caitlin smiled briefly, and with Forth tucked under her arms, she lay back out in her boat, the breeze drifting over her face. With her eyes closed, she could only hear the waves' gentle knocking against the boat. The noise of the traffic was distant. An engine of a boat hummed into the background.

'Caitlin, is it raining?' asked Forth.

'No, pal.'

'So why is your face wet?'

Caitlin squeezed Forth tighter.

*

As they neared the shore, standing astride his bike was a familiar face.

'From the class bully to the town bully,' sighed Caitlin.

'Do you want me to bite him?' said Forth.

'Ryan's nae harm. To me, that is.' With Forth behind her back, she dragged Midge up the pier's slope.

'Aye, just stand there, Ryan, nae bother,' said Caitlin as she started to pack the mast away.

'Seems like you're doing a great job yourself. Taking your wee dug out as well, I see?'

'He's no' a dog, you doughnut. He's a polar bear cub.'

'Oh, right. Should be in a zoo then. Are you teaching it to swim or sail, by the way?'

'Shouldn't you be at your secondary school? Or are you off bullying wee ones somewhere?' asked Caitlin.

'No. Training day. And in any case, it's you I wanted to see.'

'How?'

'Well, for one thing, you're the talk of the steamie right now. Everyone's on about how you kicked Sophie Wallace and then ran out of school. Go on yerself, Caitlin McGill.'

'What? Already? Well, she was asking for it.'

'Aye right. Anyway, that's not the only thing I'm here for. It's your gran, Caitlin.'

'My gran?' said Caitlin, now looking up at Ryan.

'Aye, she's down by the shore, in her goonie, with a bag or something. I've just seen her.'

'What? Is this some sort of bad joke, Ryan McKechnie?'

'No joke, Cat. Swear down. That's why I'm here. To let you know.'

Caitlin hesitated, trying to make sense of what Ryan had just said. 'Right, here, put my kit over your handlebars. You can give us a lift to her right now.'

Ryan did his best to cycle as quickly as he could. Along with a large bag at the front and Caitlin sat behind him, there was also a polar bear cub bouncing up and down on his passenger's back. Yet it wasn't that long before they were under the rail bridge. She jumped off the bike without waiting for Ryan to stop.

'Gran! Gran! What are you doing?' shouted the granddaughter.

As Caitlin ran, she couldn't believe what she could see up ahead: her very own gran, still in her nightclothes, a plastic bag in one hand and in the other, the picture. People walking past looked on puzzled and slightly amused.

'Gran, you'll freeze to death out here!' She didn't respond to her granddaughter's remark and just stared out towards the river. Her thin face was partly covered by her windblown hair, with eyes full of hope. Caitlin saw how vulnerable her gran looked right now.

'I forgot Davey's lunch, hen,' said her elderly relative. 'He'll be coming off the ferry in a wee while. I've got him some tea too,' and she passed the plastic bag to her granddaughter. In it was a plastic container with the sandwich Caitlin had made her, and a flask that when she held it felt empty.

'She needs tablets or something,' said Ryan.

'Isn't it about time you've got to go bully someone?' snapped Caitlin.

'Fine then,' said Ryan and he dropped Caitlin's kitbag before cycling off. 'Get a doctor to her. She's needing help.'

Caitlin scowled at him.

'Is this him?' asked Gran.

A boat, one that regularly carried people for trips, was making its way towards a small pier near where they stood.

'No, Gran, that's not it. Maybe we'll get him later, back at the flat. How about we get back home for a cup of tea, eh?'

'That's a shame. What will he think of me?' and she began to cry.

Caitlin picked up her bag, grabbed hold of Gran's hand and headed back. As they walked up the high street, a couple of ladies whispered, 'Shame.' Caitlin pretended not to hear and kept her head down.

'I'll make him his favourite tea: mince and tatties, so I will,' said Gran as they rounded into their street. 'Any leftovers, I'll give to your dug,' and she glanced at Forth who watched over Caitlin's shoulder.

-15-

At the top of the stairwell, Caitlin didn't need to look for her key as the door was already open.

'Gran!'

As they went in, there in the middle of the room, was Aileen. 'I've just arrived. The door was open. I thought you were in.'

The young girl didn't reply. Instead, she sat her gran in the armchair.

'Tea?' said Caitlin as she went through to the kitchen.

'Not for me, thanks, Caitlin,' replied Aileen, who followed the ten-year-old girl. 'What's going on?'

Caitlin was silent.

'I'm here about what happened today at school. Then I see you bringing your gran in, who's dressed in her nightgown and whose door is wide open to the world! So, I'll ask again, what's going on?'

'A bad day, that's all,' said Caitlin. She tried to fight them back, but tears began to fill her eyes.

Aileen sighed. 'Look, Cat...'

Caitlin carried on filling the kettle then looked for cups.

Aileen touched her arm, 'Stop Caitlin, and look at me, please.'

Wiping her eyes she looked towards Aileen.

'As I said before, you're incredible, do you know that?' said Aileen. 'You're ten and look what you do! There are not many ten-year-olds able to do what you're doing but it shouldn't be like that. And I'm concerned about your gran. Really concerned.'

'How do you mean?' said Caitlin, wiping her eyes again.

'Look, I'll have to go back to the office and see if I can

get some sort of care-package for her. And it will have to be pretty quick.'

'A care-package? What for?'

'Well, what's going to happen next? If your gran isn't trying to blow the place up with gas, she's away into town with just her goonie on. It's just not safe for her being like this, or for you,' said Aileen. She hesitated. 'Caitlin, I think there might be something else.'

'She isn't like this all the time. I mean, she's old. She's allowed to get mixed up, isn't she? Besides, I'm always here for her. I can cook. I can make her tea, do the washing and I can even iron. So I can be her carer. I can do my lessons here at home, so I can be right here.'

Aileen sighed and shook her head. 'It isn't as simple as that, Cat. I know you can do all that stuff. And if you were older, maybe that would be the answer, to some degree. But you're not. You're ten...'

'Eleven in a few months.'

'Right, but that's far too young. You need to be a child

and do what children do. You need to go to school and have friends. You need, Caitlin, to thrive and be the best you can be. Let the adults help. Let adults help your gran. And, yes, you can still help, but maybe not all the time.'

The ten-year-old girl turned round to face the sink.

'Caitlin, I think your gran is ill.'

She knew this was coming. Things weren't right. Had she been waiting to see if things would get better, that her gran would somehow improve? Or had she just denied the truth, that things would not get better, that Gran was getting older and was needing more help? The reality of the situation had been growing and was now staring her in the face. She knew it. She just didn't want to look at it. Instead, she'd tried to ignore it, pretend it wasn't there.

Caitlin slowly shook her head. 'Don't you think I know?' she said quietly and turned to face Aileen. 'She's got old age, hasn't she?'

Aileen smiled. 'Well, old age isn't an illness as such. It's just the things that maybe go with it that sometimes are. Look, just don't worry that much for now. It will get sorted.'

'Aye, right. I'll no' worry then.' Caitlin went into the living room. Aileen followed her and watched as the young girl picked Forth out of the rucksack and hugged him.

'Caitlin, I need you to go back to school, and apologise for what you've done today, OK?' said Aileen.

'It was her, she said nasty things.'

'So next time you tell the teachers, instead of running off, OK? Right, Mrs McGill, I'll see you later.' said Aileen.

'Bye for now erm... Eileen is it?'

Later, Caitlin lay on her bed, looking at the ceiling.

'So, is Gran ill?' asked Forth.

'Sort of,' said Caitlin.

'Sort-of-ill?' said Forth as he nuzzled into Caitlin's chest.

'Ill with being old.'

'Is being old the same as being ill?'

'I don't know, wee man. Maybe.'

'I'm never going to be old then. I'll just stay as a cub. So I just stay cute.'

Caitlin laughed and cried at the same time. 'Me too, pal, me too,' and she squeezed Forth as hard as she dared and let her wet cheeks rub against his soft fur.

'Are we having a cup of tea, angel?' called Gran. 'Mind, a bowl of soup too? I'm a wee bit cold.' Forth's fur got slightly wetter.

-16-

Hi Cat. Y no schwl 2 day?

Hi Grace. Gran stuff. Had to take her to Dr! She'd forget!! She doesn't even open her mail!!! ✉

Is she ok?

Old age.

???

She 4gets stuff. Gets stuff mixed up.

Sounds like me! Lol 😵 😵

Lol. She's got to go to a memory clinic!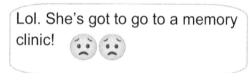

?!?!?!

Mora says it's like her gran. Her gran got put in a home

???

What if that happens to my gran?

?

3 carers a day doing stuff for gran. I cud do it but skwl

That's a gud thing right? 4 Gran? & 4 u?

Maybe. Dont no. What if she never gets better? What if she gets wurser!

?

What if she has 2 go 2 hosp or a home 4 a long time?

??? She'll get better.

Come live at ours if u want

Lol!

Forth –> i never want 2 forget I'm a pbear. Me -> I'll never let u. ʕ •ﻌ•ʔ

!Wurid!

! What will happen 2 me?

???

Gran's getting older. She'll get more old age stuff

I mite have 2 go live sum where else

110

I just want 2 b here!

Thnx pal x now 2 finish powerpoint 4 schwl!!

-17-

Polar Bear Facts

by

Caitlin McGill

(with some help from Forth)

Polar Bear – Facts

Physique

- Male polar bears weigh as much as a small car (300 - 800 kg)
- The height of a polar bear on four legs is 200 - 285 cm
- A polar bear can stand up to 3 metres tall
- The polar bear is the largest living land carnivore
- The lips of a polar bear are very dexterous
- The foot of an adult can be 30cm wide

Polar Bear – Facts
Diet

- Polar bears mainly eat ringed seals
- As well as hunting, polar bears will forage for food
- In captivity (e.g. zoo) they may eat carrot, melon, quail, fat and seeds
- Winter is the polar bears feasting season
- A polar bear once ate 1000 eggs in one meal!

Polar Bear – Facts
Life Cycle

- Polar bears normally live to 25 years for males and 30 years for females.
- Cubs are born November through to January in a den.
- Mother and cubs emerge from their den in March or April.
- In the den, mothers eat nothing for months
- Mothers cover the cub's droppings in snow

Polar Bear – Facts
Cubs

- Normally two cubs are born but there can be up to 4 in one litter.
- A new-born polar bear is among the most undeveloped of mammal young.
- It is as big as a rat, blind, only lightly furred, and helpless – it could not survive without its mum.
- It weighs only 600 -700g

Polar Bear – Facts
More About Cubs

- At birth they weigh 400-600 grams and are about 30 cm long
- A cub grows very fast after birth.
- A polar bear cub takes solid food at about 5 months old.

Polar Bear – Facts
A Polar Bear Den

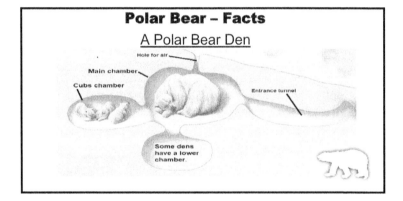

Hole for air

Main chamber

Cubs chamber

Entrance tunnel

Some dens have a lower chamber.

Polar Bear – Facts
Did you know…

- Individual bears have been recorded swimming as far as 100 km (60 miles).
- A polar bear is so well insulated that its body heat is virtually invisible to a heat sensor.
- King Ptolemy of Egypt had a polar bear parade through the streets.
- A polar bear's skin is black.

Polar Bear – Facts
Where You Find Polar Bears

| Canada | Russia | USA | Greenland | Norway |

Polar Bear – Facts
Threat to Polar Bears – 1: Climatic Warming

NATURAL CYCLE OF A POLAR BEARS FEEDING AND FASTING PERIODS IN A YEAR (BASED ON HUDSON BAY DATA)

| JAN | FEEDING PERIOD | | | | FASTING PERIOD | | DEC |

CLIMATE CHANGE AFFECTED CYCLE (BASED ON HUDSON BAY DATA)

| JAN | FEEDING PERIOD | | | | FASTING PERIOD | | DEC |

- Climate change is shortening the sea ice season and lengthening the warmer months when the bears live off their fat reserves.

Polar Bear – Facts
Threat to Polar Bears – 1: Climatic Warming

- Polar bears feed almost exclusively on the fat of seals.
- So polar bears have less time to feed and to store the fat as ice melts then refreezes quicker.
- The formation of sea ice allows the bears to hunt for the seals.

Polar Bear – Facts

Threat to Polar Bears – 1: Climatic Warming

- Warmer temperature means dens are more likely to collapse.
- Their population is thought to decline by 30-40% in next 10 years.

Polar Bear – Facts

Threat to Polar Bears – 2: Pollution

Polar Bear – Facts

Threat to Polar Bears – 2: Pollution

- Polar bears are exposed to high levels of pollutants, increasing with each step up in the food chain.
- This affects their immune system, growth, development, bone density, and organ structure.
- It may also affect cub survival and behaviour.

Polar Bear – Facts

Threat to Polar Bears – 3: Hunting

- Hunting can still pose a threat to the welfare of polar bears, but it is now well managed.
- In 1973 5 polar bear countries (Canada, Norway, USA, Russia, and Denmark/Greenland) signed an agreement.
- This restricted hunting, but meant protection of habitat, and cooperative research on polar bears.

Polar Bear Facts

by Caitlin McGill and Forth

-18-

'Well, what a great presentation, Caitlin McGill.'

'Thank you, miss.'

'What did you think, P6B?'

The class agreed. Caitlin beamed as she took Forth from the desk and went back to her desk.

'Listen P6B,' addressed Miss Bell, 'maybe we should do a project on polar bears and global warming, given all that information we've just been shown? Maybe we could raise awareness of their plight, yes?'

'We could do all the maps of where the ice is and where polar bears live and that,' suggested Brandon.

'And maybe we could write to some of the zoos or even Canada and send them some of our posters?' said Grace, who was just about standing out of her chair to get her idea across.

'They're great ideas. Right, we'll start that next week then.'

*

After school, Caitlin was walking downhill, back to her flat. In the distance, she noticed the Firth of Forth laying calm as clouds hung over the far shores of Fife.

'It doesn't sound that good for us polar bears,' said the cub from the rucksack.

'Hopefully, things will get better, pal,' said Caitlin, and she reached behind to stroke the top of his head.

'What if all the snow and ice melted? What would happen then?' asked Forth.

'Well, I guess we'll all be in trouble. It is a shame that you and all the other animals have a hard time of it because of us humans.'

'Don't a lot of human peoples like animals then?'

'No, I don't think that's it. In fact, I think there are far more that do than don't actually. Far more. It's just…I don't know. We're just mince at cutting down all our rubbish and stuff.'

'When do you think human peoples will get better at rubbish and stuff?'

'Soon, I hope. Mind, we've got a long history of being bad at making this planet a midden.'

'What's a midden?'

'A rubbish tip.'

Just then, Ryan came cycling as hard as he could up the steep hill. He bounced over the curb and stopped abruptly in front of Caitlin.

'Cat, it's your gran. Now she's in ger goonie up on the Queensferry Crossing. There's the polis and an ambulance. She's refusing to move by the looks of it. She's holding onto the railings.'

'What are you talking about Ryan McKechnie?' snapped Caitlin. 'My gran's at home with the carers, you loon.'

'Swear down. We had a trip. To the Sea Life Centre. We've only just got back. We all saw her.'

Caitlin looked at Ryan. She didn't say a word. Her head was spinning.

'Cat, here. Take my bike. Lock and key as well. Away and see for yourself.'

It must be true. Ryan wouldn't do this, to give up his bike like that. She jumped on it and descended the hill at a speed, Forth bumping up and down at her back.

As soon as they got to the foot of the steps, Caitlin jumped off the bike, hurriedly locked it and leapt up the steps then once at the top, sprinted along the bridge.

Up ahead there were the flashing lights of two police vehicles and an ambulance. Traffic on one side of the bridge was down to one lane. It crawled past the sight of an old lady, dressing gown billowing behind her. Her hands held the bridge railings as if she were staring out from a prison cell. Either side of her were two lady police officers with a paramedic in close attendance. Drops of rain began to fall.

Caitlin, still running as fast as she could, started to shout. 'Gran! Gran! What's wrong? What are you doing up here?'

Two male police officers who were monitoring the traffic intercepted her.

'Wait a minute little lady, no' too hasty mind. We don't want your gran to get frightened or upset if she sees you.'

'She's my gran, let me see her! Why are they holding her?'

The two police ladies turned to look at Caitlin.

'Just in case,' said the policeman.

'Just in case what?' said Caitlin. None of this made any sense. Why was this happening?

'Look, we can't get her to give us a name and if she doesn't let go, we'll be forced to physically move her. We're a bit reluctant but we cannae have her like this all day.'

'Let go of her, she's my gran, you big bullies. See if it were your gran, you wouldn't be too happy, would you?'

'It's not safe...,' said the police officer. 'What's your name?'

'Caitlin, Caitlin McGill.'

'Caitlin, there's a load of traffic around here and as you can see, we're quite a way up. We just need to be sure she doesn't hurt herself or anyone else, OK?'

'Fine.'

'What's your gran's name by the way?'

'Catherine. Catherine McGill.'

'Address?'

'Flat 1A, 7 The Loan, Queensferry.'

The policeman got out his radio. 'Hi sarge, still at the bridge. Got a positive I.D. It's a Catherine McGill...'

Caitlin interrupted him. 'I'll get her down, OK? Just let me talk to her and tell those two to let go of her.'

'OK but if that doesn't work, I'm sorry we'll have to use a wee bit of force. Jill, Liz.' The policeman waved his hand at the lady officers to come back.

The rain was coming in hard now and Caitlin had to push the wet hair out of her eyes. She put her hand on the elderly lady's wet, bony shoulder. Gran turned her head briefly.

'See you brought your dug.'

'Gran, what's wrong?'

'I'm no' moving, angel. Bloody polis. I'm no' harming anyone. Handy this wee bridge, though, eh? I was just away to see my Davy, down there, on the far shore. He might have been fuelling up. He'd maybe blow me a kiss, so he would. Then this lot stuck their noses in. So, I'm no' moving 'till they're away.'

'Gran, it's OK,' said Caitlin. 'Look it's wet, you're wet. Sure, Davy wouldn't want you looking like this? How about a cup of tea and a movie? Let's get a warm and a bite to eat. I'll dry and comb your hair just as you like it?'

The old lady just stared down at the water. Caitlin noticed how beads of rain ran off her hair, over her grey face and dripped all the long way down to the Forth.

'Well, my hair's a bit of a mess, right enough. I'm not wanting him to see me look a ticket. And a cup of tea sounds good, darling.'

The granddaughter took the frail hand of her grandparent.

'She'll need to be taken to the hospital. To be assessed.' It was the paramedic.

'Assessed for what?' Caitlin sighed.

'Well, she might have mild hypothermia, also she's out in her night clothes. She should be wearing her proper clothes and a jacket. That can't be right. We just need to check if everything's OK with her. I'm Hugh by the way,' and he offered his hand.

Caitlin sighed and reluctantly shook it. 'Gran, they want to take you to the hospital for a cup of tea.'

'What for? I've no' broken any bones and I'm no' sick.'

'It's all right Mrs McGill,' it was Hugh. 'We do a lovely cup of tea and they've some lovely baking in the café.'

'Really? Scones and that?' said Gran.

'Och, big as saucers.'

Gran smiled. 'Oh, very well then, lead on McDuff,' she laughed. Caitlin just shook her head as she and Hugh helped her into the back of the ambulance.

-19-

In a curtained cubicle, propped up by pillows, Gran was chatting to a nurse who gave her a cup of tea with a straw.

Caitlin disliked all this waiting. Her gran was fine now. She was off the bridge, she was warm and dry, and she seemed in good spirits. Which was what she told a lady doctor who had examined her.

'I can see that, Caitlin. What I can't see is why she was on a busy bridge, on quite a cold day, in her dressing gown. Why was she doing that?'

'She said she wanted to see Grandpa Davy. Her husband.'

'I see.'

'Only, my Grandpa is dead. He died before I was born.'

'Right. So, you see this is what we need to look at. Why is she thinking about these sorts of things when you and I know your Grandpa passed some time ago? Is that a polar bear by the way?'

'Yes, it is.'

'Shouldn't really have wild animals in the hospital,' and the doctor winked.

And now she'd left. So then there was all this waiting for some other doctor to come and look at Gran. And do what exactly? Her phone helped pass the time while her gran sang a little song to herself, eyes shut. The cubicle curtain swished back.

'Hi Mrs McGill, Caitlin,' said Aileen. 'How are we doing?'

'Och, I'm fine, just fine,' replied Gran.

'I thought your carers were there to help,' said Caitlin, still staring at her phone. 'Not to let my gran go wandering all over the place.'

'Well, yes, I'm sorry about that,' said Aileen. 'But I can't give your gran twenty-four-hour support. And to be honest, I didn't think things were this bad.'

'Angel, do you think I could get another cup of tea?' asked Gran.

Glad to be doing something, her granddaughter jumped up, picking Forth off her knees, and went to look for the hospital cafeteria.

'This hospital den feels like a sad place to me,' said Forth, from underneath Caitlin's arm.

'They're not meant to be places for a party, pal.'

'There's a funny smell to it.'

'All the disinfectant I suppose to keep it clean.'

'It smells of sadness. Sadness and tears.'

When she came back with the hot drink, a male doctor was sitting on the bed as Gran smiled and chatted away to him.

'Thank you, darling,' she said, as Caitlin placed the cup of tea beside her.

'Hi, nice to meet you, I'm Doctor McNaught,' and he shook her hand. 'Who's this?'

'Forth.'

'A polar bear cub?'

Caitlin nodded.

'Wow!' and the doctor sat on the side of the bed. 'Right, I'm just going to take your gran's blood pressure and get a wee chat with her, OK?'

Aileen signalled to Caitlin to come out for a chat.

'Doctor McNaught specialises in these sorts of things.'

'What sort of things?' asked Caitlin.

'Like what happened today. Your gran's going to need more tests, which may take a couple more days.'

'OK.'

'So...' Aileen paused.

'What is it? What's wrong?' asked the ten-year-old, who clutched Forth tightly behind her folded arms.

Aileen continued. 'It's too dangerous for you to be cared for by one adult who obviously has health issues. Your gran is your one and only carer. You've no other family, so you'll need to go into temporary foster care.'

Caitlin hesitated for an answer.

'Temporary foster care? So how long have I to be there?'

'As long as it takes. Until we can get you a more permanent setting.'

'Where and who with? Why can't I just go home with Forth? I can do everything, cook, wash, hoover.'

'You're not eighteen. You can't be left alone at the age of ten, Caitlin.'

The young girl rested her head on Forth's.

'It'll be fine,' said Aileen. 'There are lots of other children in a similar position. I've got one temporary foster parent, Mrs Paton, I'd like to take you to see. I've been back to the flat with your gran's key and I've put your clothes and some other bits and pieces in my car. And about your gran, Caitlin.'

'What about her?'

'She's going to need to be put into a home.'

'A home? What for?'

'It's a special home, where she'll get specialist care and provision, twenty-four hours. It'll be a bit like a hospital.'

Caitlin paused for some sort of reply.

'For how long?' she managed to ask.

Aileen sighed again. 'I don't know. It could be some time though.'

'Weeks?'

Aileen shrugged her shoulders.

'Months?'

Aileen nodded. 'Sorry Caitlin, but more than likely. She'll be staying in here until they've carried out further tests. It will give us time to finalise details of an available home.' She got out her mobile and made a call. 'You go and say goodbye to your gran for now, OK? Oh, hello, Mrs Paton?'

The young girl turned towards the curtain. Behind it,

the only constant thing in her life.

Trying to make sense of everything, the world she knew crumbling beneath her, Caitlin went through the curtains. Doctor McNaught stood up and left.

She kissed her gran on the forehead. The grandparent's delicate hand gently rubbed her granddaughter's arm. 'You take care of yourself, do you hear?'

Caitlin, burst into tears and walked out, smothering her sobs into Forth's furry head.

-20-

The ten-year-old girl and her social worker were silent in the car. Streets and places that Caitlin only vaguely knew drifted past. A new world awaited, and she didn't want to go there. What she was used to and what she knew was floating away. All she wanted to do was turn back and return to that familiar and happy place: the flat, sat watching an old movie with her gran.

And what was this care home anyway? Home didn't seem like the right word. It wasn't going to be like a home at all, was it? Gran would be out sometime though, wouldn't she? She just needs help remembering things. Tablets could do that. And if the carers would just keep the door locked, she wouldn't be able to walk onto bridges. And maybe the gas could be turned off when they weren't cooking somehow. Then what about the water? What if she leaves taps running? What if she overfills the bath? In that case, couldn't they get a carer that could be with her gran all day until she got home from school?

A proper home. Their home. Not a home just for old people.

She was going to miss her so much. So every day after school by bus, taxi or even walking, she'd visit her. So her gran wouldn't get lonely, confused, or worry about how her "wee angel" was doing.

And where was her home now? Whose faces would now greet her when she came in from school or woke from her sleep? Who would these people be? Not family. Not her family, just some random adults.

As the car pulled up in front of a row of terrace houses, Caitlin sighed and slowly shook her head.

*

'So, that's Caitlin's background, Mrs Paton. Or do you prefer Shona?' asked Aileen.

'I don't mind,' said Mrs Paton, smiling before taking another sip of her tea.

'Caitlin likes Cat, don't you?' said Aileen.

Caitlin just nodded. On Mrs Paton's sofa, she felt ill at ease, uncomfortable. She eyed the room again. Her temporary home, like a hotel or a bed and breakfast. Just something for the time being. She held Forth close to her.

'Have you got any questions, Caitlin?' asked Aileen, who sat beside her. She placed an arm around her shoulder. 'You're in good hands here. Mrs Paton is an experienced foster parent.'

'How do I get to school from here?'

'I've arranged a taxi,' answered Aileen.

'Can I have friends' round?'

'We'll see,' said Mrs Paton. 'Let's just get you settled first, OK?'

'Have you got Wi-Fi?'

'We do,' said Mrs Paton. 'It goes off at nine p.m. though.'

'Caitlin, this is just temporary,' said Aileen. 'Once I have sorted out a more permanent placement, you'll feel more settled. Maybe while you're here you'll get used to living in someone else's home?'

'A more permanent placement? When do I get back to the flat?'

Aileen and Mrs Paton exchanged glances.

'Caitlin,' said Aileen, 'your gran is quite ill, OK? As I explained, it's going to be some time before she gets better.'

The ten-year-old didn't say anything as she stroked Forth and looked down at his sparkling brown eyes.

'I'll get your things out of the car,' said Aileen.

Once she had left the room, Mrs Paton started to clear the cups away. 'What is that thing, by the way?' she asked, looking at Forth.

Caitlin looked at Mrs Paton but remained quiet.

'Is it a dog?' she queried.

'Polar bear.'

'I don't normally have those sorts of things in my

house: pets, furry things, or anything like it. My Ronnie has asthma. Hairs play havoc with it, so they do. Then there are the fleas or whatever germs they bring in with them.'

'Forth is a polar bear. He's very clean. I wash him myself, in the bath. There's probably more fleas on a dog or a cat,' said Caitlin, still gazing at Forth.

'Not that I mind you bringing it in. If it helps you settle, fine. Just keep it out of your bed, please.'

'So, where's he meant to sleep?'

Mrs Paton just stared at Caitlin. 'I hope you're not going to be hard work, lady?' And with that, she took the cups away.

-21-

Wide awake, lying on an unfamiliar bed in an unfamiliar bedroom, Caitlin tried to pinpoint what it was she was feeling right now.

Was it that feeling of being away from her flat, being away from that comforting normalness of everyday life? Was it sadness from not seeing her gran, not knowing how she was or what she was doing? Or was it a reluctant acceptance that this was what her life was to be like for the foreseeable future: living in another person's house, being looked after by people who aren't relatives, they are just strangers. All because you're unlucky enough not to have a family of your own.

And this ten-year-old's life was just a drawer of clothes. A birthday card from Gran when she was one that she kept in its original envelope. The picture with her mother from her third birthday party. And her mobile phone with pictures of herself with her grandparent on Christmas Day, who smiled into the camera. In her head, she could still hear her gran's words and her laughter.

'I don't like it here, pal,' Caitlin whispered.

'Neither do I,' replied Forth. 'Fleas?'

'I know. Look, I've got a plan, OK? We just need to wait a while.'

Later, with arms behind her head, Caitlin waited. Waited for the snores of Mr and Mrs Paton to rhythmically come and go. Waited for the noises outside: cars, buses, people walking by to turn from a persistent stream to a mere trickle. And when they did, she dressed, packed a few of her clothes into a holdall and placed Forth into the rucksack. Then as quietly as she possibly could she crept downstairs, unlocked the back door and went out into the night.

Her mobile phone gave her the route as she walked down unknown alleyways and dimly lit streets. She was nervous to be out at this time of night. Yet the plan she had helped settle her fears as it would set her and Forth free. A plan that would see them living out their happy ever after. A plan that gave her hope.

Eventually, Caitlin stood outside her old flat. She still had her key. They hadn't asked for hers.

Inside she was met by the familiar smell and the strangeness of being a visitor in her own home.

'Are we coming back?' asked Forth from Caitlin's back.

'No, too obvious, pal,' and she went into the kitchen. 'This is what we call "running away." '

'Running away? Away to where?'

'You'll see. First, we need food.'

Opening the cupboards, she found it odd that there were still packets of biscuits, cans of soup or opened boxes of cereal as if they would all be back some time.

Grabbing a couple of plastic bags, Caitlin started filling them.

'Knife... Fork... Tin-opener,' she said, showing each one to Forth over her shoulder, before putting it into a bag.

'Tuna?' asked Forth.

'Check,' and she took a couple more tins from the shelf. 'Oh, and my sleeping bag and the clubhouse key,' and Caitlin quickly went into her bedroom.

'Are we sailing?' asked Forth.

'Aye, we are, pal.'

Laden with bags, Caitlin made her way through the dark but known streets of Queensferry. At the clubhouse, it was a relief to be able to put all the bags down including the one on her back with a bear cub in it.

'Right, I'll not get changed, it's just a wee sail,' said Caitlin, and she looked at the waves slapping the launch way. There was quite a breeze.

With her lifejacket on, she pulled Midge on its trolley down to where all the bags lay. Forth watched as Caitlin, with ropes and ties, fastened all the bags inside the dinghy until there wasn't much room for herself. Forth, still in the rucksack, was placed right against the mast. Caitlin secured it with its shoulder-straps, the young bear looking straight ahead.

'Alright, wee man?' asked Caitlin.

'Erm, I think so,' replied Forth.

'Good. You can tell me if we're on course for Inchgarvie.'

'Inchgarvie? So, is that where we're running away to?'

'Aye but it's no' far. So we can still come back and see Gran.'

'Are there bears there?'

'No, pal. Just gulls and other birds. It's a sanctuary for them, but listen, we'll live there. And you can practise your hunting and foraging skills.'

'So, we're going to stay there for a while?'

'Aye.'

Forth was quiet for a moment.

'You OK with that?' asked Caitlin. 'I mean if you're not, just say. We could go somewhere else if you like?'

'Does it have warm water?' Forth said eventually.

Caitlin smiled, but not for long. 'Oh no! Water!' and she darted back into the clubhouse. Unlocking a door, she switched on a light. The club's bar had lines of alcoholic drinks behind a metal grille. A couple of empty plastic bottles lay on the top of a bin. She grabbed them and headed outside. In her rush, she didn't see a red light right next to the till begin to flash.

Outside Caitlin filled the bottles from a hose they used to wash down the boats.

'That's everything. Right pal, let's go,' she said, running back towards Midge.

Pushing Midge out into the water, as soon as the dinghy was free of its trolley, Caitlin quickly hauled the wheeled frame back up the launch way. The boat was turning around in the waves, the sail still wrapped around the mast. Knee deep in water, Catlin clambered onboard.

The sky was a heavy black as the moon fought to be seen. It was still a very early January morning. Caitlin, holding the tiller in one hand, opened up the sail with her other. They quickly picked up speed as the sound of surging water came from the small boat's wake.

A sudden gust hit hard. Caitlin was slightly caught out as Midge heeled sharply. Caitlin steered to right the dinghy, but a few tins emptied from the bags and sank into the waves.

'Jeez oh! You OK, Forth?'

'Is that meant to happen? Being on the side bit?'

'She just got hit by a gust. I'll take some sail in, so it won't be so bad next time.'

As Caitlin leant forward, she managed to kick a bottle of water which also went over the side. Caitlin sighed. She steadied herself as Midge skipped into the waves, which slapped against the front, sending spray over them both.

'That's not very warm,' said Forth.

Caitlin shook her head. 'Some polar bear you are!'

The young sailor glanced behind her, and there, even at this early hour, was Alan, the club Commodore, entering the clubhouse. Masked by the dark or simply because he didn't look out towards the river, it didn't look like he'd noticed them.

Moonlight briefly appeared from behind clouds as the outline of Inchgarvie grew. The odd beacon out in the wide river flashed a beam of light that struck its shores.

'Forth, we need to look carefully for a good place to land.'

'What's that?' asked the cub.

In the dim, Caitlin was able to make out a tall structure, jutting out of the water. Occasionally the flashing light illuminated its wet and shiny beams.

'Looks like an old landing jetty. A fair bit of it is missing and it's far too high. There should be paths and tracks leading to it.'

Caitlin turned Midge towards the island, ducking under the swinging boom as she did so. The sail quickly filled with wind. Caitlin pulled the centreboard out from the floor just as the shallow bottom scraped against the underside of the boat. Lifting the rudder, Caitlin let Midge drift towards land. Dozens of roosting birds sent high pitched cries out into the early morning dark and fluttered away.

'Are we here?' asked Forth.

'Yes, pal. I said it wouldn't take long.'

Pulling the bags out of Midge and untying Forth, Caitlin surveyed where they were.

'We'll leave Midge here, but first let's get these bags, and you, to the top of this slope,' she said.

With the rucksack on her back, as well as holding both food bags and her holdall, Caitlin had to occasionally put one down to steady herself and negotiate the rocky slope. At the top, Caitlin had no sooner put everything on the ground when she made her way back down the embankment.

'Where are you going?' asked Forth.

'To hide Midge,' replied Caitlin. Back at her dinghy, she took the mast out and lay it on the deck. Grabbing seaweed from nearby, she began to cover her beloved boat until only some small bits of its white hull could be seen.

Back up on the ridge, Caitlin once again loaded up with all the bags and headed along a faint shingle track.

'We've got to keep our eyes and ears open, Forth, OK?'

'My eyes already are. Can you close your ears?'

'It's just an expression. We've got to keep hidden, right?'

'Who are we hiding from?'

'People.'

'Peoples? Isn't everyone, apart from animals, peoples?'

'Exactly.'

Inchgarvie was largely covered in old relics of buildings and structures from times past. These weren't brick buildings but plain, concrete ones, the size and height of small huts. Their windows and doors were long gone although occasionally their flat roofs were still intact.

Caitlin peered into the nearest building then back over

her shoulder where the wide river lay under the strengthening breeze. The rail bridge loomed overhead, so near she could hear the wind whistling through its iron stanchions. In the distance, the road bridges were illuminated against the now inky blue sky.

'This will do,' said Caitlin.

Inside smelt damp. The floor was messy with bits of concrete from the crumbling walls and weeds that grew out of cracks. A puddle sat in the far corner. Caitlin quickly changed into a pair of dry jeans.

'OK, we can only go out when there's no-one about, pal. Before long tourists will be taking trips around here in the boats. And then there'll be the passengers on the trains.'

'Is this place also called a home then?' asked Forth.

'No. All of these are just buildings that were built during battles a long time ago. They also used them as a prison and there used to be a big cannon on here, to protect the rail bridge during the war.'

'What's a war?'

Caitlin had to think for a good, clear answer.

'It's when countries don't get on with each other. One might want the other's land or oil or gold or whatever. Or it might be a country did something bad like let off bombs or missiles. So, other countries send out people in armies, or in boats or even planes to go and kill other people so that they stop being bad. The loser is the one that surrenders or has the most killed.'

'Killed?' said Forth.

'Afraid so, pal.'

'So, people kill for a game?'

'Mmm..., I'm not sure about that. Most people don't like having one. A war that is. It's just a few important people, like prime-ministers or kings, who want it. So, because they say so, we all have to do it.'

'Why don't you say no?'

'Then we would probably get shot or put in prison.'

Forth remained quiet.

'Mostly it's really sad,' continued Caitlin. 'Mind, I'm not sure that there are any wars that are happy ones. Except if a country is being really bad. Och, it's all a load of nonsense if you ask me.'

'Human peoples are quite strange, aren't they?' said Forth, staring out towards the rail bridge. 'I mean, we would normally only kill for food.'

'We just kill each other for not being happy about something, I think.'

Forth didn't say anything but stared out from his rucksack, as if he were thinking.

'I'm hungry,' he said.

'OK, pal,' and Caitlin pulled him out and placed him on the floor. 'Soup and a tin of tuna? Och! I'm a numpty! Matches! We'll need to fetch some back with us next time. Then we can have a fire to cook and keep warm. In the meantime, it's cold soup and tuna.' She opened a couple of tins and fed herself and then Forth.

Caitlin looked out at the bridges while she ate. The

dark sky signalled another winter morning with the odd gust nudging her face.

So, this is how freedom feels. Being on an island, in the murk and rain, eating cold soup. And yet it still felt exciting. And best of all was the freedom from worry. The worry for her future and where she was being told to live. She'd sail back to see her gran. Maybe every other day. And after she'd seen how she was doing, ask her for some money then go shopping and return to the island, her new home. It would have to be dark, so no one saw her and asked questions or wondered where she'd been. That would be harder in the long summer days. She wondered if there would there be those, "Missing: Caitlin McGill Aged 10," posters. Would she be in the papers? Maybe she should have stocked up on more food, so she didn't need to return for months. But what about seeing Gran? Caitlin sighed. Being free was going to be hard work. *Then again I ask you, who is free.*

Forth broke the quiet. 'If you're ten, are you ready to hunt?'

'I don't need to hunt, although I could fish. Mind, I

probably wouldn't catch anything. It's just going to be difficult that's all: to run away and be completely free. All the food and other things we need we'll have to get ourselves.'

'Wouldn't your grown-up adults help? Just tell them you're living on this island and it's your new home and that you're ten.'

'I wish it was that easy pal,' smiled Caitlin and she placed Forth on her knees so they both could lookout.

'What shall we do now?' asked the cub.

'Well, we can explore this island, our new home but first we should… listen!' A train, lights inside its carriages and so close that the odd face could be seen, glided above them along the bridge. Caitlin moved Forth back into the shadows of their shelter.

'A wee girl with a polar bear cub on an island won't look good to passers-by, trust me.'

A sudden blast of wind came in through the entrance and the broken windows. It threw heavy drops of rain onto the floor.

Caitlin pulled the bags deeper into the hut.

'Are we going to have an explore now?' asked Forth.

'What? In this?'

'I've explored in snow and blizzards.'

'Wild or no', wee man, even polar bears need to rest.' Caitlin got out her sleeping bag, lifted Forth and placed him on her holdall of clothes. She lay her head next to his.

It was still only the early hours of the morning, but it already felt like a long day. A ten-year-old girl tried to keep her eyes open, just enough to see a young bear cub, looking outside as if he was wondering what all this was about; humans, this country and what he was doing right here on this tiny piece of land.

-22-

When Caitlin woke, it was still dark. How long had she slept?

From where she lay, she could see the lights on the bridges, car headlights and the beacons flashing over the surface of the water. The wind had picked up and drizzle swept against the outside walls. With each gust, drips fell heavily into the hut, the puddle now much larger.

Forth was already awake but he was now lying on the floor.

'I'm cold,' said Caitlin groggily, and she got out of her sleeping bag.

'So am I,' said Forth.

Caitlin shook her head. 'Right, blankets as well as matches. We can collect driftwood and store it up, so we can have a wee fire.'

'Won't people see that?'

'Mmm... you're right. Maybe if it was against a wall or something. Anyway, let me sort that out.'

'When can we go outside?'

The girl reached her hand outside. 'Now if you like. Just hang on, I want to see what the actual time is.' She looked at her phone. 'It's half-past five! Jeez oh, some sleep!' There were also six missed calls. All from Aileen. There were text messages from her as well. Caitlin didn't open them. She also saw she had two messages from Grace.

> Hi Cat. Y R U late? Ur Gran?

> Cat where r u? Police & a wman in skwl 4U Pse txt so I knw ur ok x 😟😟😟

She'd been gone less than a day and now everyone knew about it. Her phone gave a beep: Battery Low.

Caitlin shook her head. She'd maybe not miss her phone if all she read on it were texts that upset her. How could she let Grace know she was fine? If she did, would the police be ringing and quizzing her best friend?

'Right wee man, let's go.'

Holding the cub with both arms around his tummy, she stepped out and clambered up some steps, right next to their hut. At another set, she helped the cub climb them himself. At the top, gulls and oystercatchers scattered out of the way.

Although not very high, Caitlin could see all around the island. The wind and wet rushed in, pushing her back slightly. She picked Forth up and, with arms outstretched, turned full circle so the young bear could see it all.

'This is all ours, pal,' said Caitlin, who was having to talk above the gusts to make herself heard. 'No one else here to bother us. No one else here to tell us what to do. No more school, no more being sent to homes and families that aren't ours. Just me and you. All the family we could need. Until Gran gets better and then we'll go back to the flat and we'll tell her our story.'

Forth didn't say anything.

'Pretty good, eh pal?' said Caitlin.

'It's still cold. Maybe we could get a den that's out of the wind?' said Forth.

The young girl smiled. She looked into the young bear's eyes. 'It's not going to be easy. It's not meant to be. It's just us two, but that's got to be good, isn't it? Just us and ... all this.'

'Does that mean we can hunt?'

'Sure does.'

'For seals?'

'Well, we could try I suppose. I'm not sure how, mind.'

'I'm going to get the biggest one and then we won't need to eat for a few weeks!'

'You're on your own there, pal.'

In the dark, with the wind and rain, a ten-year-old girl helped a polar bear cub down to the shore. Maybe they would see seals or at least some signs of them. So when they couldn't they explored other parts where they might fish, tried other buildings to shelter in or the best places to have a fire. At one point they pretended to visit a neighbour for tea. The pair explored from one end of the island to the other, not bothered by the cold, wet and windy weather.

'How about we see if you and me can walk on that jetty?' said Caitlin.

When they got there, Caitlin noticed how old and rotten some of the planks were. What she didn't want right now was to injure herself. And there, down below them, was Midge but on her side. The seaweed camouflage had gone, and her white hull moved with the strong waves.

'Midge!' cried Caitlin. Grabbing Forth, she carefully clambered down the rugged slope. She was halfway down when the sudden loud blast of a foghorn made her stop. Cowering to the ground, she tried to position herself behind a large boulder.

'What's wrong?' asked Forth.

'It's a big navy boat.'

'A navy boat? What's a …'

'Shush!'

Caitlin raised her head very slightly to see the vessel plough past the top of the island. On it, bright lights cast shadows over its decks where a few people in uniform stood on watch.

'A big navy boat, full of navy people, who will all have their binoculars and radios and goodness knows what else.'

'I thought we were free?' replied Forth.

'Aye, but if we are spotted they won't see it like that. They'll say I'm too young or something.'

'Why? Can you only be free when you're old?'

'Perhaps when I'm eighteen or twenty-one. Maybe then they'll say it's OK to be free. We'll show them though, eh pal?'

'Yes. Especially when they know we can hunt for fat

seals, build fires and maybe make our own dens?'

Caitlin smiled and stroked Forth on his head. She cautiously stood up and with the large boat now heading further down the Firth of Forth, she carried on towards her beloved dinghy.

'Midge! What's happened?' said Caitlin. The dinghy was rubbing against rocks now visible due to the low tide. Her finger followed a crack caused by the boat continually striking the sharp shoreline. She shook her head and sighed. How would she get back to the mainland now?

'Mmm. Maybe we can quickly sail back across before she fills with water, pal. Then we'll have to borrow another boat.'

Forth didn't say anything.

Her phone beeped. Another message. Aileen. Then the phone went dead.

'Matches, blankets, sleeping bag, another dinghy and ...' The noise of another boat's engine, not far from where they were, halted her words. It was getting louder. She picked up

Forth and hid behind one of the jetty's posts.

'What's wrong now?' asked Forth.

'It's a RIB. And it's close,' Caitlin hissed back.

'A RIB?'

'A rigid inflatable boat.'

The noise of the engine continued to grow until it was suddenly silenced. Caitlin peered from behind the dark, damp wood to see Alan, in his waterproofs, knee-deep in water, now pulling his boat behind him. In his other hand was a flashlight to inspect Midge.

Only feet from Caitlin and Forth, Alan lashed his boat to a small wooden pole in the shallow water.

'Caitlin McGill? Come out from behind that post, lady.'

-23-

In no time at all, from the RIB Caitlin could see the lights were on at the clubhouse. Walking down the launch-way was Aileen, one hand in her pocket, the other trying to keep her hair out of her face.

'Is that Miss Young?' asked Alan.

Caitlin nodded.

'Wouldn't want to be in your shoes, lady.'

'She doesn't understand. No one does.' She pulled Forth out of his bag and held him tightly under her arms.

'Aye well,' said Alan, 'all those who care for you want to know is that you're safe and well. That takes priority. If you start running away, folk will only worry and that's not good. Why don't you talk to someone, rather than scaring everyone half to death?'

Caitlin stood silent. What was the point in arguing?

How could Alan or any adult know what it was like to be told, not asked, to live with someone who wasn't family? And that this was how it could be for the rest of her childhood.

Alan looked at a slightly submerged Midge, which followed obediently by rope in the RIB's wake. 'Caitlin, you're a good wee sailor. You've skills. You can read the wind so well. It'd be a shame not to reach your potential.'

Caitlin remained quiet, her eyes fixed on the shore.

Alan continued. 'I'm just saying that it might be a way to escape for you, something to focus on.'

Alan's words rang true. Caitlin knew how free she felt on the water. And for the very short time she was on Inchgarvie, she felt free. Free to not think about what was going to happen next in her life. To be her own family, just her and her furry best friend.

Yet as they approached the slipway, Michael's words came into her head: *then again, I ask you, who is free?*

She stepped out of the boat and walked towards the clubhouse.

'Miss Young?' asked Alan, as he tied up.

'Hi, yes. Aileen Young and you must be Alan Brown. Sorry about this.'

'Nae problem. Just a good job she tripped an alarm off, or I'd be none the wiser. And then with Midge missing and your phone call, I just put two and two together.'

'Thanks, Alan. Your help is appreciated.'

'Do the other services know?' asked Alan.

'Yes. I let them know as soon as you rang.'

'What's going to happen now?' and Alan nodded towards Caitlin who stood at Aileen's car.

'Not a great deal, to be honest. I've got her somewhere more permanent. I'm hoping then she'll settle down. Anyway, listen, thanks again for all you've done.'

'Nae bother,' and Alan passed her Caitlin's bags.

In the car, before she turned the ignition on, Aileen looked at Caitlin who, with Forth on her lap, stared out of the window.

'There's a piece of paper in the back. It's for you.'

Caitlin turned to pick it up. On it, was a drawing of a girl who was holding an animal under her arm. Underneath it read:

<u>Urgent - Please find Caitlin McGill</u>

Any information about Caitlin (and her polar bear Forth) – please contact Caitlin's school on this number – 0131 750991

Thank you.

From Grace Calder

'She wanted me to photocopy these and post them around Queensferry.'

Caitlin was quiet. She kept looking at the picture and reading the text. She put it back on the seat.

'So, have you got anything to say, lady?'

Caitlin said nothing but returned to stroking Forth.

'What? Not even an apology?' Aileen waited for an

answer. Caitlin continued stoking the cub.

'And that was just Grace,' said Aileen. 'Do you think your gran would be happy about it? She thinks you're on a school trip. We said that so as not to worry her when you didn't show up for visiting.'

Caitlin turned to face Aileen. 'Why did you have to tell her I was away at all?'

'Because the hospital was the first place we looked. And with how your gran has been, we didn't want to confuse and upset her.'

Caitlin shook her head and drew Forth closer.

'All of us are trying to do the best for you, Caitlin. It may not be perfect, and it may not be where you want to be, but right now this is all we can do. For your part, you just have to go with it, OK? You keep running away and they'll put you into more secure premises. And believe me, that's less than ideal.'

'You don't understand,' said Caitlin, her voice quiet and muffled as she pressed her face into Forth's tummy.

'Oh, I understand. I understand you put yourself well and truly in danger and that you were doing it all for yourself, not caring what others think, least of all your own gran.'

Aileen paused. Tears were falling steadily down the girl's cheeks.

'No, you don't understand,' Caitlin sobbed. 'I just want it to be how it was, before…before all this…this change and knowing I'll be living in someone else's houses and not mine and Gran not being there when I get home…and not having anyone who cares for me, really cares…like a mum or a dad.' Caitlin cried so much at times she had to get a breath.

Aileen sighed. 'Look, Caitlin. I've done this many times before. And in just about every case I've dealt with, it's had a good ending, OK?'

Caitlin buried her face into the cub again.

'Just promise me you won't run away again.'

'OK, if you promise me, I can live with Gran again,' came the young girl's muffled reply.

'I can't do that, Caitlin. Listen…,' Aileen hesitated.

'Your gran moved into her new home today. It all happened very quick.'

Now sitting up, from out of her window, the young girl noticed the length of the Forth shining in the moonlight. Her face was wet with silent tears. 'When can I see her?'

'Well as soon as we get you sorted out at your new temporary foster carers.'

'What?' snapped Caitlin as she turned to look at Aileen.

'Sorry, a lot of change I know, but I need to take you to your new foster home.'

Caitlin shook her head.

'Mrs Paton's husband is quite poorly and is going to need to go into hospital. So I'm going to take you to Mrs Johnstone's. She's lovely and has a lot of experience.'

'Great. Another home. More people I don't know.'

-24-

Aileen knocked on the black door. Caitlin looked around. This was a part of Edinburgh that she didn't know. Cars and taxis, their headlights on, rattled over the cobbled road. Opposite, fenced and floodlit, was a small park.

The door was opened by a lady older than Caitlin expected.

'Well hello there, Aileen,'

'Hi, Annie. Thanks for doing this at this time of day.'

'And you must be Caitlin? How are you?' asked Mrs Johnstone.

'Fine thank you.'

'Well come in, come in.'

In a tall room, a small dog leapt off a chair and with its tail wagging, started sniffing at Caitlin's feet.

'This is Billy, as in Silly-Billy. He's a bit daft but very friendly.'

Caitlin crouched down to stroke him. 'Hello, Billy.' The dog eagerly licked her face then sniffed at her rucksack with Forth in it. Billy barked then crouched back, cocking his head to one side as he looked at the cub.

'Oh, and who's your friend there?' asked Mrs Johnstone.

'Forth. He's a polar bear cub.'

'Well, I never. Seems like Billy's taken a liking to him. That's what he does when he wants to play.'

Billy yapped again, tongue out, still looking at Forth. Caitlin smiled.

'Right, let's get a pot of tea,' said Mrs Johnstone. 'Juice Caitlin or is it Cat?'

'I don't mind, either and tea is fine, thank you.'

Billy ran after Mrs Johnstone as Aileen sat herself down and Caitlin took Forth out of her bag.

'Well?' asked Aileen.

Caitlin nodded. 'Yeah, she's nice.'

'Good. Mrs Johnstone, Annie, has been fostering for a long time. She's lovely.'

She nodded again. 'Thanks.'

'Maybe you'll stay here then?'

'Maybe,' said Caitlin, smiling.

'Don't even joke about it, lady,' said Aileen. 'This is only temporary. Until I find a more permanent place, this will have to suffice.'

'What about school?'

'I've arranged a taxi for you again. Maybe a slightly earlier start but at least then you'll still see your friends.'

'OK,' and she placed Forth on her knees.

Moments later Billy came in, just in front of Mrs Johnstone who carried a tray. The dog jumped up next to Caitlin and began to lick Forth who didn't seem to mind.

Aileen talked to Mrs Johnstone about Caitlin. The ten-year-old added bits to her story but she was more content to stroke both Billy, who was now lying next to her, and Forth. She'd heard her own story many times now.

'How about you take Billy a wee walk in the bit of park out there, before his bedtime, while I get a chat with Aileen, OK?'

'OK.' Caitlin quickly sipped at her tea, put Forth back in his rucksack and took a lead from Mrs Johnstone. 'See the gate, it's at the top there,' said Mrs Johnstone pointing out of the window. 'And here's the key.'

'A key?'

'Yes, all the residents have one.'

Inside the small park, Billy busied himself in the bushes and ran around groups of trees.

'Billy's very friendly Forth, eh?' remarked Caitlin.

'His breath was rotten.'

'Still, he does like you.'

'I suppose. He's not going to be sleeping with us, is he?'

'Ha! I don't think so, pal, but he seems cute, mind.'

'Cute? But he can't build a den, can he?'

'Jealous, pal?'

'Jealous?'

'Never mind. Mrs Johnstone seems nice.'

'She does. Is she our new gran?'

'Kind of. And kind of not. There's only one gran. And however nice she is, it's not the flat. It's not *our* home.'

'So, what do we do?'

'Well, we'll wait until Gran gets better, I suppose. Then maybe I can look after her, along with the carers back at the flat. She might get all her memory back and that. So, it'll be just like before. Just like it should be.'

'Our own den again. And our own family?'

'Exactly, pal.'

A little while later, Caitlin and her two furry friends

arrived back at Mrs Johnstone's to see Aileen get in her car and go. She waved out of her window and sped away.

'Enjoyed that? Billy seems very happy with himself.'

'Yes, thanks. He did his toilet.'

'Forth or Billy?' said Mrs Johnstone, laughing.

'Oh, erm, Billy sorry,' said Caitlin, also laughing.

'Right young lady, shower and a glass of milk? I was thinking we should go see your gran tomorrow, don't you think?'

'Aye, definitely,' agreed Caitlin, as she stepped inside. 'I don't know the last time I didn't see her for more than a couple of days.'

'You've no school until you've had a few days here. So, we'll go straight after breakfast.'

Caitlin smiled.

'Oh, and maybe you can tell me about your furry friend before you go to bed?'

'Sure,' and she ran upstairs to look at her new bedroom.

-25-

Forth could see the bear's large incisors, could smell its hot, rank breath. He pushed. Nothing. The adolescent bear nosed in at him then roared. Being so close it stung Forth's infant ears. It inched back to give itself room for one fatal bite, all it needed to despatch the cub.

From out of nowhere, Forth's mother, up on her hind legs, swiped at the young adult bear's back. It gave an agonising yelp.

Forth looked up at his parent who fended away the badly hurt and enraged bear. The cub noticed marks on his mother: where she was pristine white, she was now flecked with red, more so on her chest and neck.

The younger bear's stamina and strength, for all its injuries, were exhausting the mother who was not long from her lengthy fasting in the birthing den. She lunged out and *hit the bear hard on its jaw. The bear lost its balance and clumsily staggered against the carcass where Forth lay, still trapped. The bulk of the dazed bear knocked and nudged against the heavy, bloodied remains. The weight eased slightly on the cub's back. Quickly squeezing out, Forth moved away from the ensuing fight.*

The other two bears, previously unconcerned with the conflict, now rounded up on the female.

As she fought the first bear, Forth, scared and unsure as to what to do, let out a growl followed by a sorrowful cry. The cub's alarms aroused his parent's instincts: a need to nurse and protect her offspring. The mother looked towards him. In that instant, one of the pair rose and dealt her a severe blow to her head. She staggered, and as she fell, she looked towards Forth. The pair were on her in a flash.

Forth froze. He cried out in the hope of some sort of reply. One of the attacking bears swung round and snarled in the direction of the cub, who gave another cry. Still no answer. Angered by the cub's persistence, the bear started walking heavily towards him.

Forth turned and ran.

The Arctic fox, not that far ahead, sat as if he'd been watching and waiting. As Forth approached, the fox got up and also ran. Forth looked back. There was no sign of the wounded bear. And there was no sign of his mother.

Ahead, Forth noticed that the fox had stopped again. Yet as soon as the cub drew closer it continued to run.

Forth couldn't be sure, but did the fox want him to follow? Was this animal something he could trust, something that would keep him safe? Right at this moment, the cub didn't have any other choice. So, he ran behind the fox who was now moving at a more sedate pace.

Very soon the ground underneath Forth changed. It grew harder. Where once there were inches of continuous snow, the land was now covered with cracks and fissures. Some were big enough for the dark water of the sea to seep through.

The fox nimbly jumped over the gaps, the bear cub following in the paw prints of his leader. Unnervingly, the gaps differed in size and the fox's trail avoided some of the larger cracks.

The land was changing again. Forth could smell it. There was now as much sea as there was ice. Some of the larger pieces of drift-ice carried snow, banked and sheer sided. The fox chose to ignore these, sticking to the smaller pieces and often springing across to navigate the larger splits.

As Forth followed, he paused to get his breath. Up ahead he could see three or four dark objects laying on a larger piece of the floe. Their dark bodies shone and glinted in the bright sun. The fox was sniffing in their direction. Unable to make out their definite shape, Forth noticed their movement. They simply slipped into the water and disappeared.

Was this why the fox wanted Forth to follow him? Was he trying to tell him something by leading him here?

Forth was tired and he lay down, keeping an eye on the other mammal who was steadily making some distance on the cub. The young bear only wanted to rest a short while, just to summon up enough energy to carry on. How much further were they to travel? How much longer of the day would this take?

Forth stood to carry on. The shifting current, the slight breeze and now the tide were moving the floe, not speedily but enough that the ice he was on, shifted. The gap had now widened.

Forth hesitated to cross. Could his small stature make the crossing? He stepped back. He could still see the fox, some way ahead now. He had to try, or he would be alone once again in this unforgiving and hostile place.

He ran and jumped. His front legs met the other piece of raft ice, but his rear did not. Levering himself up with fur wet from the sea, he was slippery and couldn't get any purchase to struggle on to the safety of the ice. He waited for a moment, the water cool beneath him, his front legs rigid so *he could hang on.*

Maybe he could let himself go, drop into the water, turn back and try again? To swim was a skill he wasn't sure about, a skill he'd not been able to copy in the short time he was with his mother. Forth was once again having to think for himself, having to make decisions with no instruction or support.

The ice was still moving as he held on. He felt uneasy. And he looked vulnerable.

Forth weighed up his best option: swim or try to haul himself up one more time? He was about to try and pull up again when out on the horizon he spotted a great grey shape. Forth could tell it was large. Extremely large. What could it be? More danger?

Forth tried again, but once more his frantic scrambling failed to bring him out of the water. He'd have to swim. He turned his head to see where he could get to. As he did the gentle sound of breaking water followed by the rasp of blowing air, came from his right-hand side. He turned to see the outline of an object that broke the water and, behind it, a smaller identically shaped one. Forth could see their shadowy black and white bodies just beneath the surface.

The giant grey object was now coming directly towards him. Forth watched how large sheets of ice broke and moved out of its way where it pushed through with its large nose. What was it?

A rasp of air came again, only this time it came from behind the section of ice Forth was desperately holding. The monochrome shadows had returned. Could they feel Forth's struggles vibrating through the water? Did they recognise how defenceless he was right now? Forth felt anxious, a feeling of impending danger. The outlines under the dark, calm water, circled him now.

The huge, grey beast was now so close, Forth could hear the deep sound of its guts churning and rumbling. From the creature's back came a thin wisp of black mist that Forth could taste as he sniffed the air. It wasn't a taste he liked. It was acrid and clung to his throat. The beast was suddenly silent, and it slowed, still gliding towards the small bear, ice buckling at its front, the cracking noise sharp and piercing.

The cub felt something touch him below the water on the back of his legs. The sudden shock made him find an inner strength and in one movement he was lying on his stomach, out of the water and on the ice. He noticed the smaller finned body turn away. Had it just been nosing him out of curiosity? The dark shapes, the white of their flanks quite clear below the surface, headed away. Now the grey hulk, blocking out the light, loomed over the cub's sprawling body.

There was a pause, a stillness. Forth could hear his heartbeat. All around him were threats and menace. What was he to do?

The young bear turned his head ever so slightly to see where the next danger was going to come from. A large fin was cutting through the icy water. It was heading straight for him. He hadn't noticed its black and white body turning back, regardless of the colossal, grey animal close by.

Only inches from the water, if the whale breached the

ice, Forth could easily be grabbed and dragged into the deep.

He dug his claws into the ice. A rasping sound told him how

close the whale was now. Then something fell on him.

-26-

The following day, inside the entrance of the home, Mrs Johnstone signed Caitlin and herself in, then asked where Mrs McGill was. Once told, the ten-year-old made straight for her gran's room and found her in a large armchair, still in her nightgown. A smile grew on the elderly lady's face as she raised her head from a magazine.

'Hi Gran,' said her granddaughter as she kissed her on the forehead, then lay Forth on the unmade bed. 'How's you? Taking your pills? Eating well? And how are you sleeping? It'll be going like a fair round here on a night, I expect?'

'Sorry, dear? What was that?'

'Sleep. Are you sleeping OK?'

'Och, fine, just fine. Now nurse, could you tell me when my husband is coming? I need him to pay for the tea delivery.'

Caitlin looked around her. 'Gran?'

'Aye, you're a cheeky one all right. Gran? I'm no' your gran lassie! I'm no' even a mother! Gran indeed!'

'Gran, it's Caitlin.'

'The tea will need paid for, sure it will. Anyway, thanks now.'

'Gran, it's Caitlin,' and she lay her hand on her gran's arm. 'What's wrong? Is this a game?' and she gently shook her grandmother.

'Look, lady,' and Gran gave her a fierce look. 'Take your bloody hand off me or I'll have the polis on you, so I will, do you hear me? Now, scoot!'

Caitlin had never seen her gran like this. She couldn't even remember when she last shouted at her. Blinking back tears, she grabbed Forth from the bed, and keeping his heavy body close, she ran out of the room, bumping into Mrs Johnstone as she did so.

'What on earth is the matter?' she said, as she steadied herself after Caitlin collided with her.

Not answering, the young girl ran all the way back to the car, leant her back against the door and sank to the ground.

What was wrong with Gran? Why wasn't she acknowledging who she was? Was she on new pills? Had she been away too long? Two days and now the person that she had known all her life had forgotten about her only granddaughter. Was this how it was going to be? The person who brought her up, who she came home to, who was there when she woke, watched TV with on an evening, and finally kissed her goodnight, was she now slipping out of her life?

Tears came easily. Forth nudged into his upset friend, as she held onto him, her face hidden in the fur of his tummy. There was a tap on her shoulder.

Caitlin looked up. Crouched beside her was a man in a white short-sleeved top like that of a nurse. Mrs Johnstone was with him.

'Hi, I'm Matthew. I think you're upset about seeing your gran this morning, am I right?'

Caitlin shrugged.

'I'd like to talk to you about your gran if that's OK? About what's happening to her. Let's say we do that inside though.' Matthew took her hand and lead her back, Mrs Johnstone following.

In a small room, Matthew opened a cupboard.

'Juice? Biscuit?'

'Yes please,' sniffed Caitlin.

'Tea, Mrs…?'

'Johnstone. No, I'm fine thanks.'

'And what does your pal eat,' and Matthew nodded at Forth, who was behind Caitlin's folded arms.

'He's fine.'

'Here, have a chair and there you go, juice and a biscuit. Caitlin, your gran has got something going wrong with her. This has been confirmed with the results we got from her appointment at the memory clinic. You went with her?'

She nodded.

'So, your gran is getting old and the older you get, you start to lose more and more cells from your brain. These don't get replaced which can often lead to a thing called dementia. Your gran's memory and how she is begins to change.'

'So, she'll never know who I am?' said Caitlin.

'No, not necessarily. They'll be days when she knows exactly who you are. Then there will be days when she doesn't, like today for instance.'

'So, she'll get better? Her tablets will fix her brain, won't they?'

Matthew sighed. 'I have to be honest with you so that you don't get upset any other times you visit. The fact is your gran won't get better.

With tears rolling down her cheeks again, Caitlin spoke slowly, 'so she's going to get worse?'

Matthew nodded his head. 'Yes. We can help her, and we can give her medicines that might slow the process down a bit. Sadly, there is still no cure. I'm being cruel to be kind to you. And now you know the truth there'll be no more nasty shocks like this morning, I hope. Och, there'll be sad times but there'll be good times as well. It's going to be hard, Caitlin.'

The young girl didn't know what to say.

'You're going to be so important to your gran though,' continued Matthew.

'I am? How?'

'You're family and looking through Mrs McGill's notes, you're the only family she's got. A known face in this new world of different ones is going to be extremely important to your gran.'

Caitlin nodded. She understood that.

'When you're visiting just be you, obviously, but top tip here: when your gran starts talking to you like you're not her granddaughter, just go along with it, OK? Saves her getting even more confused.'

'Like today? She thought I was a nurse.'

'Right, so you just pretend to be a nurse asking her how she is and that, like you would anyway. No giving her any jags though?' smiled Matthew.

'OK,' and Caitlin gave a quick smile.

'Great. You all good now?'

She nodded.

'Listen, how about you go and pop in to see your gran now? See how you get on after our wee talk here?'

'You alright with that?' asked Mrs Johnstone.

Caitlin got up holding Forth, and without saying a word, she walked quickly back down the corridor to her gran's room.

At the door, she hesitated before stepping inside. There was her gran, this time in her bed, opening her eyes at the sound of the door.

'Och, my wee angel, so glad you're here, darling. And you've brought your wee dug. How was your holiday?'

Caitlin sighed with relief and jumped on the bed, clutching Forth and lay so she could rest her head on the grey-haired lady's shoulder.

'It was OK. Just wished you'd been there, pal.'

'Och, I'd only slow you down. So, what do you know then?'

'Cup of tea first Gran, eh?'

'Aye, that'd be good '

Caitlin got back up leaving Forth on the bed.

'Has your wee dug grown?' Gran said.

'Maybe,' and she laughed.

Outside Mrs Johnstone was stood with Matthew.

'Well?' asked Matthew.

'All good. She's wanting a cup of tea.'

'Excellent. I'll go get it.'

Caitlin smiled at Mrs Johnstone. 'Thank you.'

'Thought you might need it all explained,' and she patted the girl's arm.

Returning to the room, Caitlin once again lay beside

her grandmother. And, grabbing hold of Forth, she told her how she'd gone on a school trip to an island but that it was bad weather and boring.

'Och,' said Gran, 'you didn't need to have gone with your school, wee hen. Your Grandpa could have taken you.'

Caitlin sighed and tucked in as close as she could to her grandparent, whose eyes were beginning to close, so she didn't see her granddaughter smiling and wiping her eyes.

-27-

Srry G. Didn't like 1st hme. I suck @ running away BTW 😔 now @ another foctor home!!!! 😔

Hi. Me wurid! Gld ur OK. Mist u. Y new hme???

Last fosterer ill & in hosp. Now further from SQfy

😔😔

Hows 4th?

Gud. He wants a family 2.

iii Runaway to Iceland! 😊

195

Iceland has 0 P bears!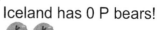

Zoo?!

No way!

There's that
park up North?!

Yip. Will c. I'd miss him
sooooooooo much!

Me 2!

!!LOL! xx

Byeee

-28-

During the night, Caitlin woke to the sound of talking and shouting outside. Was it going to be like this most nights? The flat back in South Queensferry wasn't the quietest with people moving about their rooms, but it was quieter outside than this. She turned over to try and get back to sleep. Now someone was knocking at the door. She sat up as she heard Mrs Johnstone go and answer it.

There was more talking at the door followed by someone, perhaps a girl, shouting and swearing.

Creeping across to peer through a slight gap in her bedroom door, Caitlin could only see Mrs Johnstone's back. The front door then shut and a man, who was holding a struggling teenage girl, could be seen at the foot of the stairs.

'Get off of me, you eejit!' and the teenager spun out of his hands.

'It's for your own safety, Amy, and that of Mrs

Johnstone here.'

'I'll report yous, you big lump ya,' said Amy.

'Whatever. Just get up to your room,' said the man.

'Same room as before, Amy, OK?' said Mrs Johnstone, calmly.

'And you can get stuffed as well, you b…'

'Enough Amy! Away up! Sorry, Annie, it's an emergency placement, OK? I was unlucky enough to be the on-duty tonight.'

'You're fine. I've seen it all before. Especially with that one. Shame.'

Amy, who Caitlin guessed, was about fifteen or sixteen, stomped as loudly as she could up the stairs. Still watching from behind the door, she was spotted.

'What yous looking at? What, scared of me? Well, you ought to be!' The teenage girl spat out her words.

Caitlin took a step out.

'Pah! Yous wanting a piece of me? Square go then, yer wee spuggie!'

The younger girl just stood there, holding herself and then without reply, stepped back into her bedroom and locked her door.

'Ha. Thought so,' and Amy went inside her room, slamming the door as she did so.

From her bed, Caitlin could hear the angry teenager knock stuff over in her room and grumble loudly to nobody but herself.

*

Up and dressed quite early, Caitlin made her way downstairs. In the kitchen, she placed Forth into a chair then switched the kettle on. She had set the table and was hunting for the cereal when her temporary foster parent came in.

'Och, you don't need to do that but thanks. Morning by the way.'

'Morning. I normally do jobs and that first thing anyway.'

'Right you are. That's very kind of you. Like our new guest?'

'Amy?'

'Aye, she's been here before, in fact, a couple of times now.'

'What happened?'

'Not sure. A full report will be sent through after an emergency meeting later today. No doubt she ran away.'

'Ran away? Ran away from where?'

'Och, I shouldn't say. Just don't mind her ways. It's all for show. I'll better get her up. Amy! Amy, you need to get up and get your breakfast! Caitlin's got it all ready for you.'

Caitlin had nearly finished her meal before Amy wearily entered the kitchen.

'Morning, Amy,' said Mrs Johnstone.

'Morning,' said Caitlin.

Amy didn't answer but scowled at them both then lay her head on the table.

'Do you want some juice?' asked Caitlin, about to pour her some.

'Aren't you a goody two shoes? No, I don't want juice,' said Amy, her head still on the table.

'Cat is just being nice, Miss Sinclair. No need to snap at her like that.'

Amy was silent. Mrs Johnstone went to answer a ringing phone.

'Annie said you've been here before?' said Caitlin.

'She's a witch. And what if I have? What's it to do with you, Spuggie?'

'Just asking.'

'Well don't.'

Amy sat up. 'So, what are you making me for my

breakfast?'

Caitlin shrugged.

'Porridge with jam. The bear wants honey,' and the teenager lay her head back down.

'He doesn't like honey and there are packets of porridge over there. I'm no' sure where the jam is mind,' said Caitlin between mouthfuls of toast.

'You're quite old enough to make your own, lady,' remarked Mrs Johnstone, coming back into the kitchen.

Amy looked furiously at Caitlin as she rose off her chair. She picked up a sachet of porridge and dumped it into a bowl. Putting it into a microwave, she pressed buttons until it lit up and turned on. Then she rested her head on the worktop next to the microwave.

'What about your milk?' asked Caitlin.

'What about it?' said Amy, and she went and grabbed Caitlin's sleeve and pressed her face so close that the ten-year-old could see the sleep still in her eyes.

'You need milk, you doughnut,' said the younger girl, calmly.

'To your room, Amy,' said Mrs Johnstone. The teenager still held Caitlin's shoulder. 'I mean now.'

Amy slowly released her grip. 'Good. I can get back in my scratcher and get some sleep,' and she sulked off upstairs.

A little while later, Caitlin surprised Mrs Johnstone by asking if she could take Amy's breakfast up to her room.

'Are you sure?'

She nodded. 'As my gran would say, she's all bark and nae bite. Besides, it'll be a peace offering maybe?'

'Well, OK, but be careful.'

Caitlin knocked on the bedroom door and without waiting for an answer she pushed it open.

'Your porridge.'

Amy was lying on her side, mobile in her hand. She ignored Caitlin as she placed the bowl by her bed.

'Get out,' said Amy quietly without looking up. Caitlin who was now sat on her bed didn't respond.

'I said, get out!'

'You can't read, can you? The porridge?'

'Get out! Unless you want me to batter yous?'

'You can't read too well. So you get angry that you can't. You get angry at people who make you read, like teachers or other adults, so then you get angrier and run off or run away or just scream and shout.'

Amy was quiet for a moment then went back to her phone.

'What are you, Sherlock Holmes' wife or something, Spuggie? Now get out.'

Back in her room, Caitlin wondered what she would do for the rest of the day. As she stared into her laptop, there was a knock on the door.

'Spuggie, Mrs Holmes, whatever, are you in there?'

'Sorry doll, no one in here by that name.'

'Away you wee bampot. Let us in.'

'Aye, I will do but not until you say Caitlin and say please.'

'What?'

'You heard.'

'Jeez oh! Can you no' just let me in?'

'Let me in what?'

'Please. Sakes!'

Caitlin took Forth off her knees and unlocked the door.

Amy, wrapped in her duvet, waddled over and onto the bed.

'I got this Cat-Flap.' She showed Caitlin her mobile phone. 'I can read some of the words but not all of it. She uses long words not like, you know, text words which I can read.'

'She?'

'My mum. She's a doctor. She knows loads of long

words. Think she puts them in a message just so I can't understand what she's on about.'

The long text was immediately read by Caitlin. She stopped at one point and hesitated. 'Erm, that word isn't a nice one.'

'Never mind, skip the bad words. What is the other stuff?'

The message was explaining to Amy that she wasn't welcome back to wherever this person lived due to her "foul and abusive mouth," and her "destruction of costly valuables and household appliances."

'I thought as much,' said Amy, and taking the mobile off Caitlin she threw it against the wall. Still intact, it landed harmlessly on the bed.

'Amy, me and Forth are going out. So you can stay in my room if you want.'

'And why would I do that, Spuggie?'

'It's up to you. Just saying. Maybe we'll get a chat when I'm back?'

'You're not bothered if I might like, nick stuff?'

'No, because I know you won't.'

Caitlin got her rucksack and helped Forth into it.

'A polar bear in Scotland, eh? How did you come by one of those?'

'Finders keepers.'

'Right enough, Spuggie. What's his name?'

'Forth.'

Amy smiled. 'Hi, Forth.'

'Hello, Amy. Is this your new home too?'

Amy smiled. 'Aye for a wee bit, pal. Cheers, Cat-a-log.' With that, she turned over and pulled the duvet over her head as Caitlin and Forth quietly went out.

-29-

It was Friday, and Caitlin arrived back at Mrs Johnstone's to find Aileen there as well.

'Hi there, young lady. I'm just about to go, actually. I was just delivering a bit of news.'

Caitlin, who had Billy running around her feet, put Forth, still in the rucksack, onto the sofa and sat down. She could tell by Aileen's tone that this was going to be serious.

She spoke quietly. 'It's Gran isn't it?'

'No, no, your gran is fine Caitlin,' replied Aileen. 'It's your mum.'

'My mum? What's happened?'

'Nothing bad, Cat,' reassured Mrs Johnstone.

'Annie's right. She's requested contact with a view of you going to live with her,' said Aileen.

Caitlin hesitated. In her tummy, a knot formed and started to tighten, yet in her head: excitement.

'Nothing is finalised here by any stretch of the imagination,' continued Aileen. 'We need a meeting and we need to see why the request and why now? I will be speaking with her support workers down In Manchester to find the best way to go forward with this.'

Caitlin noticed Annie rubbing the back of her neck. The knot was getting bigger. Family.

'Annie needs to be informed, Caitlin, as she is your primary carer right now, OK? So, I'll let her read the information and also all your other details.' Aileen nodded to a file on a small table. 'Right, I think that's me. Take care,' she stood up to go. Mrs Johnstone got up too and they both walked out.

Quick as a flash, Caitlin went and flipped open the file. Turning over a couple of pages she found the details she was after, photographed it with her phone then sat back down as soon as she heard the front door shut.

'So, what are you wanting to do this weekend, Cat?'

asked Mrs Johnstone as she came back into the room.

Caitlin shrugged. 'I'm not sure. I still don't know it that well around here, Mrs Johnstone, I mean Annie.'

'Well, we could get a bus. Maybe we could go into town for a while?'

'We?'

'Aye. I've done the risk assessment with Aileen.'

'Oh.'

'Sorry, but given your recent history, Caitlin. Besides, I can't let a temporarily fostered ten-year-old out and about in Edinburgh on her own now, can I?'

Caitlin didn't answer as she thought it over.

'I hope I don't bring your street cred down or whatever you call it,' smiled Mrs Johnstone. 'And we're good for cakes, aren't we Billy?'

Caitlin smiled. 'Is Amy coming as well then?' she asked.

'Well, I hope so as we can't go if she puts her foot down

and does her stubborn act.'

'Shall I go tell her?' said Caitlin.

'Aye, why not.'

Caitlin ran upstairs knowing there was a good chance, a really good chance, Amy would say yes.

-30-

Her knock was soft. 'Amy, it's Caitlin.' She spoke quietly into the crack at the edge of the door. 'See tomorrow, do you want to run away?'

There was no answer.

'Amy, it's…'

'Runaway?' said a bedraggled Amy, opening her door.

'Aye.'

'What do you know about running away, Cat-sick?'

'Well, I've done it before.'

'Jeez oh! Wee Spuggie the runaway!'

'So?'

'When?'

'Tomorrow. We're going to Edinburgh.'

'Right, nae problem.' And before Caitlin could say anything else, the door closed.

That night, Caitlin looked at her mobile phone. The picture she had taken was of her mother's address. Her phone gave her a street map of where she lived.

She couldn't wait to speak to her gran about it; that they could now be all back together. They'd move Gran down south to be with them. And sure, it wasn't Scotland and she'd miss her friends, but they'd all be together. All of them a family, together, with a polar bear cub as a pet.

Caitlin looked at Manchester, its history and its famous landmarks. After all, this was a city she was now going to be living and growing up in. She read some of the details to Forth who seemed quite interested.

'So, is it like we're running away again?' he asked.

'Shhh. Yes,' whispered Caitlin. 'Want us to get found out pal, eh?'

Whispering, Forth continued. 'Although this time we're going where there is someone, not nobody, and its someone we know?'

'Well yes, but it's another adventure. And this time, for longer.'

'Man-chester?'

'That's right. So, I can live with my mum. Then that will be a real home. Not this pretending type thing we're in right now.'

'But what about my mum and my family?'

'I've no' forgotten, OK? You are family, Forth. And once we're settled, we'll sort something out, so you can get time to be with other polar bears. Maybe there's a park or a zoo down there.'

'But I like Annie.'

'So do I, pal. She's nice but I can't ask her if I can go stay with my mum. She'll just say no. And so will everyone else. This way, if I'm already down there and happy, they'll have to say yes.'

Caitlin quietly squeezed a few things into her rucksack.

It could only be just a couple of t-shirts and pyjamas. For part of the day she was going to be with Mrs Johnstone, so carrying a big bag of clothes was something of a giveaway. Maybe she'd get new clothes with her mum?

She gave Forth a kiss on his head. Squeezing the cub tightly under her covers, she fell asleep with images of her holding her mother's hand in a shopping centre and then going to a new school or sitting on a sofa watching TV, her mum still holding her hand.

In the morning, Caitlin was putting Forth into the rucksack when she noticed someone watching her. Amy was at her door.

'Are you not taking anything?' asked Caitlin.

'Got everything right here,' and Amy pointed to her head.

'Ready when you are Mrs J,' said Amy as she and Caitlin came into the living room. Then putting on an American accent she added, 'raring to go around lovely old Edin-burg.'

Mrs Johnstone frowned. 'Really? Excellent. I'll just get Billy's lead.'

On the top deck of the bus, Caitlin sat with Amy whilst Mrs Johnstone and Billy could only manage to get a seat a few rows behind them.

On her mobile phone, Caitlin typed out a message to Amy, then silently showed it to her.

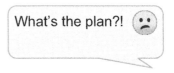

Amy just tapped her nose.

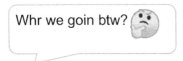

Stepping out into the hubbub of Edinburgh's Princess Street, Amy asked Mrs Johnstone if she could take Billy by the lead.

'OK Amy, thank you. Be careful with him now. He's a bit funny with all these people about.' Amy smiled and they walked in and out of the crowds.

At a zebra crossing, on the opposite side of the road, a large dog was leading an old man struggling to keep his pet close. Billy gave a growl followed by a bark.

'Billy!' snapped Mrs Johnstone.

'Perfect,' Amy muttered quietly. Only Caitlin heard and instantly had a notion of what Amy was about to do.

As they crossed over, Billy strained at the lead. Amy let go.

'Stop it Billy!' cried Mrs Johnstone.

'Now!' cried Amy and she began to sprint off, with Billy leaping about the larger dog who also broke free from his owner's grasp.

Caitlin looked at Amy then back at Mrs Johnstone who was trying, in vain, to get Billy's lead. The two dogs were leaping about each other, without taking any notice of their owners.

'Caitlin, let's go!'

Caitlin hesitated. She looked once more at Mrs Johnstone whose focus was on her dog.

'Caitlin, now!'

She was still frozen to the spot as Mrs Johnstone got a hold of the lead.

'Now!'

She started to run. In only a matter of moments, the pair of them were running down steps that led into the mouth of Waverley Station. Amy panting, hands on her legs, looked up at the big board.

'Platform eleven..., there! Look! Come on.'

'Tickets?' shouted Caitlin.

'It's fine, come on!' said Amy and Caitlin followed.

Still panting, Amy began a fake cry. 'Mum! Mum! Don't go without us! Mum!'

'You alright?' asked an official-looking man at the barrier.

'She's only got on the train without us two! I know we were in the shops too long and she was getting like mega-crabbit and that. So now she's taken all our bags and all our food and all the tickets! Mum, come back, please! Mum!'

'Och, look, you're fine,' said the man, 'calm yourself, the trains not due to leave for another ten minutes, here,' and he opened the barrier for them both. 'Now can you remember the carriage number you're on?'

'Erm…yeah, that one!' and Amy ran towards the train with Caitlin in hot pursuit.

Seated, and both still panting, the girls laughed with Amy giving Caitlin a high-five.

'See Cat-a-pult, a master at work.'

Caitlin laughed, and she was still smiling as the train pulled away. She sat Forth on the small table, so he could see outside. She was still thinking about Mrs Johnstone. 'What will Annie do now?'

'Oh, probably ring the polis, the social services and the zoo!'

'The zoo?'

'Yeah – see if they have space for a polar bear. And us two eejits.'

Caitlin laughed but she still had mixed feelings about leaving Mrs Johnstone like that. 'And what if we get caught?'

'Probably just a more secure place.'

'Prison?'

'Ha. No, but pretty much like one. They're all prisons to me. So, who's at Manchester then Cat-a-list?'

'My mum.'

'Nice one.'

'I hope so.'

'What do you mean?'

'Well, she left me when I was three. I just hope we get on and that.'

'Och, she's your mum. They'll be days when you will and days when you won't.'

Caitlin liked that. She looked out of the window. 'Just like a proper home then?'

'Maybe,' said Amy. 'Mine would kick me out as soon as she set eyes on me.'

'Really? What about your dad?'

'No thank you,' and Amy started biting her fingernails. Caitlin decided to change the subject.

'So, where are you aiming for?'

'Anywhere and…everywhere.'

'Ha-ha! Nut-job!'

'Tickets please, girls.' A uniformed lady held her hand out.

'Sorry hen, but mum has got them all. She's away to

the loo.'

'Right, well I'll just wait here then, *hen*,' said the lady, eyebrows raised.

'It's just she may be a wee while. She's got, you know, tummy stuff?'

The lady looked at Amy blankly.

'You know,' said Amy, and she leaned over to whisper something to the woman.

'Right, well, I see. I'll be back mind, OK?' and with that, the lady went further down the train.

'See?' said Amy.

'Master at work, alright,' smiled Caitlin. She grabbed hold of Forth who was gazing at all the buildings flashing by.

'It's like we're going somewhere, but we're just still and everything else is rushing past us,' said Forth as he stared out of the window.

'Shh!' said Caitlin, looking around. A man, walking down the aisle, holding a baby, smiled at her.

Amy laughed, 'And I'm the nut job!' and she sunk into her seat. 'So, where did you get your wee furry friend from?'

Caitlin told her the story of when she first met her polar bear cub friend, tangled amongst a submerged tree's branches in the Firth of Forth.

'Well, how did he get to be here? I mean all the way from Lapland or wherever?'

So Caitlin explained.

-31-

'Milo! Now! Further Over! Quick, Orcas!'

'OK, OK. I'm doing it, Luka!'

'Quickly! Quickly! Bystrei! Bystrei!'

The net covered a struggling Forth. Yet the more he grappled the more he became entwined. One of his back paws was entangled and then a front paw. He bit the mesh, but its tough, sinewy feel wouldn't give to the young bear's fine teeth even with his firmest bite.

A splash of water. A rasp of air. The snow-covered ice tipped violently towards where the whale had now breached. The orca's bulk tipped the ground more and more towards its large, pink mouth. Then the world changed.

Forth felt weightless as the whale shrunk in size and the view below him began to turn.

'That's it Milo, good, good. Easy now, easy! Good. Now down Milo, down!'

'Luka, I'm doing it, I'm doing it! Sheesh!'

The cub could see the whale, now swaying heavily from side to side, as it moved backwards and slipped into the water.

'Slowly, Milo. Over yes? More. More. Now drop it behind this container. We don't want Cardo seeing it, yes?'

Forth tried to look at where the noise was coming from. A couple of strange animals on two legs stared at the cub as the world came up to meet him. One of these animals crouched down close by. Forth struggled and let out a pathetic cry.

The animal, which was now on its knees, began to slowly take the net off the cub.

'Easy now little man. Milo, the bucket.'

Milo handed a bucket to Luka.

'Here, little man, yesterday's catch: fresh beluga. Nice, no?'

Forth sniffed at the piece of blubber. Then he licked it and carried on just licking it. It tasted good. His stomach told him to eat some.

'There you go. See, Milo?'

'What? A bear on a boat? Sheesh!'

'Ah, but Milo, not any sort of bear. A white bear. And, my friend, not only that, a bear cub!'

Milo raised his shoulders. 'So?'

'And all he says is, "so." So! Think, Milo. Who would not want a sweet, small bear like this one, eh? A real live toy. One that eats and drinks?'

Milo shrugged.

'A child, Milo, a child, eh?'

'I guess.'

'And what child do you know who would be so thankful for such a gift?'

Milo frowned. Then his face changed into a bright smile. 'Alyana!'

'Exactly!' said Luka, and he stood and patted Milo on his shoulder. 'Our boss's daughter, right? And surely such an oligarch would smile favourably on a crew who brings back a present for his daughter, eh? And a crew that thinks about their bosses' daughter?'

'Holidays?'

'What? Holidays? Holidays! Money, Milo. Den'gi! Den'gi! Much money, eh? Big bonus, no?'

'I get it Luka, but where do we put it? If Cardo finds it…sheesh!'

'That lazy, fat oaf couldn't find his backside in a storm! A container. The furthest away.'

'And feeding it for the next few weeks?'

'Simzar! Kai! Here! Bystrei! Bystrei!'

Two other men appeared from a metal stairway. They both frowned when they saw Forth.

'What's the matter?' said Luka, 'never seen a white bear cub, eh? Ha! Possibly not in your countries, eh?' He fished a piece of cord out of his pocket. 'Now, easy little bear, easy.'

Forth was too busy chewing the food to notice until Luka pulled the looped cord tight. The cub shook his head strongly, the blubber still in its mouth.

'There, there, easy now. Simzar, here,' and Luka placed a scrap of blubber into Simzar's hand. 'The brown container, first hold, port side, eh? Now, go.'

Simzar stood his ground.

'Look, den'gi, den'gi! eh?' and Luka rubbed his fingers together as if holding bank notes.

Simzar, without saying a word, took hold of the cord. Forth pulled against it, his strength taking Simzar by surprise. He placed the whale fat in front of Forth's nose. The cub stopped pulling and sniffed at the scrap and attempted to eat it. Simzar lifted up the whale fat and taunted the young polar bear with it. Forth moved as Simzar lead him away.

'Milo, you go with Simzar, yes? And Simzar,' said Luka, and Simzar had to stop again. 'If it dies...' he used his hand, pretending to cut his neck, then pointed to Simzar who just shook his head as Luka laughed. 'Right, I tell Cardo, no whales here, yes?' and he walked away.

Milo led the way down into the first of the ship's vast holds. At one point, Simzar had to lift and hold the cub while they negotiated the ship's many sets of ladders and steps.

'Ha, the bear is already a pet, look how he lets you hold him,' said Milo observing the cub who continued to look for the scraps of blubber in Simzar's clenched fist.

As they approached the container, Simzar opened up his hand as Forth gratefully licked it and began to eat the remaining fatty morsel. Milo unlocked the heavy container doors and Simzar lead Forth inside its dark metallic space.

Simzar quickly walked out as Milo shut the container doors.

Darkness. The only sound was that of the beast's guts churning below him, a slight vibration in the ground. Forth could make out a faint light at the edge of the door. He moved about warily, not knowing what was in front or behind him. Was this a den? The darkness and cold were a reminder of his.

In the gloom, he occasionally stretched out a front paw to locate where the edges of this place were. Finding it, he sat and began scratching at the solid wall that was as hard as pack ice. It didn't give as Forth continued to scratch, his claws not making any impact apart from scuffing its surface. The cub sat and panted with the effort. He let out a small cry. Where was he? What was this? What were those strange creatures that made noises he'd never heard before yet gave him food? And more than anything else, he wanted to know where his mother was. He wanted her guidance, her security, *just the warmth and feel of her company.*

-32-

Caitlin woke up to Amy nudging her. 'This is me, Cat-a-ract,' and she offered Caitlin a high five.

'Where are we?'

'Carlisle. My get off.'

'Carlisle? Why?'

'Because… I can,' and Amy winked.

Caitlin sat up, leaned over, and gave her a big hug. 'Take care, and thank you,' she said.

'Eek! Don't get all soppy on me now, Cat-a-pillar,' said Amy smiling. 'And bye to you, Forth.' And she gave the cub a quick rub on his head.

'Adios, amigos!' and with that, Amy jumped up and was suddenly outside waving, smiling then sticking her tongue out. The train nudged away as Caitlin, head turned right round, strained to watch. Amy was soon gone, running up some steps and away.

Caitlin felt sad for a moment. She'd only just got to know this mad, teenage ball of energy. Yet she was as worried as she was happy for her.

'Is she going so she can go get freedom?' asked Forth, from his friend's lap.

Caitlin smiled then looked to see if anyone was listening. Two girls sat opposite her, but one was asleep and the other had headphones on.

'Maybe, wee man,' she said quietly. 'I just hope she's OK.'

'Has she a den?'

'I don't know.'

'She'll survive though?'

'She will. It's hard in a city, all alone. In some ways it's nearly as tough as being in the North Pole. I'm sure she'll be OK.'

'Do you think we'll survive?'

'Aye, wee man. At least we've got a mother to go to.' And with that Caitlin hugged Forth tight and watched the countryside roll by.

*

At last, signs for Manchester drifted past Caitlin's window. Where there was once trees and fields, now buildings, tower blocks and roads filled with traffic formed the landscape. The ten-year-old looked at the photo of the letter she had. She typed the address into her phone. It was a forty-five-minute walk from the station.

In no time at all, after using Amy-like tactics to avoid showing a ticket at the barrier, she was out into the bustle of the big city.

'Right, pal, let's go.' Caitlin had butterflies in her stomach. She couldn't get across the many busy streets quick enough.

'What do you think your mother will say when she sees you?' asked Forth.

'I think, she'll grab hold of me and maybe cry a bit but then be happy.'

'Are you still mad at her for leaving you?'

'I don't really know. Maybe she had her reasons.'

'My mother would never leave me. Not until I was old enough, that is,' said Forth.

'It's different for a polar bear. By the way, do polar bears cry?'

'I don't know. Maybe their eyes would freeze up. I never did. I can cry out, like this, RRRRRRAAARRR!'

'Hey, you! Shh!' smiled Caitlin, as the bear's cry was lost in the noise of cars, double-decker buses and the odd tram racing by. The cry of a polar bear in Manchester city centre.

Once at the front door, Caitlin checked herself. Her heart was racing. She looked at her reflection in her phone and noticed her ginger hair, the freckles and her eyes. Would her mother recognise her ten-year-old daughter? Would Caitlin recognise her mother? Flattening down her top, she drew in a short breath.

Her finger hovered at the bell. What was going to happen? What if this was a mistake?

She is my mother. I'm her daughter. And this is us starting again. A new chapter. No, a new book.

'Are you not going into the den?' asked Forth.

'Just hang on a moment.' Caitlin shuffled Forth under her arm. She sighed. 'Here goes.' Pressing the bell, she could hear it ring somewhere deep inside. There was talking then the door opened.

-33-

'Yeah?'

Caitlin faltered. She wasn't expecting a man to answer.

'Hi, it's Caitlin. Is my mum, in?'

The man shook his head.

'Jeanie McGill?' said Caitlin.

The man stood quietly for a moment. 'Jeanie, there's someone here for you.'

'Who?' answered Caitlin's mother.

'Caitlin.'

'What? Caitlin? My Caitlin? What the…'

Her mother appeared as the man stepped back inside.

'Caitlin? Caitlin! Look at the size of you now! Oh my God! What on earth are you doing here, honey? Who sent you?

How did you get here?'

'Surprise mum!' and Caitlin gave her a big hug. Holding her parent's hands, she stood back to look at her.

This was her mum, slightly different from the photo she had of her, but nonetheless her mother. The long flowing hair of the photo was now shoulder length and red, lipstick-red in fact. She hadn't remembered how small her teeth were and how shrill her voice seemed. Yet stood, right in front of her, her mother.

Caitlin moved to hug her, to hold her parent again.

'But why are you here in Manchester, I mean?' said Jeanie McGill, holding her daughter by the shoulders. 'Who did you come with? Does anyone know you're here?'

'No, I'm on my own. I just thought... we could maybe... live together? You know, maybe start again. I'd heard about you wanting me to move down here to be with you.'

Jeanie glanced back inside, then speaking quietly, 'Aye, well right enough. News travels fast, eh?'

'Mum, I'm grown up now and do lots of stuff on my

own and that. So, I'd be able to help out, nae bother. Then we can maybe bring Gran down later, eh? So, it'd be you, me, Gran and my polar bear,' and she nodded to the cub. 'A family, all together.'

'But...well... erm...'

'Five minutes, Jeanie, we need to be there. I told them three o'clock, right on the button. Let's get a move on.'

'Can I come in?' asked Caitlin.

'Yes, yes. Erm...of course, but I need to go out darling. Come on in.'

'Oh. Right. I thought...'

'Jeanie! Three o'clock!'

'OK, OK. Come on through, Cat.'

In the front room, the curtains were still drawn, and ashtrays were full of cigarettes. The smell of their smoke lay heavy in the air.

'Just stay here until we're back. Then we'll maybe get a chat, eh? Just make yourself at home. Juice?'

'Oh. OK,' said Caitlin. 'I'll get it, it's nae bother.'

'Och, hang on, maybe we've just got tea actually.'

'That's fine.'

'Look, I'll have to go. I should only be a couple of hours, OK?'

Her daughter nodded.

'Just help yourself, darling.'

'You look pretty, mum.' Her mother was wearing a short crop-top and a short leather skirt with long, shiny black boots.

'Pretty? Really? Thanks, darling,' and she stroked Caitlin's cheeks. 'Who'd have thought you'd come all this way to see your wee mum, eh?'

'Jeanie, now!' said the man, who appeared holding car keys.

'Is this your boyfriend, mum?' The man laughed.

'That's Danny,' replied her mother. 'Right. Must go.

Put the satellite TV stuff on, alright?'

Caitlin went to kiss her mum.

'Och, sorry doll, the lippy! We'll get a chat when I get back. Bye, darling.'

'And don't answer the door, got it?' said the man.

Caitlin nodded and with Forth close to her chest, she lay on the sofa and listened to her mother's boots striking the path, their car starting up and then fading away. An ambulance broke the silence. It was as if she had travelled all this way just to be in an unknown house, with people she didn't know.

'It's like being at Mrs Johnstone's,' said Forth, as if reading the girl's mind.

'That was my mum. So, this is like being with family.' Caitlin snatched at the remote and used it to switch on the television.

'So why has she left you again? I think if I get to meet my mum, she'd stay right beside me and let me curl up next to her.'

'She's busy.'

'Then we'd go and hunt and explore or...'

'She's busy, OK?'

The night drew in and the room was illuminated by a cartoon that no one was watching. She looked at the time on her phone. Unread messages were adding up. She ignored them all.

'Are you wanting some tea, pal?'

'Aren't you going to wait for your mother?' replied Forth.

'No, we'll just get ours, like she said.'

A garden gate clinked open. Caitlin couldn't hear the distinctive sound of her mother's heels. She turned off the television. The dark from outside was now in the room. Remembering Danny's words, she grabbed Forth and hid behind the sofa.

There was a knock followed by a voice speaking through the letterbox. 'Miss McGill? It's the police, are you in?'

The police? Caitlin held the cub tighter.

'Miss McGill, it's about your daughter. Can you answer the door please?'

Did they know she was here?

'Miss McGill, if you're in, it's in your best interests to let us in and speak to us, or we'll be back later with a warrant.'

Even with the police outside and behind the locked front door, Caitlin breathed as quietly as she could.

There was some muffled talking. A radio sounded and was answered. Then their footsteps trailed away before a car engine started and melted into the night.

'Why are we hiding?' asked Forth.

'So the police don't find us. I'm not meant to be here without people knowing. And if they do find out then they'll want me back in Scotland.'

'Why are you whispering?'

Caitlin shook her head, picked up Forth with both arms, and lay him on the sofa and went into the small kitchen.

Putting on a light revealed a sink full of pots with more to the side. She began to wash them. Then she wiped down all the worktops followed by tidying up the inside of the fridge. The kettle was filled, and she lined up three cups. Eventually, she made Forth and herself a snack.

*

Caitlin sat up from her sleep, her neck stiff from the arm of the sofa, as she heard the front door open and voices.

She smiled and held Forth as her mother and Danny stumbled into the room. They didn't switch on a light and were laughing at something then kissing, then laughing again. Caitlin smiled at their antics. Then she watched as her mother opened another door and just about collapsed through it. She could just make out a bed that caught her mother's fall. Danny looked straight at Caitlin then, without saying a word, closed the door behind him.

The room was still dark, but now it felt quite cold. The

muffled voices and the odd laugh coming from the bedroom suddenly stopped. Catlin could only hear her own breathing and the odd sniff as she wiped her eyes. A siren broke into the quiet.

'If my mother left me,' said Forth, 'when she got back, I bet she'd lick my face and sniff me to see if I was well.'

Caitlin nodded then reached for her jacket and her rucksack.

-34-

Outside a steady drizzle fell. There was a quiet feel to the city compared to the daytime busy noise of people and traffic.

Caitlin only had a vague notion of where she was going. She didn't use her phone; she didn't want to. She wanted to get even more lost within these unknown streets, to disappear and not be found. Ever.

Her mind raced. What now? As soon as she stepped into her mother's house, things didn't feel right. This wasn't at all how she imagined it would be. She'd travelled all that way to be with her parent, for what?

Caitlin searched and searched for a scrap of something her mother did or mentioned in the brief time she was with her. Something that said she wanted her, that meant she'd missed her so much, that she wanted to put everything right. One scrap of evidence was all she needed for her to go back and feel loved by her own flesh and blood, loved by the person who brought her into this world. Something that said, "You're mine and you are so important to me." Tears, along with the fine rain, wet her cheeks.

She still had a mother, just not the mother she wanted. Maybe it was just a bad day for her? Maybe she should have called her first, made sure she was free? She wasn't used to having a child wandering about the place, just that boyfriend of hers. A call to say she was coming, and she could have had a mother all week: shopping, going out on a bus, getting a burger somewhere or even just snuggling up on that sofa to watch the TV. All those hopes and dreams. Yet what she got was nothing much at all from a parent who hadn't seen her daughter for seven years.

So, when she searched, really searched inside herself to find the truth, she found what she already knew: her mother didn't care enough. There just wasn't enough proof to tell Caitlin that her mum wanted her and would stop everything just to be with her. There was no big fuss when she saw her. No dropping of everything to be with her only child. And she was a mother. Her mother.

Something inside Caitlin was extinguished, lost: that hope that she could have a life with her mum and with Gran there too.

So, the question she now asked, did her mother truly love her?

A taxi slowly drove past and then came to a stop just ahead of Caitlin. As she approached, a window rolled down.

'Need a lift, love?' asked a lady taxi driver.

'No, thanks,' said Caitlin, and she walked on.

'Are you sure?' said the lady. Her large, hooped earring bobbed as she spoke.

'Yes, thanks,'

'It's an awful night.'

'Sorry, I've not a lot of money.'

'Don't worry love. Look, you just pop yourself and your rucksack on the back seat with your furry friend there.'

Caitlin paused then went and opened the back door.

'So where are we going, darling?' asked the lady, talking into the rear-view mirror.

'Erm, the train station.'

'Right you are,' and the lady spoke into her radio. 'Rita to base, train station with a young one and a..., is it a polar bear, love?'

'Aye,' said Caitlin and she tried to wipe the wet out of Forth's fur.

'And a polar bear.' A voice laughed on the other end of the radio. 'It's not safe, a young girl your age, out on the streets at this time in the morning. So you must promise me to go straight home, you hear?' smiled the lady.

'I will,' said Caitlin. Then she frowned. 'How do you know this isn't my home?'

'Rita knows a lot of things, love. I know your accent isn't from around here. And also...I guessed,' and she winked.

Caitlin wanted to tell her that she thought Manchester was going to be home. Instead, she looked at the streets and lights of the city. She noticed the taxi's meter.

'Look, love,' said Rita, 'the deal is a free fare, but you've to get back home and get back to those who will be missing you, OK? By the way, is a train to Edinburgh any good to you?

'Perfect,' said Caitlin.

'Grand,' and Rita turned the meter off.

At the station, Caitlin noticed they had driven into a 'Taxi's Only,' zone. The car parked only feet away from a platform and a waiting train.

'Right, little lady,' said Rita, getting out of the car, 'just need to find Bob. Follow me.'

They walked to the very end of the train where a sliding door pulled back and out stepped a uniformed man.

'Hi, Bob, love. I need a favour, for this little girl. Sorry, darling, what's your name?'

'Caitlin.'

'Caitlin here is needing a lift up to Edinburgh. Think you could help?'

'Right, leave it to me Rita, honey. Caitlin and…, who's

your friend here?'

'Forth.'

'Right, let's see if there's a spare seat for you both then, eh?' and he smiled.

'Now you go straight home,' said Rita, 'and sort out whatever you need to sort out, you hear?'

Caitlin nodded and hugged her. 'Thank you.'

'Don't mention it. Look after yourself,' and Rita went back to her taxi.

On the train, Bob took Caitlin to a seat and showed her how a small curtain could be pulled across if she wanted to sleep.

'You'll be pretty cosy in there.' Then Bob presented Caitlin with a ticket. 'You'll need this to get off the platform.'

'I haven't got much money on me, but I do have some.'

'Don't you worry about that. This is a one-off. Just do as Rita asked, OK?'

Caitlin nodded. 'Thanks for doing this.'

Bob nodded his head and walked back down the aisle to see to other passengers.

As they set off through the dark shadows of northern England, it wasn't long before the girl fell fast asleep, while the young bear stared out into the darkness of the early morning.

When Caitlin opened her eyes, Forth was awake and Bob was by their seat, curtain pulled back, holding a tray.

'Breakfast, madam? Here's a bit of toast and some juice. I'm not sure what Forth has, a kipper?'

'Toast is fine,' smiled Caitlin. 'Where are we?' she asked as outside the countryside blurred past in shades of green and brown.

'Just past Lockerbie. About an hour from Edinburgh,' and Bob left them to their meal.

Caitlin continued to stare out of the window. In a way, she was proud of herself for doing what she had done: to travel down the long-distance on her own and find her mother. If she could do that surely she could go anywhere and survive. She glanced at Forth, another survivor like herself, and stroked his head.

What was she going to do when she got back? It was odd and sad at the same time; to think that she wouldn't be going home, going back to the flat in South Queensferry. She'd go back to Mrs Johnstone's and no doubt Aileen would also be waiting. There would be the cross words, their questions and some sort of punishment for running away yet again. Then what? A life living with people she didn't really know, of being in her, "pretend" type family.

A nag pulled on her stomach. Her gran. She missed her. She had so wanted to tell her that they were going to live with her mum in Manchester and that she could move down there with them and be a proper McGill family. That wasn't going to happen now.

It warmed her when she thought of seeing her elderly relative, maybe doing her hair or just sitting together, watching TV, silently drinking tea. Right now her grandmother was being fed and being well looked after and, in a way, Caitlin missed that. Missed that one consistent face in her life.

'Will Gran be better now?' asked Forth.

'I don't think so, pal,' said Caitlin, still watching an indistinct world rush by.

'When are we going to see her next?'

'As soon as we get back.'

'Could we stay at the home with Gran?'

'No, you doughnut! It's for old ones. It's where you go when you can't look after yourself. Eat your toast.'

'What happens when you get old?'

'Och, I don't know really. Your skin gets really wrinkly and your hair goes grey. I think your joints get all stiff so you can't walk very far.'

'Then what happens?'

'You die, I suppose.'

'Die? By what?

'Old age. Old age makes you die. I think. My Grandpa died of cancer which is a really bad disease. Other old folks just die when they get too old.'

'When do you know you're too old?'

'When you get tired of your pals asking too many daft questions.'

Forth was quiet for a moment as Caitlin pushed a slice of toast under his nose.

'When I'm too old to explore and hunt,' said Forth, 'I'm going to make a big den. Then I'm just going to sleep. I'm going to sleep for a really long time and dream about all I've done.'

'About us?'

'Yes. They will be my best dreams'

Caitlin lifted her best friend onto her lap, kissed his head and looked back out of the window.

-35-

The train came to a lurching stop into the hectic morning that was Waverley station. Bob was at the door as Caitlin, with Forth at her back, stepped out.

'You got everything, Caitlin? Rucksack? Bear?' he smiled.

'Yes, thanks.'

'Right love, you take care of yourself, and straight home, you hear?'

'Will do. Thanks again, Bob,' and she gave him a small squeeze.

On the platform, a shop was selling all the day's newspapers, displayed in see-through cases.

'Look!' said Forth, whispering.

Caitlin had already seen what he was looking at. There,

on the front page of one of the papers was the headline:

IS IT A BOY?

FIRST PICTURES OF POLAR BEAR CUB

AT THE SCOTTISH HIGHLAND SAFARI PARK

'Wow!' said Caitlin as she hurried over to read some more.

Staff at the Scottish Highland Safari Park are delighted that both mother Agnes and her cub, are doing well. Polar Bear expert and park employee, Alastair Miller, told the Courier that at first sight it may well be male. It will take a routine health check once the cub explores outside the birthing den, to confirm this.

Mr Miller went on to say, 'We got a pretty good first look last night on our hidden cameras, but it's quite dark in our specially made den. So, to make 100% sure we will check when the cub goes outside. It's good that Agnes and the cub are looking healthy.'

And a name for the cub? 'We're going to let the public decide. We'll let them send their suggestions by email.'

'Another polar bear cub like me, in Scotland?' said Forth.

'Aye pal, but maybe not as cute as you, eh!' Caitlin looked at the newspaper again. 'Now Agnes has got her wee one, maybe we should go and see if she could look after two cubs?'

'Really? So, its mother and I could teach the young one? I could teach it about trains and picnics and computers?'

Caitlin laughed. 'And what about hunting?'

'Yes, that as well.'

A young couple walked by and smiled at Caitlin and Forth.

'You know them?' said the young man in an American accent, pointing at the newspaper.

'No. Not yet anyway.'

'Hey, maybe they'll get to be pals,' this time it was the young lady, pointing at Forth as they carried on walking.

'Aye, maybe,' and Caitlin read the article again. The safari park was up north, near the town of Aviemore. She scanned a big board above her head that showed all the destinations and platform details.

'Platform thirteen, Forth. That'll get us to where we need to be.'

'What about going home?' questioned Forth.

'We are, but maybe we'll go the long way round, OK? Besides, do you think we'll just hang about at our pretend home when there's a chance we can get you to see other polar bears as well as a baby one?'

'So am I going to be fostered?'

'Well, actually young cubs and adults don't mix that well. But maybe a mother would like a new cub? So, you need to get to know your new family first. Maybe we can do a couple more visits after this, then that'll be you.'

'Then what will happen to us?'

Caitlin hesitated for an answer. 'Och, I'll be still coming to see you, don't you worry about that.'

'So you'll be in a foster home and so will I. I hope we're near each other.'

Caitlin wasn't sure what answer to give Forth. Perhaps not. And could she be parted from her best friend?

'Look, let's just get up there first,' said Caitlin. 'Who knows what's going to happen.'

'And then we'll see Gran when we get back?' said Forth.

'Yip. Look, it's still quite early, and it's what, two and a half hours to get there? So, we'll be back for tea-time, nae bother, OK?'

Forth didn't reply. He looked at all the people milling around, all looking like they had important places to go and explore.

This time, instead of her Amy-like antics, Caitlin bought a ticket with the last of the money she had in her purse. As their train inched away, Caitlin watched as people on other platforms stood waiting for their trains or ran, shouting and waving as they arrived late. Like the man running towards her carriage that she vaguely recognised. It was the American, now without his bags and his partner. He noticed Caitlin through the window and started to point at her. As the train gathered speed, he stopped running and started speaking to a member of the railway staff whilst still pointing at the train.

It wasn't long before the pair were watching, once again, the rolling landscape, the blurred images of small stations flashing by, and the sudden blast of passing trains. There was great independence in what Caitlin was doing and she liked it. She knew this freedom wouldn't last forever and that she had to get back if only to see her gran. And with that came the life as a fostered child. Whatever that was.

*

The sharp fresh air bit into the young girl's face as she walked out of the small quiet station. Relieved that no one had asked her age or more surprisingly, even for her ticket, she turned on her phone for directions, ignoring notifications of missed calls and unread messages.

After a short walk along the side of a busy road, Caitlin, with her bear-cub companion on her back, came to a large sign that indicated the entrance to the Highland Safari Park. A driveway went uphill to a small hut where a man pulled back a sliding window.

'Can I help you, miss?' he asked.

'Erm, my mum's already in. She was in that last car. I'd been car sick, away down the road there and erm, my brother he'd you know, pooped his nappy and...'

'Well, is that right?'

'Aye.'

'Well, whichever adult that was, she hasn't paid for you, or at least I didn't charge her for you so you've still to pay.'

'Erm, she's maybe stressed out of her nut?'

'What? So that she forgets her daughter? And is that a polar bear cub?'

Caitlin nodded.

'How old are you?'

'Ten, nearly eleven.'

'Listen, off you go and find your mum. You pay me when you leave, understand? I'll be looking out for you by the way, OK?'

Caitlin nodded, and ran off shouting, 'Mum, you doughnut! You forgot about me!'

Once out of sight, Caitlin began to laugh. 'Think Amy would be impressed eh, pal?'

'I'm not sure,' said Forth, who was already looking ahead to see if he could see any polar bears.

One pen housed beautiful white and black marked snow leopards while at another were some sort of large deer. Caitlin read the sitemap on a display board. And there, next to a gravel path that went behind some trees, was a large cut-out figure of a white bear, standing on its hind legs.

Without saying anything, Caitlin ran towards it and followed the small track that descended towards a large wire fence. Grabbing Forth from his bag, she pressed her nose through it and held him up so he could see too, but there were no polar bears to be seen. And no artificial den that the newspaper had mentioned. The enclosure was big and the field in front of her stretched away up to a hill on one side, and down to the park entrance on the other.

A man in overalls carrying two buckets was walking towards Caitlin with a crowd of adults and children behind him.

'So, this is where I'll be feeding them from. If you'd like to gather around here so that you can see,' said the man. 'Er, excuse me wee lassie, back from the fence, the polar bears will be here shortly.

Caitlin took a step back. *So, where are they?*

'Sandy! Jonah!' shouted the man and he banged the buckets together.

'Is Agnes still in her den?' asked Caitlin.

'Aye, but that's away over the far end of the park. She and her cub are still inside and probably both sleeping the now.'

'It's for my pal here, Forth. I wondered if Agnes could possibly take on another cub?'

A few people in the crowd laughed.

'Have you got a licence for that polar bear lady?' asked the man. 'I mean an approved licence that you get when they distribute polar bears into captivity?'

'Erm, I didn't know you had to have one?'

More laughter came from the crowd.

'And you are complying with the AZA Care Manual regarding polar bears as well I take it?'

'Care manual?' replied Caitlin.

'Diet, playthings, size of the pen, all that sort of stuff?'

'No. He seems OK though and I feed him regularly.'

'What on?'

'Tuna.'

'Fresh?'

'Tinned.'

The man sighed. 'I think we're going to have a wee chat at the end of the feeding, miss. And about your pal, Forth, being a second cub? I think Agnes has got quite a bit on at the moment. And we can't put him in with Sandy and Jonah. Male adults and a young cub would be a recipe for disaster. You know that don't you?'

Caitlin smiled and nodded. 'Sorry, Forth,' she whispered but the young bear was quiet as he was staring into the enclosure.

The man shouted again. 'Sandy! Jonah! Come on now!'

Caitlin scanned every yard of ground in front of her. Still nothing.

One of the children in the crowd was the first to spot them. 'Look!' Caitlin followed where the young boy's finger was pointing. Coming over the brow of the hill, side by side, were two large, lumbering white bears.

-36-

Caitlin held her breath right up until the bears were only a matter of feet away from the fence. She didn't say anything. Forth's eyes were also fixed on the pair.

The man threw some of the contents of his buckets over the fence. A melon landed near the feet of one of the bears who pawed it like a football, then with one bite crushed it and began eating.

'It's sometimes nice to give them a bit of challenge when they feed,' said the man. 'They also like quail and these are fat balls full of fruit and seeds.' The man kept throwing the food into the pen.

The polar bears continued to eat without much acknowledgement to the crowd who were watching and photographing them.

'Hi there, my name is Caitlin, and this is Forth.' The young boy laughed as did a couple of the adults in the crowd.

'Which one of you is Jonah and which one of you is Sandy?'

It was the man that answered. 'Well Forth, that one closest to you is Sandy and so that one there is Jonah.'

'Do they eat quail in the wild?' asked the young boy.

'Well...' the man was about to answer but Caitlin, still staring at the bears, interrupted.

'No, they mainly eat seals. Ringed ones mainly but also bearded and banded seals. Oh, and hooded.'

'Is that all they eat?' asked the boy.

'Not always,' said Caitlin. 'They'll eat anything they can catch, like small rodents such as lemmings or even stranded whales.'

'Is that right?'

'Yip. And did you know,' continued Caitlin, 'they can smell seals underneath the snow? Their sense of smell is so good they can smell a seal that may be up to three metres deep.'

The small crowd were now listening to this seemingly very knowledgeable young girl, one with a polar bear cub at her back.

'Do they know you've got one of their own in your rucksack?' laughed the young boy's dad.

'No, Forth's mine,' replied Caitlin.

'How big do they grow?' asked a girl.

'Well, the males, who are bigger than the females, measure up to two point six metres from its tail to the tip of its nose. Stood upright they can measure up to three metres tall.'

'And how much do they weigh?' asked the young boy's father.

'About four hundred and fifty kilograms but a big male can reach up to six hundred and eighty kilogrammes. So, say if a pet cat weighs three and a half kilograms you would need about one hundred and ninety cats to weigh about the same. That's a load of moggies.'

The crowd chuckled at this before they began to disperse as the food quickly disappeared, so the bears started to wander back up the hill.

'Are you trying to take my job?' said the man with his now empty buckets.

Caitlin shrugged her shoulders. 'I just found out a lot of things about polar bears, when I found my pal, Forth.'

'I'm Mr Miller, by the way, Alastair Miller,' and he put out his hand to shake Caitlin's.

'Caitlin McGill and, well you know who this is by now.'

'Aye. He's a cute one by the way. Listen, I'm Head Keeper, in charge of looking after the carnivores, and I have to say I was impressed by how much you know, lady.'

'Thank you.'

'So where's your mum and dad then?'

'Erm, it's just my mum. She's got, erm... a wee bit of a tummy problem and that,' said Caitlin.

'Oh, right. Interesting. How do you fancy a wee look at the cub then?'

'Really?'

'Well, I need you to text your mum and tell her where we are as we'll need to go back to the office. Mum and baby are asleep in their den. We've some cameras set up so you can have a look-see on the computer.'

'Wow! Thank you. And yeah, I will do,' and Caitlin pretended to use her phone. 'What about that licence and the manual stuff?'

'Well don't say I didn't warn you,' and he winked at Caitlin. 'Right, let's go see the cub.'

Inside, Mr Miller introduced Caitlin to a couple of women who were drinking tea and eating biscuits. They glanced at each other, but Caitlin didn't notice. Her eyes were fixed on a computer screen that was divided into four dimly lit views of the inside of Agnes' den.

'Now, just keep your eyes on this area down here,' and Mr Miller pointed on the screen to a patch of straw underneath Agnes' stomach. Nothing was happening as Caitlin watched, not daring to blink in case she missed something. Was that the straw moving? At first, it was just the black part of its nose, but then came the pure white fur, which contrasted sharply with its mother's duller coat.

Caitlin laughed with excitement. She grabbed Forth out of the bag. 'Look, pal, there's your tiny brother!' The two women smiled as they headed out of the office.

'Well, we're not sure if it's a he or she yet,' said Mr Miller.

'It's nearly as cute as me,' said Forth.

Mr Miller laughed. 'Well, it's a close call, wee man.'

Caitlin gazed at the screen. She watched the cub nose its mother still sound asleep. The cub, undeterred, continued to play with its mother's head.

'Come on mum, I want to be fed,' said Caitlin.

'I think mum's tired just now,' said Mr Miller. 'Anyway, I'll get my cup of tea and a wee read of the paper.'

'They can't survive without their mother, in the wild that is,' said Caitlin.

'That's true. Mums, parents, family; they're pretty important, and not just for polar bears I reckon. What do you think?'

Caitlin continued to stare at the screen.

'Mmm...,' said Mr Miller, 'now that's interesting. Amazing what you can find in the news,' and he shook his paper.

Caitlin didn't move a muscle. She couldn't believe that she was watching a cub, smaller than Forth, playing with its mother.

'Mmm...not much on this page. Nothing as interesting as the first bit.' Mr Miller shook his paper again and coughed slightly. This time it got Caitlin's attention and there on the front page, a photograph of herself.

Queensferry girl aged 10 –

missing for over 24 hours.

-37-

Caitlin stood up and put Forth back in her rucksack and made to leave.

'Caitlin, where are you going?' asked Mr Miller.

There was no reply.

'Listen,' said Mr Miller, 'I'm not going to give you a row, but I must report this to the police. You're reported to be missing, a missing ten-year-old girl. People are going to be concerned and quite worried, to say the least.'

The young girl in question was still silent as she zipped up her jacket and opened the door.

'What would your gran say? It says here that your gran hasn't been told due to health concerns.'

'I was going home tonight anyway. Thank you for letting me see the cub.' Caitlin walked outside followed by Mr

Miller.

'Well, in that case let me help you get home?'

Caitlin proceeded to walk, speeding up not just to get away from Mr Miller, she also had a train to catch.

'Caitlin, just stop and listen, please. How about you and I call in at the police station? Better than letting them race round here in their cars once I've telephoned them, don't you think?'

She was almost running now. Mr Miller walked quickly to catch up.

'Look, come down to the police station, and I'll make sure you can come up again and see the bears and the cub for free. I promise'

Caitlin stopped in her tracks and turned around. 'Aye, right.'

'I'm not one for making empty promises, believe me. You've got to honour your side of the deal though. You need to call in at the police station with me, then you need to get back home, understand?'

'I don't have a home.'

'Well you're not homeless, are you? That's not what the paper said. Some people are anxious about your whereabouts. People that obviously care about you. And besides, you want to come back and see the cub, don't you?'

Caitlin nodded.

At the police station, a sergeant put down his mug and greeted Mr Miller with a smile.

'Hi Al, someone been stealing your cub?' he said, glancing at a worried looking Caitlin with Forth under her arms.

'Campbell, this is Caitlin McGill, she's been reported missing?'

'Really? Well, well. Just glad you're safe and sound. Really glad. You've scared quite a lot of people, Caitlin, so you have.'

'You're not angry then?'

'Not for me to be angry miss. I'll let someone else do that, eh? I would ask you not to do it again, mind. Now, I'll need to make a few phone calls to get you home. Over at Edinburgh, aren't you?'

'Campbell, how about I take her down the road?'

'OK Al, nae problem. I'll just make sure there's someone at the other end to get her. Have you a contact down there, miss?'

'Yes, erm ... my social worker, Aileen Young.'

'Right, I'll contact her. And Al, give me a ring when you're there and Caitlin has been picked up, OK?'

'Cheers, Campbell, will do.'

*

As Mr Miller drove, Caitlin leant her head against the window with Forth on her lap. She wasn't sure what punishment would be waiting for her back at Mrs Johnstone's. Being notified to the police as well as being reported missing and being in the paper, maybe she would end up in a more secure place as Amy warned.

'So how long have you been away from home then?' asked Mr Miller.

'Just a couple of days. You knew all along, didn't you? Who I was and that?'

'Aye. As soon as I saw you and wee Forth. Where were you before you came up here?'

'Manchester.'

'Manchester?'

'Yip. That's where my mum lives. I wanted to live with her.'

'I see. Well, that didn't last long then, did it?

'Well, maybe I shouldn't have been there anyway.'

'True. A ten-year-old running all the way down to

Manchester isn't too clever.'

Caitlin smiled, then added, 'Mind, I'm no' sure she wanted to see me.'

Alistair sighed. 'Well, these things happen, I'm afraid. Sad but true.'

'She's my mum.'

'Well, I'm not sure there is always a clear answer to something like that. Not one that helps, anyway.'

'She didn't even ask what Forth's name was.'

'Really? Now, I'm sorry to hear that.'

Caitlin shrugged and looked out of the window.

'I get it you know,' said Mr Miller. 'Not having a home with your proper family. Being cared for by people who you don't really know. I can see how that can be tough.'

'I just want to have it like it was,' said Caitlin, still looking outside.

'Time moves on. We grow up. We can't live in the past.

279

Time doesn't let us. Things change.'

'It's all these things changing that I dinnae like,' she said, her head pressed against the window.

'Aye, change can be hard sometimes, but you can make things change so *you* can be happy. Is Forth OK by the way?'

'Aye, he's fine, aren't you, pal?' Caitlin noticed they were passing a loch. The wind was wrinkling the surface of the grey water that held a couple of sailing dinghies. 'I wish that was me out there.'

'That's Loch Insh. So you sail?'

She nodded. 'I need to get back to it. Start of the season soon.'

'Is that right? Forth will no' like it though?'

'He does actually.'

'Well, I suppose he can swim if he topples in.'

'I'm not sure. He didn't have much time with his mother. I don't know if he was shown how to. I mean he didn't even know what a seal was, eh pal?'

'So listen, how did he get to be in Scotland?'

'He was captured.'

'Captured? Really?'

'Yes, the crew of one of those big ships in the Arctic.'

'Oh, a factory ship or maybe even a whaling boat?'

'I think so. Something like that anyway.'

'So, what happened?'

-38-

The blizzard hit hard and hit fast. Visibility was now only a matter of inches in front of Forth. Using his juvenile sense of smell, he tried to see if he could get the trace of something, anything. Then as quickly as the snowstorm had come in, it eased away to the odd flake. And there, lumbering towards him and picking up speed, was his mother.

He gave out a yelp of surprise and she replied with a satisfactory roar.

They ran towards each other, both Forth and his parent gathering speed. In moments Forth would be within the safety of his mother, perhaps laying against her warm belly or tucked away between her hind legs as they walked great distances together.

Within only a few more steps of being reunited, a large fissure appeared as the ground between them split.

Forth and his mother stopped abruptly. From the deep gash, seawater sprayed upwards, and a great wave showered them. The heads of two, three, then four killer whales came up from the water and broached the ice, waggling heavily forwards towards Forth. Their pink mouths and white teeth were coming ever closer. Bang!

'Hello, small one,' said Simzar. 'So sorry to wake you. The doors, they are heavy.'

Simzar crouched down beside Forth, who lay, head between his front legs.

'Here, eat and drink,' and Simzar placed two bowls by Forth.

'You look sad, and Simzar knows why. Like me, child bear, you wish to be free. I watch the seabirds, I watch the dolphins; all free, all living just as they wish. And that is how it should be. One day, you and I will both be free to go as we please. So, I beg you to stay quiet, stay strong and get through this, just like me. And Simzar here will see that, at our journey's end, we will both follow our destinies.'

As he said this, Simzar stroked Forth's back gently. Forth didn't move but let the warmth of the hand slide over his body. Somehow, although it was an animal he didn't know, the cub liked the feel of it. It felt comforting. It felt safe. It felt like this was an animal he could trust. Forth sat up.

'Good. You eat, for strength and for making you happier, little one.'

Over the next few days, Simzar would make regular trips to feed Forth, more often on his own but occasionally with Kai. When time would allow, and when Luka wasn't shouting at him to do some mundane job, Simzar, with the cord around Forth's neck, would take him for a walk around the lower container deck. And because of the young cub's trust in this animal, he would willingly oblige. Cardo rarely visited below deck, so the two friends had time to wander around the many large, metal crates.

On his walks, Forth got used to the sounds of the big, grey beast. The sound of the waves banging against its sides. The sound of it creaking and groaning as the containers *pitched and pulled on their chains.*

Simzar was just about to put Forth back when he heard footsteps.

'Simzar, Simzar! Luka comes!' hissed Kai from a nearby gantry.

'So?' shrugged Simzar.

'He's sad, not happy. Trouble.'

Just then, Luka barged past Kai, as if he wasn't there, to get down the ladder.

'So, Simzar. Exercising the bear, eh? Good, but what is this?'

Luka went over to look at the cub. 'You feed him too well, Simzar?'

Luka got closer to Simzar as he spoke. 'He's not going to be too cute when we present him to Alyana. What would she want with a big, fat white bear? And if she's scared, no gift of a bear and if no gift, no Den'gi, eh?'

Luka was right in Simzar's face now. Simzar made sure he didn't look afraid of him and stared back, hate hiding in the back of his eyes.

'And if no Den'gi, Luka very sad, Simzar, very sad, so sad he might get angry, eh? And you won't like an angry Luka,' and he stabbed a finger into Simzar's stomach.

Luka turned to go. 'Ha, I'm thinking you like the bear cub, eh?' and he turned back to face Simzar. 'Like you, no family, far from a home? Far from anybody to help, or to maybe even remember you eh, Simzar? You think about that. No more food Simzar. Milo feeds, Milo walks.'

Luka quickly went back up the ladders while Simzar stood, breathing heavily. He unclenched his fist and stroked Forth before taking him back inside the container.

*

Days passed as the ship journeyed south towards the

North Sea. Simzar made a point of hiding to spy on Milo walking Forth every day. Simzar noticed that Forth looked grubby, his white hair now tinged brown from the ship's dust and oil. And he looked thin. The next day at dinner, Simzar realised why.

'Luka, the bear's not eating. That's four days now,' said Milo.

'When it's hungry, it'll eat,' replied Luka.

Simzar pretended not to listen. The cub missed him. He looked at Kai. Kai nodded slowly as if he knew.

The next day the ship was toiling in a rough sea. A gale was blowing right across their path causing huge waves to crash over the deck. Too dangerous for the crew to go anywhere, Cardo ordered every crew member to be in the shelter of the bridge so they could all be accounted for.

'Sheesh!' said Cardo, 'only fools like us would be out in this.'

Just as he finished his sentence a freak wave, a great

wall of churning water gaining height, approached from the side.

'Port Cardo! Port!' shouted Milo.

Too late. The ship listed heavily. All the crew, apart from Cardo who held the wheel, staggered across the floor of the bridge.

'Hold on!' shouted Cardo, the visibility gone as the wave immersed the whole of the large ship.

The large vessel righted itself by slamming down into the trough left by the great surge of water. The crew helplessly stumbled about, holding on to anything that came to hand.

A loud bang, followed by several other smaller ones, came from below the crew's feet.

Luka and Milo glanced at each other. Simzar knew exactly what he had to do. He made for the door.

'No Simzar!' shouted Cardo. 'It's not safe. Something's let go, so? We will just have to get by until the sea levels out. Until then, you stay here, and you pray.'

'If the fool wants to leave, let him, I say,' said Luka, knowing what Simzar was more than likely going to do. A dead bear wasn't worth anything to a small girl.

'Captain sir, I was just going to see if I could fix?' said Simzar.

'What? And have one of those waves over us again?' exclaimed Cardo who was concentrating hard on navigating the mountainous ocean.

'Captain sir, Simzar is careful. I look, see if wanted fixed.'

'Insurance Cardo, eh? Fish and whale meat gone too rotten is no cargo, yes? A door just needed shut, a chain just needing tightened, what harm eh, Cardo?'

Cardo looked out at the sea in front of him and shook his head. 'You go Simzar, you look. If too much time needed to fix you come back, you hear?'

Without waiting for Cardo to finish his sentence,

Simzar picked up a handful of tools and made his way down to the container deck.

As soon as he got to the bottom of the ladders, Simzar could see the havoc the wave had caused. A great line of the heavy containers was stacked up against each other like a line of toppled dominoes. Two of the end crates had borne the brunt of the weight from the others and lay severely dented. One of them was Forth's.

Simzar hurried to survey the damage and see if the young bear had survived. It wasn't easy for him to walk quickly without sliding and tottering on the smooth, damp floor due to the turbulent sea. He clung to the front of each container, making his way steadily to the end. Forth's container had one of its doors bent so badly it had curled and buckled, leaving a gap a small bear could get out of. Simzar, knowing that trying to open the door properly was futile, poked his head through the gap. In the dim, there was no sign of the cub.

'Little one? Where are you? Little one, it is your

friend, Simzar.'

He looked around the back of the container. He then looked behind the one Forth's had folded against. Still no sign. More worryingly though was the red liquid on the floor that had faint paw prints leading away from it.

-39-

The Queensferry Crossing was lit up as they crossed it. Mr Miller parked in a nearby hotel car park. Caitlin could see two women standing at the hotel entrance: Mrs Johnstone and Aileen.

'Just stay here a minute, OK?' said Mr Miller, as he got out of the car.

Caitlin watched as the three adults talked for several minutes.

'Are we going home now, I'm quite hungry,' asked Forth.

'Aye pal, we're going home. I'm hungry as well,' answered Caitlin. 'Mind, we'll probably be on bread and water.'

Mr Miller waved for Caitlin to come out of the car. Carrying Forth and her rucksack, she walked sheepishly towards them.

'Listen lady, I've talked with Aileen and Annie here and we've come to some sort of deal. And as I said, you've to fulfil your side of the bargain, agreed?'

She nodded.

'So, over the next two weeks your attendance at school needs to be one hundred per cent and no running away, in fact not even late to school, understand?'

'Yes, I understand,' said Caitlin, who couldn't help thinking that Mr Miller sounded just like a teacher.

'You do that,' continued Aileen, 'and you can go to work at the Highland Safari Park.'

Hugging Forth, Caitlin's face broke into a smile.

'I'll need to be there for the first couple of trips,' continued Aileen.

'One foot out of place mind, and we start again, for another two weeks,' added Mrs Johnstone.

'I'll do that. It'll be no problem, I'll just…'

'I don't know what you were thinking. How you could be so selfish, if you…'

Mr Miller interrupted Aileen. 'I think you know you've done wrong, Caitlin, don't you? You learn from it, you hear? I hope to see you and Forth in a couple of weeks then,' and with that, he patted the ten-year-old on her shoulder and walked back to his car.

The drive back to Mrs Johnstone's was quiet.

'How's Gran?' asked Caitlin.

'Oh, so you want to ask about your gran now?' said the driver Aileen, who shook her head.

'We'll pop in and see her tomorrow, OK?' said Mrs Johnstone.

Caitlin then asked about Amy.

'We were hoping you'd be telling us!' said Mrs Johnstone.

'She's returned to her first foster home in England if you must know,' said Aileen. 'You just worry about you.'

The young girl stared at Forth, who was on her lap, looking out of the window. 'How is she though? My gran?'

Aileen looked at Mrs Johnstone in the rear-view mirror, then back at the road ahead.

'Like I said, we'll see her tomorrow,' and Mrs Johnstone glanced back at Aileen.

Uncomfortable with the distinct lack of details, Caitlin rested her head on Forths. 'Sorry.'

Mrs Johnstone sighed whilst Aileen slowly shook her head.

-40-

The following morning brought drizzle. Caitlin stared through the hypnotic window wipers of Mrs Johnstone's car as they swiped to give a brief, clear glimpse of the world outside.

In the home, they walked quickly down the corridor. Matthew, the nurse, came out of a door to meet them.

'Caitlin, can I have a quick word?'

'Aye. What is it?'

'Listen, your gran's not been too well.'

'With what?' and she pulled Forth close to her.

'She's not eating.'

'Not eating? What, anything?'

'That's right. Cups of tea seem to be not so much of a problem. It's the fortified drinks we make to supplement her diet which are a bit of a hit or miss.'

'Right.' Caitlin pulled Forth tighter and stood there not sure what to say or do.

'We can't force her to eat, so sometimes we just have to respect their wishes and dignity. You can still see her, it's just she may seem a bit tired and weak?'

'How long?' Caitlin asked, looking down the corridor.

'Three days now.'

'It was me, wasn't it? Me not being here, Gran not knowing where I was.'

'No, no. Listen,' and Matthew lowered himself to Caitlin's height. 'I'm sure your gran didn't know where you were or what you were doing. So, as you're here, see if you can get a chat with your gran, see how she responds to you. Remember how important you are in her life as well as how important she is in yours, OK?

Caitlin didn't say anything but walked down the corridor with Mrs Johnstone.

Inside her room, Gran was sat up, her gaze fixed on the television. Her head didn't move as her granddaughter climbed onto the bed. Forth sat on a pillow.

'What we watching, Gran?'

Her question got no answer or any noticeable acknowledgement of her being there.

The ten-year-old lay closer to her grandmother and stroked the hair back off her forehead. She looked at the girl.

'Davy's away this morn. Whistling his way down the street, so he was.'

'Aye? Is that right?

'Aye. Whistling away. Quite the thing. Might need to get him a poke of birdseed, eh?'

'Ha. Maybe's. He'll be back in no time though. Hey, remember that time the wind and snow came down in buckets and his engine stopped, halfway out on the Forth?'

'Och, aye. And all he said was, "I'll need my big coat on for this!" Ha! Him floating downstream with all the passengers wondering what on earth was going on. And he's just a-whistling down by the engine. Aye, he's some boy that one.'

'So he is. What was his play piece today?'

'Chocolate tea-cake.'

'And I bet you've got something good for his tea.'

'Stovies. He'll need something to warm him up, so he will.'

'You'll sit with him then, eating and having a blether?'

'Aye. My heart warms as soon as I set my eyes on him, so it does.'

Caitlin's eyes filled. 'So how about a spot of lunch, before you get started on his tea, Gran?'

'I'll Gran you!' And the elderly lady smiled. 'Aye, right enough. I'll see what I've got in.'

'Don't you worry Mrs McGill.' It was Mrs Johnstone. 'I'll make you it,' and she put a thumb up to Caitlin and went out.

'So, what are we watching then?' asked Caitlin.

'Watching?'

Her granddaughter pointed to the television.

'Och! I didn't know it was on. Shall we see if there's a film on?'

Caitlin passed her the remote and kissed her on the cheek.

-41-

It was a mixed reception for Caitlin as she walked back into her class.

Glad to see her back, a few of the children called out her name, as well as Forth's, and Grace excitedly ran over and gave her a big hug. There were also the whispers from certain pupils who, after their mumblings, just stared at Caitlin as she went to her desk. She was about to take Forth out of her rucksack when Miss Bell spoke.

'Right class, quiet please and you all know what you have to do. Grace Calder, could you maybe show Caitlin what you and some of the others made for Forth?'

Grace smiled and took her friend over to a corner of the class. There, on the floor was a large metal cage and inside it were a few cushions. It was hemmed in by a couple of bookshelves.

'My mum and dad donated the cage thing. We had it

for our dog when it was in the car.'

Caitlin smiled at her friend and placed Forth onto the largest cushion. She noticed the bowl of water and also a colourful sign, "Welcome Back Forth from P6B."

'Thank you, pal,' and Caitlin put an arm around Grace as they returned to her desk.

'So what does Forth think of it then?' asked Miss Bell.

'Perfect.'

It wasn't long until Caitlin felt like she had hardly been away. Yet trying to do her best, as Mr Miller and Aileen had asked her, was going to be quite difficult. There was the trying to do her best at the hard maths. There was the trying to do her best to keep her attention when the teacher was talking to the class for a long time. There was the trying her best not to turn around to see if Forth was settling into his new pen. And then there was the trying her best not to daydream about being up at the Highland Safari Park and watching the polar bears. Hardest of all though, was at break time and the trying not to run over to Sophie Wallace and give her a piece of her mind. Sophie looked at Caitlin, then began whispering to her crowd of friends.

Grace, with Forth on her knee, also noticed.

'Pay no attention, Cat. We've all been told by Mrs Reid not to mention what happened.'

'No doubt she's talking about me though.'

'Och, she'll soon stop if I was to tell Miss Bell. Anyway, I guess she isn't the only one talking about you.'

'Aye but not to my face. Which is fine, I suppose. I mean there's not that much to say. I ran away to an island and then had to come back. Then I went to my mum's in ...'

'Manchester,' interrupted Grace. 'But then you ran away. Again.'

'Aye, well just to see the polar bears.'

'It still counts,' smiled Grace.

'I suppose. Mind, I'm rubbish at it.'

'What I mean is, I think you were brave, Caitlin.'

Caitlin raised a shoulder.

'Brave but a wee bit stupid, maybe?' added Grace.

Caitlin smiled. 'You're right, pal. It was like I just needed to though. I don't know where home is right now. So anywhere could be home. An island, under a bridge, on top of a mountain...'

'You did get to see your mum.'

'I did. Before though, I had all these nice thoughts about how it might be? Now they're all gone. So now sometimes I wish I hadn't.'

'Really?'

'I just... I just never felt like I was a daughter and that she was really my mum.'

'It would be hard. I mean, it might take time and that.'

'I suppose. I don't know. It was...weird? Just not right I guess.'

'I was worried about you. And why didn't you tell me? We're friends, aren't we?'

Caitlin sighed. 'Aye, of course. I think I wanted it to be

a secret. And besides, they'd only ask you all sorts of questions, your mum and dad, the teachers, the polis.'

'Least you're here now. And Forth. He's just too cute.'

'Enjoy your holiday, Caitlin?' It was Sophie.

'Yes, thanks.'

'Oh, really? I heard you met lots of nice new friends. Like social workers, wild animals, oh, and policemen?' Sophie's friends giggled.

'Mind, I have another friend. The one who was a lot like you.' A bell for the end of break sounded.

'What cute and adorable?' and Sophie shook her hair for effect. Her friends laughed again.

'No, she was a seal. Fat, slimy and with bogging breath.' And with that Caitlin picked up Forth and headed to line up with the rest of her class.

*

The week for Caitlin dragged itself slowly to Friday and home time. She felt exhausted as she waited for her taxi. Mrs Reid noticed her.

'Well Caitlin, I've just come off the phone to your social worker.'

'Aileen?'

'Yes. And I was glad to report that all is well, and Miss Bell is also pleased with your efforts. Keep it up lady, you're more than capable. Have a nice weekend.'

'Thank you, Mrs Reid. I will.'

It was hard to carry her grin into Mrs Johnstone's with the tiredness she felt. She flopped onto the sofa, Forth wrapped in her arms. Billy wagged his tail as he tried to get up to her and the cub.

'That bad, eh?' observed Mrs Johnstone.

'Just glad it's Friday.'

'All good though?'

'Yip. My headteacher is pleased.'

'Great. That's all you have to do. Then you'll be park bound come next Saturday.'

'Aye, we can't wait can we, Forth?' and she looked into the cub's eyes. Billy barked.

'No room for dogs, Billy. Sorry,' said Mrs Johnstone as she sat on the arm of the sofa. 'Er, Caitlin, Aileen was on the phone earlier.'

'About school?'

Mrs Johnstone sighed. 'No. Your mum. She's still pushing for contact and custody of some kind.'

'Right. So, what does that mean?'

'It means lots of meetings and discussions. And it will also mean you'll be involved at some point. Maybe even being in a meeting with your mum present.'

'OK.' Caitlin was looking at the ceiling, holding Forth to her chest.

'Are you alright with that?'

'Am I meant to say something at this meeting?'

'Don't worry about that. Aileen, and whoever else is there, will just ask you questions. And you've just to answer as best as you can, you hear?'

Caitlin didn't reply.

'Listen,' continued Mrs Johnstone, 'it's not for a couple of weeks yet, so you just think about next Saturday and your trip. I'll go start tea,' and Billy followed her out.

Caitlin tried her best to concentrate solely on getting up the Highland Safari Park. Seeing those incredible polar bears, maybe even helping by feeding them. Yet the sunny, exciting day she wished for was slowly turning cloudy as a storm was forming on the horizon.

-42-

The following week, Caitlin only had one thing on her mind: the weekend. She counted down the days and the hours until it finally came.

And when it did come, she could hardly contain her excitement which spilt over in the car with Aileen. She talked ceaselessly about her favourite animal; facts and figures and even the history of them.

Aileen could only smile. 'I hope you keep this up, miss. The days at school that is.'

Caitlin answered with a nod.

'It's nice to see you so happy,' said Aileen. 'This is quite a treat let me tell you. So, use your time up here wisely. Maybe you'll learn some things you can use when you're older?'

Caitlin didn't answer but wondered what would be in store for her when she got there. Would she be washing the bears? She'd seen elephants been washed at a zoo on television. Maybe she'd use a long hose to clean them up, so they looked pure white. Or would she see them up close if a vet was in and had to cut their nails or something like that; a great big adult polar bear lying out on a table. She'd seen that on the Internet. For the young girl, the car couldn't go fast enough.

*

'Right,' said Mr Miller as he appeared from the office. 'I'm going to start you in the shop today, Caitlin, OK?'

'The shop? I thought I would be helping with the polar bears, cleaning them or something.'

'Cleaning the bears? They're wild animals, they're no' guinea pigs! I need someone to help Morag run the shop. Up for it?'

Caitlin sighed.

Mr Miller smiled and winked at Aileen. 'I'm asking you

to work in the shop as you seem to know so much about polar bears, I thought that would come in handy. Besides, the polar bear gifts contribute to a charity that helps conserve the bears.'

Caitlin felt only slightly appeased.

'I know what you'd really like to do, but actually, this is a compliment,' said Mr Miller.

'OK, which way to the shop?'

'Erm, the big sign there that says, shop? And make sure no one thinks a polar bear cub is for sale, alright?' and Mr Miller nodded at Forth, sat in the rucksack.

'Right,' said Aileen, 'I'll come for you later, I'm away to see some old friends,' and with that, she left.

Morag was unpacking small boxes as Caitlin placed Forth safely behind the counter.

'Hi, Caitlin isn't it? Mind giving me a hand? Keyrings. Hundreds of them,' she said. And the new member of staff started hanging them up.

It was a quiet day in the shop. Any customers that came

in were served by Morag whilst the shop's newest volunteer went about tidying the shelves.

A young boy ran to the children's book section and poured over the polar bear books.

'Mum, bears! White bears.'

'Polar bears,' said Caitlin.

'Polar bears? Awesome!'

'They are very awesome. Do you know how tall they are?'

The boy shook his head.

She pointed to a ceiling light. 'Stood on their two hind legs, their head would be touching that bulb.'

'Awesome! What do they eat?'

'Seals mainly and other things like small mammals.'

'So, they eat meat?'

Caitlin nodded.

'Awesome! Do they eat people?'

'Aye, they've been known to.'

'Mega-awesome!'

'Caitlin! Don't scare the wee man,' said Morag, from behind the till.

'In fact,' Caitlin whispered, 'they're known to start on a human's head and are capable of crunching the skull with one bite!'

'Mega! Mum, can I buy this book?' The parent smiled and took it to the counter.

At her break, the ten-year-old went and sat on a bench that looked over the polar bear enclosure. The day was cold and bright and away in the distance were the two bears. Jonah lay on his back whilst Sandy explored a couple of tyres that were attached to a tree.

'This is what it would be like back home, back living in polar bear country,' said Forth, sat next to his best friend.

'Aye, I guess so. You could just wake up and there would be a couple of adult bears on the horizon.'

'Do they go and hunt every day?' asked Forth.

'No, they've no need to. They get fed.'

'Mmm... I wonder if they miss hunting?'

'Maybe. It must be nice not to have to. Think of all the time and effort it saves.'

'Polar bears like hunting though don't they? After all, we're good at it.'

'True. Do you miss it, pal?'

'I think so.'

Caitlin looked at her friend then back at the adult bears and sighed.

*

In the office at the end of her day, Mr Miller and a few other staff were crowded around the computer that showed inside Agnes' den.

'Well Caitlin, how did you like your first day?'

'Great, thanks.'

'And Forth?'

'Loved it. He thinks he's home!'

Mr Miller smiled, as did the other members of staff.

Caitlin looked curiously at the computer. Despite the dimness, she could see the polar bear cub trying to get his sleeping mother's attention by chewing on her ear.

'So Miss McGill, Archie or Mirren? What do you think?'

'Archie?'

'Well, if it's a boy. Mirren if it's a girl. They were the email winners. We can do a health check on the cub once it's out in the open. Then we'll know.'

Caitlin still couldn't take her eyes off the screen. 'Mirren sounds all kind of grown-up maybe, but Archie sounds cute?'

'Well, true enough. Oh, by the way, just while we're waiting on Aileen coming back for you, remember you were telling me about how Forth got to be with you?'

'When he was on the ship?' said Caitlin, as she sat down on the computer chair.

'Aye, that's right, except there was a storm.'

'That's right.'

'So, what happened next? We'd all like to know, wouldn't we folks?'

Everyone nodded.

-43-

Simzar noticed how the paw prints trailed away through a gap between the containers. The rope that Forth had been attached to swung rhythmically with the ship from the side of the container. A clanging sound came intermittently from somewhere not far from where he stood.

The gap was too low for Simzar to stand in, so dropping onto all fours, he dragged himself into the dark void and moved towards the light at the far end.

Reaching the other side, he called out, 'So, where are you? Come, it is your friend, Simzar,' and he slowly stood up. His call came out of hope rather than it being satisfied by any sort of reply.

He noticed the damage to some of the other containers, their metal walls curved in or their doors misshapen. He also noticed the fainter paw prints that went towards a spotlight at the foot of a stairwell. Slowly, and using the large containers nearby to steady himself, Simzar followed. Below the spotlight was a small metal door that opened then clanged closed as the ship pitched and plunged.

Pulling it back, there, lying on the floor, was a polar bear cub with bright red patches on its white coat. He crouched by its side.

'No! No! No! Young one! What has happened? Not this? To die so young and to die a prisoner.'

Simzar surprised himself as tears welled up in his eyes. He ran his fingers through the young bear's fur, a smudge of red sticking to his fingers. He continued to stroke and began reciting a prayer, whispering it under his breath. The cub opened an eye.

'Young one! What is this? Some sort of miracle?' and he gently stroked the polar bear's side.

Forth got to his feet, slowly and gingerly, looking to this other animal for food.

Simzar wiped his face with his sleeve then smelled his fingers. He licked them.

'Sauce? Sauce! Ha, ha, ha!'

Forth didn't understand the two-legged animal's behaviour. It was not a noise he knew. He tilted his head as he watched the animal slap itself on its legs then sit down and stroke him, all the time making the same noise.

*

Washed, Simzar dried the cub with a clean rag, then sat back to look at the now whiter young bear.

'Friend, you are fine. Very fine. Now here, food. And here look, there's so much more, a container full of tinned fish! Even one full of your sauce, ha! Not a word to the boss-man. Promise?'

Simzar placed Forth back in the container as he

hammered the door back so it would shut, not perfectly, but enough so the cub couldn't get out.

'Simzar! The noise, eh? What is that you do?' It was Luka, shouting down from the stairs.

'Fix door. Cub is fine.'

'Good. Now back up. Sea is flatter. Cardo wants us. Remember, Milo walks, ...'

'Milo feeds. I know it,' said Simzar, as he pushed past Luka resentfully.

'Hey, you watch Simzar, because Luka watches you, yes?'

Simzar turned to stare at Luka, then carried on up the stairs.

In the bridge, Cardo looked over sea-charts on a computer.

'Christmas in Shotlandiya, OK? Refuel. The containers, Simzar?'

'Five, six, maybe more, need fixed.'

'No. We replace. Rosyth, Shotlandiya, a Firth of Forth,' and he pointed with a pencil to the town, north of South Queensferry.

'How long at this, Rosyth?' asked Luka.

'Two weeks,' replied the captain.

'Fourteen days? No. Three at most,' replied Luka, crossly.

'Two weeks. Holiday, yes? Christmas. Two weeks. Fix and repair.'

Luka rubbed the back of his neck and shook his head.

Simzar noticed. A polar bear cub would grow in fourteen days. Maybe not by much but it would grow. And they were still nowhere near home. Was that why Luka was worried?

'Anything else?' said Cardo.

'Gasoline,' said Simzar.

'Gasoline?' replied Cardo.

'For the ribby boats.'

'Yes. Simzar, you go. As soon as we get there sort out hired van to collect gasoline, OK? It is the Christmas times. Go before everything closes, yes?'

Simzar nodded as a plan formed in his head.

'More pay?' asked Luka. 'Fourteen days more pay, eh?'

'Yes, yes, Luka. Money, money, eh?' said Cardo, shaking his head.

Luka didn't say anything but walked out of the door.

*

That night, with Kai in the top bunk, Simzar knelt by his bed and whispered a prayer.

'A prayer? What good are these prayers, Simzar?' asked Kai.

'A man who wants his freedom must pray for it, no?'

'Freedom? What is that my friend? Are you free from needing money, free from needing shelter, somewhere to live? No. You are not.'

'It is what I wish for. A freedom that makes me happy, not this sadness that I carry, day after day my friend,' and Simzar slipped into his bunk.

'Freedom lasts not long. Freedom is like rum. It's nice when you drink but when you stop, the world is not changed.'

'I want freedom without the drink. Every man should strive for freedom. A freedom he believes in. I wish it for myself.'

'You're a fool for wishing such a thing.'

'I wish it for me as I wish it for every living thing.'

'Hmm. Night Simzar.'

In a container, a young bear was sleeping soundly. He dreamt of being with his mother running through a blizzard. Running through it with no particular place to go. Just running into all the whiteness.

-44-

Being back at Mrs Johnstone's gave Caitlin the comforting familiarity and routine of being with her friends at school and seeing her gran regularly. Normally she counted the days down until she was back at the park but for the last few days, the countdown was for something else.

It was the day of the meeting and Caitlin pulled off her rucksack and placed Forth onto her lap. She sat on a plastic chair in a long, white corridor.

'What happens now?' Forth said, staring at the door.

'We've to wait for Aileen,' Caitlin replied.

'So, your mum is behind there?'

'Yes.'

'If it were my mum behind there, I'd be scratching and biting at the door. Then my mum would just knock it down to get to me.'

'Well, if I were allowed, I'd just open it and go see her, so I would.'

'Allowed? You're not allowed to see your mother?'

'I know. I'm just having to wait. They're maybe talking or writing things down. I don't know.'

'It seems funny, having to wait to see a mother.'

'It's more complicated than that, Forth.'

'Human peoples are complicated all the time.'

'You're not wrong there, pal.'

'My mother wouldn't wait, she'd look for me, she'd search for me, she'd protect me, she'd...'

'Look, it's fine,' interrupted Caitlin. Something Forth said pricked her.

'Do you want me to start scratching the door, it wouldn't take long and …'

'No, it's fine I said.'

'Or I could growl, so then someone would come?'

'No!' Caitlin sighed. 'I… I just want to sit here.'

Forth didn't say anything. Caitlin pulled him closer.

'I'm nervous, OK?'

'Nervous of your mother?'

'No, it's not that. I'm just … I'm not sure if… I don't know.'

Forth didn't say anything but kept looking at the door.

There was a big part inside Caitlin that wanted to just get up and go, walk out, leave and never come back. Surely the adults could sort all this out. What if she said the wrong thing? What if she didn't know the right answer or if she didn't know what to say when she was asked?

'Well hello, Caitlin and wee Forth,' it was Aileen. 'How are we?'

Caitlin was silent.

'So, just to say that for the purpose of this meeting, I and your mother's caseworker Mrs Ferguson, will record how things go. You can ask or say anything you like. Don't be put off just because we're there.'

Caitlin nodded.

Aileen sat next to her. 'Are you alright with all this?' she asked.

The reply was a sigh.

'Listen, I know all this is a bit emotional, but she is your mum, and it seems she is interested in caring for you. We've at least to give her a chance to air her side of the story, OK?'

'Fine.' And with that, Aileen led her and Forth into a small room. In it were just a few chairs and a table. And there, sat smiling, was Caitlin's mother, clutching at a paper cup.

'Hello Cat, my wee darling. How are you?' she said. Miss McGill stood and reached out to her daughter. Caitlin just sat, smiled, and put Forth on the table. 'Who's this, darling?'

'Forth. Don't you remember?'

'Och aye,' said her mother, looking at Aileen. 'Well, a

wee dug, eh? I love pets, so I do.'

'He's a polar bear,' and she looked at her mother while she stroked Forth's head. There was the cigarette smoke she smelt in the Manchester house as well as the lipstick red hair that draped over her sallow skin.

'Well, is that so?' said Miss McGill, who laughed with her cackle. She looked at Aileen again. 'Polar bears or dugs hen, it disnae matter to me,' and she laughed again.

'So,' said Aileen, 'this is an observed meeting between, Caitlin McGill and her mother Miss Jeanie McGill, Mrs Ferguson, Jeanie's caseworker and me, Aileen Young, Caitlin and her gran's, social worker. Right Jeanie, thank you for coming all the way up from England. So, here's your chance to say what you'd like to say to Caitlin.'

'Right, erm..., well darling, you know I love you, don't you? Sure, I'm your mother, eh?'

Caitlin didn't say anything but gave Aileen, who was writing something down, a glance.

'Well Cat angel, because I love you and that, I want to

make it up to you, so I do, for all those years I've not been about.' Her parent took in a sharp breath and paused. 'I wondered if you'd like to come down to Manchester and we get a house for us both? A brand-new house that is. It's no' even been built yet.'

Her daughter noticed Aileen look at Mrs Ferguson.

'So,' her mother continued, 'we can both choose the colours and stuff for your room and...'

'Will he be there?' asked Caitlin. 'Your boyfriend?'

'Danny?' replied her mother. 'Och, no darling.'

'Can I ask, Jeanie,' said Aileen, 'for our notes, who is Danny?'

'Her boyfriend,' said Caitlin, looking straight at her mother.

'Boyfriend? Ha! He's just a pal, angel.'

'He went into your bedroom though.'

'Can we have his full name please, Jeanie?' asked Aileen.

'Erm, well aye, I suppose. Daniel Aislewood.'

'Address?'

'Why do you need to know all that?' asked Miss McGill.

'Jeanie, if Caitlin here is going to be in Daniel's company, we need to make relevant checks, OK? Caitlin's welfare is the priority here.'

Mrs Ferguson passed Aileen a piece of paper.

'Right, got it all here, thank you,' said Aileen.

'Look Cat,' said Miss McGill, 'don't worry about Danny. He's no' going to be living with us, OK?' She reached out for her daughter's hand who still held on tight to Forth. 'It'll be a new start, angel. Just you and me darling. Wouldn't you like that?'

'What about Gran?' asked Caitlin.

'Mum? Well, we'll pop up now and again to see her, so we will.'

Caitlin frowned and noticed Aileen's surprised

expression.

'Och, she's well looked after,' continued her mother. 'So you could write, sure you could.'

'Have you been to see Gran yet?' her daughter asked.

'No, not yet, darling. I'm only up for the day. I've trains to catch and that,' and she looked at Aileen and then back at Caitlin. 'I'll go see her next time, so I will.'

'And what about Forth? Can he stay too?' and she continued to stroke the cub's head as she spoke.

'Aye. Och, well, I'll need to get a bigger freezer, so I will,' and her mother gave another cackle as she looked at Aileen.

Caitlin didn't smile. 'You didn't even say hi to me when you got back that night.'

'I…erm…sorry…I must have forgotten or something. I maybes thought you were sleeping, eh?'

'You'd not seen me in seven years.'

Her mother was quiet.

'When I was three, Gran said I asked where you were about a hundred times.'

'I'm sorry angel, it's just…things were hard…and things were different then.'

'Gran said I kept asking right up until I was seven.'

Her parent didn't reply, her eyes heavy with tears.

'So,' continued Caitlin, 'how do I know if I lived with you, that you wouldn't want me again. And maybe you'd just go. Like before.'

'I won't darling. Not this time. I promise.'

Caitlin with tears falling her voice was hesitant. 'I… I was so looking forward to seeing you, mum. I wanted to talk, to chat… to… I wanted to ask you like a million questions… about what you've been doing and what I was like when I was a baby. I just wanted to call you… mum or… mummy. I wanted you to say, "I'm so glad you're here." I wanted you to say, "Stay, Caitlin". I wanted you to…pick me up, hug me, anything…to tell your boyfriend to go away, to tell me we're going to watch a movie or go shopping because that's what a mother does, that's what family does.'

Her mother sat silent. Tears fell off her cheeks and onto the table. She looked for something to say as she smeared away the teardrops.

'It was…' said Caitlin, 'it was just like being with someone who I don't really know and they… they don't know me. And that's because…because… they don't really want me.'

'No, darling, no that's no' right, I'm your mum.'

Caitlin paused. She looked at Aileen who was still writing things down. Then she looked back at her mother who was staring at her. She took it all in: the colour of her mother's eyes, the slight lines that ran from each of them, the odd freckle on her nose and cheeks. Her pallid skin looked shiny under the small room's lights. This was her mother. Yet it could be the face of anybody.

'See when I have children,' said Caitlin, 'I am going to be there for them. Always. And see when it's their birthday or when it's Christmas, I'm going to wake up with them or maybe they'll run into my bedroom. And see at the end of a school day, I'll be at the gate. I'll wave at them and then take their bags and walk them home where there'll be one of those big TV's waiting for them.'

Her mother reached her hand out towards Caitlin across the table. 'We can have all that, darling. And I'm here now, aren't I? And I want you now, so I do. A new start, angel, eh?'

'Why now? After all this time? And to have that Danny guy coming in and out? He doesn't even like me.'

'He does. He doesn't know you, that's all.'

Still in tears, Caitlin spoke. 'I want to go now,' and she picked up Forth.

'Hang on, Caitlin not just yet. Two more minutes and then you can go,' said Aileen. Caitlin hesitated. 'Please,' and Aileen nodded at the chair.

Sitting back down she held Forth on her lap. Mrs Ferguson passed her a box of tissues.

'So, Jeanie,' continued Aileen, 'how did things go when Caitlin came for her, let's say, unofficial visit?'

'Well actually, I was a wee bit busy and not knowing she was on her way down, I … I had plans and that.'

'So, you hadn't seen your daughter in how long?'

'Aye, a few years.'

'And when you say you were busy, what do you mean, Jeanie?'

'I mean, it was a total shock, so it was. A total surprise, but…well, I erm… had to go out and that.'

'So, did Caitlin come with you?'

'Erm, not exactly, no.'

'No?'

'Well, it was…you know adult stuff, no' for kids. She'd be bored.'

'So, where was Caitlin then, while you were busy?'

'At the house. I told her to no' answer the door and I left her food and that.'

'So, you left a ten-year-old in the house?'

'Aye, but she's all grown up, so she is. I mean ten in age, but she'd just got a train all the way down to see me. Sure, I didn't even do that when I was her age?'

'Jeanie, she's ten. We need to take all things into consideration. We're looking at your skills and abilities as a mother to be able to care and provide for your daughter, Caitlin, your feelings and input here have also been very important as to whether the panel decides to let Jeanie, your mother, be the best person to be your primary carer. Jeanie, I will also need to look at paperwork from your Social Worker in Manchester, OK?

'Right.' Miss McGill shook head and sighed. 'All I want is my wean back.'

'Jeanie, it was never going to be that simple. Think of where you've been for the past few years. And why.'

Caitlin's mother rolled her eyes upwards.

'And you say you have got a new house for you both?' asked Aileen.

'Aye, it's the truth. It's just about finished.'

'I'm just concerned, and so will the panel, that having Caitlin with you is a means that will give you priority on any housing list.'

'And?'

'I'm just saying. That may also be judged by the panel as a negative issue as much as a positive one.'

'What does that mean?' asked Caitlin.

'I'll explain later,' said Aileen.

'I just want Caitlin back, OK? I'm her mum. She's my wean. I've got rights.' There was a noticeable anxiety in her voice.

'It's been seven years, Jeanie,' replied Aileen.

'Seven, aye. No' seventeen or seventy.' Jeanie sat back in her chair, folded her arms, shook her head and stared into the distance.

'Why didn't you come back?' asked Caitlin. 'When I was three, why didn't you come back home and see me. I wondered why a mum would leave without saying goodbye.'

Jeanie bit her lip, kept her arms folded and just shook her head, crying silently.

'I mean, if you loved me and you knew how much I loved you, you'd come back, wouldn't you? Because you'd miss me so much. You'd want to hold me and take me down the play park or into town. That's what mums' do, isn't it? I just…I don't understand why you'd do that?'

'Caitlin honey,' her mother suddenly put her hand out. This time Caitlin held it, tears filling up her eyes again. 'It was…just difficult. You know…I wasn't right…I couldn't give you a good happy home. I had …lots going on. And darling, it was the hardest thing I've done. Believe me, sweetheart. It was so hard. Back then I thought mum, your gran, would do a better job of being a mother than me. Do you see?'

Caitlin let go of her parent's hand.

'Come on darling, I'm your wee mum, so I am.'

'I'd like to go now.'

'Right Caitlin,' Aileen replied, 'if you want to just go and wait outside, I'll be with you in a few minutes.'

-45-

Back at Mrs Johnstone's, Caitlin, on her bed with Forth lying on her tummy, was taking stock of the day's events.

'What does your mum do now?' asked Forth.

'I don't know.'

'Will we go find her again?'

'Not now, pal.'

'Will she run away to try and find you next time?'

Caitlin slowly shook her head. 'I wouldn't have thought so.'

'Is Mrs Johnstone going to be your new mum?'

'No. Well, in a way she is I guess. Mind, she's not someone I'd call, "mum" though.'

'Who do you call your mother then?'

'My mum's, my mum. She's... well, she's just a mum I have that's not living with us right now.'

'Will she become your mother later on then?'

'What? No, and shh! I'm thinking.'

'Do peoples think on their bed lots?'

'I've nae idea and stop your yap!' and Caitlin grabbed Forth and folded her arms around him.

Her mind was trying to clear itself of the muddle it was in. That feeling of a daughter saying that she wasn't wanting to be with her mum. After all this time of wishing to have her one parent as her family, could she be really saying that?

She'd always have a mum. There was no way of getting out of that. Yet she was here, on a bed with a polar bear cub, in a house that she didn't know too well. A house far away from her mother.

Who knows, when she was old enough, she'd maybe visit her parent. Maybe even have a few days with her. As long as that boyfriend wasn't there. To live and grow up with her though? That wasn't going to happen now. Caitlin slowly shook her head. All the wishes she had for all these years had faded and blown away like dust.

So now her real family would be just her and Gran like it always had been and perhaps was always going to be. Or would it? What would happen if her old, ill gran was to ...? She pulled Forth even closer. She breathed in his furry smell. She couldn't go through with her thought. That thought of losing the only person she'd ever known. It was like the feeling of being at a cliff's edge: scary and unsafe.

'Are you thinking to run away to another den?' asked Forth.

'No, wee man. We're staying here, OK. For now. Remember, Aileen said this was only meant to be a temporary home. She's trying to find one where we'll always be and grow up in. Besides, we still want to get up to the park, don't we?' Caitlin gently lifted Forth off her chest and reached for the laptop.

'Will you miss your mum?' the cub asked the ten-year-old.

'Not sure,' she said switching her laptop on. 'Maybe.

Sometimes. It's just... och, I don't know if you can miss something you've never had. So maybe but not as much as I did before.'

'So really you're like a polar bear. Your mum left when you were young.'

'Sort of. Mind, I wonder how hard it is for a mother polar bear to leave their cub?'

'Mmm... I suppose if she knows I can hunt then she'd be fine.'

'You wouldn't see your mum again, either?'

'That's true, but then I'd be an all-grown-up polar bear.'

'Adolescent even.'

'Yes, and I could growl better.'

'Yeah? How?'

'Like this, GRRRRRRRRRRRRRRRROWL.'

'Go on yourself, Forth,' Caitlin laughed, and she typed

in a search box, "living with foster parents."

-46-

The next morning, Caitlin was, for once, looking forward to going to school. Working towards another day at the Highland Safari Park was a good distraction, a distraction from the turmoil in her head.

And two weeks passed quickly. The after-school routine of returning to her new temporary home, taking Billy out for a walk, going into Edinburgh with Mrs Johnstone, or just lounging about the house on her laptop, became a new way of life for Caitlin. There was no need to make cups of tea, no need for her to make meals, provide snacks or even fill the washing machine. That wasn't to say she wasn't always willing to help. It was just Mrs Johnstone would wave her away. So much was new and different.

They'd also go see her gran every other night. Sometimes she was sleeping, sometimes she treated Caitlin like a nurse, and sometimes she'd put on that well-known smile as soon as she saw her granddaughter. And many a time, Caitlin with Forth on her lap, would lay beside her and talk about what she'd been up to at school or at Mrs Johnstone's. And Gran, on her good days, was always interested to see how she was doing.

Then it became a Friday, one where the schools were shut for teacher-training and one when Aileen drove them north to the park. The excitement of looking forward to seeing Mr Miller and the bears seemed to shrink all thoughts of her mother or what was going to happen in the future. Right now, she was a ten-year-old girl who was being driven to a place that kept polar bears.

'I know you like this Caitlin,' said Aileen, as she drove. 'But I'm thinking they must like having you up there as well.'

'What, the bears?' smiled Caitlin, as she stroked Forth, who was lying on her legs.

'Ha, no. Mr Miller as well as the rest of the staff.'

'Well, they seemed happy enough having me about the place.'

'So what about when this ends? How will you feel then?'

Caitlin hadn't given it much thought. 'Why? Is this the last one?'

'No, it's not ending just now,' reassured Aileen. 'But you like Mr Miller and maybe you'll keep in touch with him?'

'Well, I'd like to, right enough,' and she rubbed Forth's head.

'Great. I mean, that's good. Mr Miller letting you come up and giving you jobs, at a place you love, it shows he likes you, Caitlin. And more importantly is that he's ready to trust you, so…just be good, OK?'

Caitlin frowned. 'Why?'

'Why what?'

'Why are you making so sure that I'll be good?'

'Well, Mr Miller rang me at the office the other day. He was asking about you and what I was doing to help you and your gran.'

'OK,' said Caitlin, slightly puzzled. 'Why?'

'He's just interested, I guess. So, this trip maybe isn't just about the bears. Or the other staff. Or even about the park.'

'Oh, it's about being on my best behaviour and all that? Sure, we'll be good, won't we Forth?'

'I know that. It's about Mr Miller having faith in you and doing this to help you, Caitlin.'

'I know.'

'So…well, let's just see how you get on OK?'

'You don't want me to run away, right? That's it isn't it?'

'No Caitlin, that's not it, honestly. I know you're not going to run away from somewhere you like. It's just, well, good first impressions and maybe who knows, you might get more visits up here.'

'Yes, that would be good,' and Caitlin stared at the road ahead.

What was it that Aileen was really trying to say? Just to be good? She was being good at Mrs Johnstone's so why should she be any different at the Highland Safari Park? She let go of her curiosity as soon as they drove into the car park.

When Caitlin walked into the office with Aileen, standing next to Mr Miller was a teenage boy.

'Morning Miss McGill. Morning Forth. Ready for a day of hard work?' said Mr Miller and he gave her a wink. 'This here is Stefan, and he's going to help you because your first task is to prepare the food for all the animals, OK?'

Caitlin smiled.

'And then,' continued Mr Miller, 'there's a secondary school coming from down your way. Recognise it?'

Caitlin looked at the piece of paper that Mr Miller was holding.

'I don't believe it! There's a boy called Ryan I know goes there and it's his year group.'

'Really? So are you OK to show them to the polar bear pen with Morag?'

'Nae problem.'

'Right, off you go you two. I'll see you both later. Aileen, before you go back down the road, can I have a wee word?'

Caitlin followed Stefan out into a large shed. Inside were crates of fruit and vegetables along with sacks of seeds and nuts. There were freezers, large sinks and a long wooden table.

'Right, think you can cut and chop these?' asked Stefan.

'Course,' and Caitlin put Forth and the rucksack onto the floor, took a large knife from a holder and began chopping up some carrots.

'Is Forth OK? He's not going to start eating all the food and stuff?' smiled Stefan.

'He's fine. He'll just stay near me.'

'OK,' said Stefan as he glanced at the young bear. 'Is this the start of your Easter break too?'

'Aye. So are you staying here for your Easter holidays?'

'Ha. Not really.'

'So, are you here because you've been good as well?' asked Caitlin.

'What? No.'

'Oh, so you like just helping out?'

Stefan laughed. 'You could say that, aye.'

Caitlin frowned.

'I get paid,' said Stefan.

'Really?'

'Aye. I get paid pocket money.'

'Pocket money?'

'Aye. Mr Miller, Alastair? He's my dad.'

'Ah, right. I didn't know.'

'No worries. So you're the bad one then?' smiled Stefan.

'Aye, right. Because I run away and stuff?'

'Well, yeah.'

'Yeah, I'm bad Stefan. I do all sorts of crazy stuff,' and she wielded the large knife around.

'Woah! I'm messing.'

'Good. So am I,' smiled Caitlin.

'Dad said you were a loon,' and Stefan smiled again.

'He's right,' said Caitlin, laughing.

'Well, fair play to you, I've no' runaway or anything or travelled around the country on my own and that. And what are you, ten?'

'Aye. Well, there you go. I didn't mean to…I mean I did…it's just…it's just what I had to do I suppose.'

'Och, you don't need to explain. I heard.'

'Really? What, everything?'

'Yeah. I just thought it was…well, kind of sad.'

'Sad?' said Caitlin and she stopped chopping.

'Yeah because I know I'd never run away. And I'd never

runaway because this is where I want to be.'

'You're lucky. To have all this, the park and that, and a mum and dad.'

'Well…,' and Stefan paused.

'Well? Well, what?'

'I…I, erm… look, it doesn't matter but you're right. I am. Very.'

Later, Stefan loaded up a cart with buckets of chopped vegetables, fruit and seeds. There was also chickens and joints of meat that were left whole. Some of the park's other keepers came up to the cart and took a few of the buckets. One of the keepers was Morag.

'Hi Caitlin, out of the shop this week like me then, eh?'

'Aye.'

'Right you two, oh sorry, and Forth, let's go and feed the bears.'

A small crowd of people had gathered up ahead. Stefan began shouting for Jonah and Sandy who were already lumbering towards them.

Morag started her talk. 'OK, so in twenty-five years or possibly earlier, we're going to lose more of these magnificent animals.'

'Numbers,' interrupted Caitlin, 'may decrease significantly over the next forty or so years, and this is mainly due to global warming. Which puts the polar bears in a very vulnerable position.'

Morag nodded, acknowledging Caitlin's fact.

'Wow! She's got the polar bear cub in her backpack!' observed a member of the crowd.

'No, he's Forth and he's mine,' said Caitlin and a few people laughed. 'Forth is lucky. Although he doesn't have a parent, he has me. In the wild females can starve due to the lack of seals meaning their cubs will also die. And there is also the risk of the dens that the mothers build, collapsing because of the rising temperatures. This can also kill both the mother and her young.'

'Go on yourself, Caitlin,' said Stefan afterwards. 'You

know your polar bear stuff.'

'It's all on the Internet,' said Caitlin.

'Still, I'm impressed. Maybe my dad should pay you as well.'

'You think?'

'Why don't you ask him?' and Stefan nodded in the direction of Mr Miller who was approaching with Aileen by his side.

'All OK you two?' asked Mr Miller.

'Aye. And you're right dad, total loon.'

'Told you,' winked Mr Miller.

'She can chop carrots, mind,' said Stefan and he began stacking the empty buckets onto the cart.

'Aye, she knows about polar bears, Alastair,' said Morag.

'Well, Caitlin, I can't put you on the payroll. Not yet anyway,' said Mr Miller. 'I have asked Aileen here though, if you, and Forth, can do an overnight here. Thought you might like some extra time at the park? Are you OK with that?

'Really? Sure.'

'Good. As long as you keep up the attendance and good work, that is.'

'I'm happy with this as well, Caitlin,' said Aileen. 'It's a nice offer and I'm only too happy to oblige as long as you stick to your word, OK?'

'Oh no,' said Stefan, 'not a girl staying? Can she no' sleep with the snow leopards?'

Mr Miller and Aileen laughed as Caitlin frowned and nudged into Stefan.

'Sorry,' said Stefan, 'I didn't mean the leopards…they don't poop as much as the bears do.'

'Hang on,' said Caitlin, 'in a few weeks, it's my birthday!'

'Really,' said Mr Miller, 'well then, what about having it at the park?'

Caitlin nodded and grinned. She felt different. She felt happy and the noises and troubles in her head seemed quieter now.

-47-

Later, Morag and Caitlin were stood waiting in the coach park when the school's bus pulled in.

Ryan spotted Caitlin through the window and pointed at her. 'Someone said you might be here,' he remarked as he stepped off the bus.

'Name please,' asked Caitlin.

'The Duke of Edinburgh,' replied Ryan.

'The doughnut's arrived then,' said Caitlin and she smiled as she ticked him off the list.

'I see your wee bear friend's here too. Shouldn't it be in a cage?' and Ryan pointed to her rucksack.

'Is that your girlfriend, Ryan?' said one of a group of boys.

'Get lost!' said Caitlin.

Ryan walked back to his pals.

'Ryan and Caitlin under a tree, k-i-s-s-i-n-g,' sang another of the boys.

'Get away you, Dale' said Ryan.

'Hello S1, let's go this way please,' instructed Morag. 'It's the polar bear's second feed.'

'Take no notice, Cat,' whispered Ryan.

'I haven't,' she replied.

At the enclosure, Morag began by introducing the adult bears, Jonah and Sandy, who were strolling towards the group.

'And this is Caitlin, who will now give you a bit more information.'

'Miss, that's Ryan's girlfriend, so it is,' shouted Dale.

'No, it's no',' snapped Ryan.

'Enough Dale and you, Ryan,' said one of the teachers.

Caitlin did her best informative voice as she addressed

the group. 'Right I hope the rest of you are listening as those tubes clearly aren't.' Most of the group laughed.

Caitlin continued. 'At the moment, the world's population of polar bears is threatened by the current warming trend of the world's climate. Ice packs are retreating giving bears less chance of hunting for their favourite food, seals. That's why places such as this are important: to teach and show polar bears to the public. By showing how incredibly beautiful they are, people will maybe understand that it is important to help lessen the effects of global warming to enable their survival.'

Morag then followed on with the talk.

The polar bears were getting closer, so Caitlin began to throw items of food from a bucket over the fence.

'Is that the wee one?' shouted Dale, pointing at Forth.

'Shut up!' hissed Ryan.

Caitlin ignored the comment. 'The Highland Safari Park's baby bear is in a separate enclosure and is still inside the specially built den.'

'Right S1, now we need to go this way,' said Morag.

Caitlin stayed put as she threw over more items of food. Dale and two other boys came over.

'So, Mrs Ryan, how come you've got a baby bear then? Why is he no' in with his pals?'

'Polar bear cubs shouldn't be put in with adults, especially males. They have to stay with their mother for at least two years.'

'Is that right?'

'It would be too dangerous.'

'How?'

'They would be eaten.'

'Really?' Dale looked at the other two boys who were grinning. 'Like, really eaten? Their own, wee bear?'

'Aye.'

'Och, that's so sad,' said Dale, sarcastically.

'Right, you no' joining the others, you clown?'

'Aye, we will but we love nature, so we do. Isn't that right boys?' The other boys nodded.

Caitlin just shook her head and, with a bucket in each hand, set off.

Dale winked and in one quick move, the two boys held Caitlin while Dale viciously pulled Forth out of his bag, hurried to the fence, and flung the cub over it.

Everything seemed to go so slowly; Forth falling through the air, landing on his back, then that gradual realisation of what was happening.

A scream: loud and horrific. The school group turned to see.

Caitlin, the buckets dropped, ran at the fence, screaming, desperate with clumsy attempts to try scale the wire and metal posts between her and her best friend.

Ryan appeared. 'What've you done, Dale? You absolute...'

'Down Caitlin, NOW!' ordered the approaching Mr Miller.

The young girl was still full of screams, still trying, however vainly, to get to her friend. She could only get so high, before slipping back to the ground. Then she tried again, her hands cut and bleeding. She attempted to push her hand through the mesh, as if Forth could be summoned by her outstretched, beckoning fingers. To just get up and walk to her. To be out of harm's way. To be safe. To return and be folded up in her arms.

The adult bears were now curious. They nosed the air towards where Caitlin was crying out, loud and desperate, 'Forth! FORTH! Come here! Come here, please! Please, Forth! Hi you, Forth! Come on! Hurry! Please, Forth. PLEASE!'

'Caitlin, get down from that fence now, I swear to…' It was Mr Miller, only a yard or two away now.

Ryan grabbed Dale. 'You total eejit,' and he threw him to the ground.

Her cries were more desperate. 'Forth! Forth! Please, pal! Please! PLEASE'

Jonah was first to sniff at the ground, inching towards Forth.

'Forth move! Look he's not moving, he's just not moving! FORTH!'

Mr Miller grabbed Caitlin around the waist and dragged her off the fence.

'No! NO! Forth! FORTH!' She punched and struck and did everything she could to get out of the adult's strong grip.

'It's OK Caitlin, it's OK,' and Mr Miller hugged her, wrapping his big, thick arms around the ten-year-old girl, whose punches and kicks became softer, like the rain easing after the anger of a storm. She cried into his shoulder.

Mr Miller let her down gently and still holding a hand, tried to walk her away. Yet Caitlin wanted to turn around, see what fate was to befall Forth. Maybe the bears would be disinterested, and leave him be? Caitlin resisted the adult's intentions so she could still witness what was going to happen.

With only the slightest of movements, a slight prod of Jonah's paw was more than enough to cut through Forth's belly. And when he did, a piece of stuffing came out and on the breeze, landed in long grass. The large male bear sniffed at the ripped material then nosed in at it. Sandy approached and also inspected it with an inquisitive lick as pieces of thread and fluff flapped or skated across the ground, the draught casting them towards the watching girl.

'Forth,' she whispered.

'It's just a toy, you dafty,' Dale responded, as he picked himself up off the ground. 'It's no' real. It's just a big teddy for wee girls, like you.'

Caitlin's whole body shook as she wept. Mr Miller placed his arm around her shoulders.

'Right, you! Here. Now!' Mr Miller was speaking to Ryan. 'Look after her, OK?'

Ryan nodded, and without being asked, slowly wrapped himself around Caitlin. Still sobbing, the girl's head fell onto his shoulder.

'Sandy! Jonah!' Mr Miller shouted. He had hold of the buckets and banged them together, to get the bears attention. They both looked up and lolloped towards him as he emptied the remaining contents over the fence.

'Right, which one of you did this?' said Mr Miller, looking at the boys.

Ryan let go of Caitlin and pointed to Dale.

'Where's your teacher, pal? You're banned, understand me?'

Dale shrugged.

A teacher appeared and took hold of Dale by his shoulder. 'McPike, back to the bus, now!'

'And I haven't finished there either,' said Mr Miller. 'I'd like a few more words with him if you don't mind?' said Mr Miller.

'By all means,' said the teacher.

Mr Miller got out a walkie-talkie. 'Hi, can Martin and Lesley get the holding pen ready? Aye, just briefly. We need to remove a ...well, a foreign object from the main bear enclosure, over.'

Caitlin walked slowly to the fence, wrapped her fingers through it and looked at the tattered remains of her friend.

Another piece of stuffing crawled along the ground on a slight breath of a breeze.

'Forth,' and she let her head rest against the cold metal.

*

As Mr Miller drove Caitlin home, he gave her an occasional glance.

'Are you going to be OK?' he asked.

'I suppose,' replied Caitlin, her head against the window.

'We'll still see you again in a couple of weeks for your birthday?'

'Aye, I'd still like to help out and that.'

'Nae problem.'

'It's just…it's not going to be the same. Nothing is.'

'I know. It's always going to be hard losing your best

friend. Do you know what might get you through?'

Caitlin shook her head.

'Memories. Sometimes they'll maybe give you a wee tear but, now and again, they'll also put a smile on your face.'

Caitlin gave a quick smile then fought back tears as she bit her bottom lip.

*

Stood by her car, Mrs Johnstone didn't even get a chance to say hello as Caitlin opened the door and got inside.

'Can we see my gran?' she demanded.

'Erm…OK then. No Forth?'

There was no answer. Mr Miller slowly shook his head and got into his car.

Caitlin's gran was oblivious to her granddaughter coming into the room or even lying beside her on the bed. The young girl kept silent whilst her gran lay gently breathing as she slept.

Mrs Johnstone stood at the door when, Matthew, the male nurse, popped his head in.

Caitlin was already asleep and so she didn't hear the door click shut or the conversation with quiet words outside.

'It's fine Mrs Johnstone. I'm on nights and I'll let the other staff know.'

'Oh, OK. I'm not sure what's happened but she's come back from the Highland Park without Forth.'

'Oh, dear. Well listen, if there is a problem, we'll give you a ring, OK?'

'Right, I'll have my phone by my bedside. And I'll come and get her tomorrow.'

'OK, Mrs Johnstone, see you then.'

-48-

When Mrs Johnstone next saw Caitlin, she was sat up with her gran, eating a slice of toast.

'So how are we both?' asked Mrs Johnstone.

'OK,' said Caitlin.

'Could we have more tea please, nurse?' asked Gran.

Mrs Johnstone smiled. 'I'll see what I can do,' and she went out of the room.

'So, where's the dug?' asked Gran.

'He's …erm, he's just gone.'

'Gone? Gone where?'

'Erm…the North Pole.'

'Is it Christmas?'

'No gran,' said Caitlin, who couldn't help but smile.

'It's actually Easter. I'm on my holidays the now.'

'Och, but he'll be cold.'

'Who will?'

'Your dug! I would have made him a coat so I would. A wee tartan…'

Caitlin grabbed a hold of her gran before she could finish and gave her a squeeze.

'Och, you're a soft tattie, so you are,' said Gran, and she kissed her on the head.

'I miss him,' came the granddaughter's muffled voice as she was still wrapped around her grandparent.

'Aye. And that's fine. It's good we miss those that we love. Shows we cared about them. And you'll have all those photos of him, all the ones in your head I mean,' and she stroked the young girl's hair.

Back at Mrs Johnstone's, Caitlin was in her room, staring into her laptop, when there was a knock on her door.

'Yes?' said Caitlin, and Billy bounded straight in and

onto her bed.

'Thought you might like some company,' said Mrs Johnstone. 'We're away out later. Fancy coming?'

'OK,' and she stroked Billy whilst still looking into her laptop.

'Interesting?' asked Mrs Johnstone.

'Just watching polar bears. There's a website that tracks tagged ones out in the wild.'

'Really? Great thing the Internet, eh? So how are you feeling now?'

She shrugged.

'Look, I know it's hard. All this. Living with people you don't know and then on top of that, losing your best friend.'

Caitlin was listening as she still gazed at the screen.

'But this bit, being alone, or feeling like you are. It won't be forever; you know that don't you?'

No reply.

'You'll be given a permanent foster place and that will be with people who want you to be part of their family.'

'What if I don't like them?'

'Well there are no guarantees, but then there are no guarantees in life, Caitlin. Rest assured though that Aileen and her team, as well as the fostering agencies, will be trying hard to match you to a foster family that is the best for you.'

'And what if they don't like *me*?'

'Listen, these people, the people that want you to be in their family, they're not doing what they do to pick-and-choose and maybe then hand it back. They're doing it because they think they can help.'

'I quite like it here though?'

'Well that's nice Caitlin, but that's not what this is about. Surely you want to be looked after by a mother and a father? And maybe they'll have sons and daughters too. So, you'll be part of a family. And be their family when you're all grown up.'

'Adopted?'

'No. That's slightly different. And it's a decision that Aileen will need to look into. I think you would still want to have some sort of contact with your mum, am I right?'

'Yes, I suppose. Perhaps letters or birthdays cards?'

'Well, even given that limited contact, fostering is going to be the best option for you.'

'Still, maybe I'd be better off here. At least you know I'm happy enough, just being here with you?'

Mrs Johnstone didn't answer but instead left Caitlin with Billy on the bed. A little while later she returned and in her hand was a large folder.

'Thought I'd show you this. My photo album. It's all the children that have stayed with me over the years. May I?'

Caitlin nodded and shut her laptop as Mrs Johnstone sat on the edge of the bed.

The pages were covered by dozens of photos of girls and boys, brothers and sisters, all of different ages and all smiling for the camera. All that is apart from one.

'Amy?' asked Caitlin.

'Aye. Think that was the first time she stayed here.'

Mrs Johnstone pointed to a picture of twins, 'Now they were wee roasters, so they were,' and she laughed. 'Mind, they got a foster home and they're doing so well. Their foster parents are special school teachers. Just what they needed.'

'Do you get sad though?' asked Caitlin. 'When they leave you after staying?'

'Yes, I can be. I have to tell my family not to come round as I'm quite upset for a few days. Then before you know it, Aileen will ring and another girl or boy needs foster care. And off we go again.'

Caitlin was quiet as she continued to browse through all the pictures.

'Point is Caitlin, just about all of these have gone on to a more permanent type of care.'

'Just about?'

'Amy. Out of all these pictures, she's the only one. She

is a slightly different case though. She gets to go back to her home. But as you saw, when that placement breaks down she ends up going back into care.'

Caitlin had to admit that there was a lot of children who had stayed.

'Do the parents get to choose?' she asked

'No. It's not like that. They're picked specially. There's a trial period, you know, a few getting to know you sessions. Then that's it.'

'Will they look after my gran?'

'No, Caitlin. Your gran is in the best place for her just now. You'd still see her though and that's something to take into consideration as she's your family. Your only family,' and with that Mrs Johnstone shut the folder. 'Right, I'll see you downstairs. Ten minutes? A two week holiday, Caitlin. Got to keep you busy, eh? And we'll post your birthday invites. Who is Michael Vagabond of Princes Street Gardens, by the way?'

'Just a pal. I'm not sure he'll get it, but we'll see.'

'Mmm... OK. Anyway, ten minutes?'

Once Mrs Johnstone left, Caitlin stretched out on her bed and stared at the ceiling. What was this feeling? A feeling like the ground beneath her was moving, that nothing seemed stable anymore. That she was being guided along by some big, powerful river, like the Firth of Forth, one which she was unable to halt or steer herself. Was it the feeling of change? That life would be very different from the one she was used to? And if it was, the young girl couldn't be sure if she liked it or if she feared it.

-49-

Hi Grace. Bday party nxt wk @ the Highland S Park. Yaaaaay!

Oh yesssssss! 👍 🎁 😎

Who else?

Mrs J + Billy + invite back from Aileen!

LOL! Kwl

& remember Ryan McK?

Yes. Y?

& him.

Just a friend!

Lol.

ς •ﻌ•?

???

Forth has gone.

???

Ring me!

2 sad C U @ schwl 2mrw

-50-

The first day back at school after the two-week holiday was always going to be hard. Not just because of the going back to lessons, but her best friend, the friend that made her feel special, wasn't by her side. Then there were the questions.

'Where is he? What happened? Why is he not here?' asked Grace, her questions fast and demanding.

'He's...gone.'

'Gone where though?' replied a crestfallen Grace.

'Just gone, where all polar bears go.'

'Iceland?' suggested Brandon.

'Iceland doesn't have polar bears,' said Caitlin.

'Ikea?' said Brandon laughing.

'Aye right, numpty,' replied Caitlin.

Miss Bell came in. 'No Forth?' she asked.

Caitlin shook her head.

'We'll maybe turn his space over in the corner to something else then. How about something in memory of the school's first polar bear cub?' offered Miss Bell.

Caitlin sighed as she glanced at the empty cage with its sign and surrounding cushions.

Just then Sophie walked past to take her seat. Caitlin braced herself. *Just one silly question.* Yet Sophie didn't say a word and carried on without even acknowledging or noticing that a young, white bear was not in class.

At break time, Grace and Caitlin were sat having their snack.

'You could always get another?' said Grace.

'What? Another polar bear cub? How?'

'A shop?'

'No, not now. I'd be telling it all the stories about Forth and what we did. It wouldn't be fair. Besides, I don't know if

I would feel the same about another polar bear cub. It just wouldn't be the same.'

Grace sat silently.

'And,' continued Caitlin, 'I'm going to be eleven next week.'

'I know. Thanks for the invite by the way. Mrs Johnstone rang my mum. What's this with Ryan McKechnie? Wit-woo!' smiled Grace.

'Away and raffle your doughnut, you. It's just being eleven, you know? Soft, cuddly teddy bears or polar bears or any other toys really, maybe that's all behind me now?'

Just then, Sophie wandered up to them both.

'Here it comes,' whispered Caitlin.

'Keep calm, Cat, keep calm,' Grace whispered back.

'Hi, Caitlin. Grace,' said Sophie.

'Go on, say what you've been wanting to say. Say something rubbish about Forth not being here,' said Caitlin, who stood up.

'I was…erm…just going to say…' responded Sophie, uncomfortably.

'What?'

'Sorry. And about losing Forth that is.'

Caitlin was a bit taken aback. 'Is this a joke, Sophie Wallace? Because if it is, I'll…'

'No. It's not a joke. Max, our Labrador. He died during the holidays. We've had him since I was wee.'

Caitlin paused for a moment. 'Oh, I see. Well, I'm sorry to hear that.'

Sophie pulled her mobile phone out of her pocket. She showed Caitlin and Grace a slideshow of pictures of her dog from when he was a puppy to him having grey hairs around his muzzle.

'He's cute,' said Grace, '*was* cute,' she quickly added.

'Aye, he seems a nice dog, Sophie. Friendly?'

'He was. And daft, and he was so gentle,' and Sophie's eyes began to fill.

'You'll have a load of good memories though, eh?' said Caitlin, remembering Mr Miller's and also her gran's words.

'Aye. He was such a good dog. Such a good pal.' And with that, she walked away with her friends still by her.

Grace pulled a face of disbelief. 'Wow! OK, I wish I just had recorded that. You know what you'll have to do now, don't you?'

'No? What?'

'Invite her to your party.'

'OK.'

Grace laughed, 'I was kidding.'

'I know. But I wasn't.'

-51-

On the morning of Caitlin's birthday, there wasn't time to rip open parcels or read all her cards. Instead, they all got bundled into a small suitcase, along with all of Caitlin's other bits and pieces.

From the back of the car, Mrs Johnstone was directed to Grace's house who, once inside, sat beside Caitlin and a panting Billy. Mrs Johnstone instantly became their chauffeur; listening and watching through the rear-view mirror, as the girls chatted incessantly throughout the journey.

Once at their destination, they parked beside Aileen, who was stood with Ryan and Sophie.

Ryan nervously handed Caitlin a card and wished her a happy birthday.

'Thanks, Ryan and for all the other stuff.' said Caitlin.

'Like what? Pushing Dale over?'

'Well, aye and you've looked out for me over these last few months. What with my gran and all.'

Ryan just nodded as Sophie also passed Caitlin a card as well as a small present.

'Thanks, as well, for doing this,' she said.

'Nae problem,' replied Caitlin.

Sophie nodded. 'It's cool.'

Just then Mr Miller, along with Stefan, came out of the office.

'Right, is this your gang, Caitlin?' he enquired.

'Aye.'

'If you pop all your bags and things inside here. Oh, and is the dog yours Mrs Johnstone? I'm afraid he'll have to stay in the office, OK?'

'Not a problem,' said Mrs Johnstone.

'Right,' continued Mr Miller, 'we have a big surprise for all of you.'

Caitlin was slightly puzzled but guessed it was a cake or something else to do with her birthday. When the four of them came back out, now standing with Mr Miller, were three other men all holding large cameras.

'Right folks,' said Mr Miller, 'if you'd like to follow me.' And so, the small group followed.

'What's going on?' Caitlin asked Stefan.

'You'll see,' said Stefan.

It didn't take long until it dawned on Caitlin what may be happening. The large wooden birthing-den came into view as they headed towards Agnes' enclosure.

Up ahead was Morag, stood by the fence. Caitlin suddenly felt her heart race and she ran towards her, looking into the den.

'Ladies and gentlemen,' said Mr Miller, 'here is, Archie!'

'Archie!' said Caitlin, as there, in amongst long reeds that bordered a small pond, was the brilliantly white, polar bear cub.

'A boy, Archie?' Caitlin asked.

Mr Miller laughed. 'Yes, Archie, a male polar bear cub.'

'Archie, pal!' and Caitlin fell onto her knees as if the baby cub would come trotting up to her like a puppy. The small bear stayed near his mother.

'I've been waiting so long to meet you. Me and my pal, Forth but... sorry, he can't be here...' As she spoke, Caitlin's voice faltered slightly.

'Are you OK?' asked Stefan.

'Yeah, it's just... there's no Forth here to see it and it's nice...you know...Archie just following his mother around. Like a child would.'

'Hey, Caitlin, don't upset yourself,' it was Mr Miller, and he crouched down beside her. 'You know it won't be too long before we've to put Archie in his own pen or even another park, did you know that?'

Caitlin nodded.

'Then he's to stand on his own two feet. Sorry, four

feet,' joked Mr Miller.

Caitlin managed to give a quick smile and, with her sleeve, brushed the dampness off her cheeks.

'Up until then,' continued Mr Miller, 'maybe we should enjoy Agnes being a mum and Archie, well, being a pain, eh?'

'He's too cute to be a pain,' replied Caitlin.

'Ha, I know. And we, the park that is, are so lucky to have him. So, we'll enjoy them both, eh? And enjoy that they're lucky to have each other, agreed?'

Caitlin looked at Mr Miller. 'Sure. And thank you.'

'What for?'

'Well saying all that and letting me be here. Thanks.'

'Nae problem, lady.'

The photographer's cameras clicked and flashed at a blissfully unaware Archie, who investigated the reeds, and the ponds muddy shore, all the time keeping close to his mother's side.

'Aye, early hours of this morning,' said Morag, 'he took his first steps outside of the den. So, we did a quick check and yes, Archie is a boy!'

'Well, what do you think folks?' said Mr Miller.

'So cute!' said Grace.

'Really cool,' said Sophie.

Ryan nodded.

The photographers lined the four friends next to the fence.

'First visitors to see the baby polar bear cub,' said Mr Miller, as if reading a newspaper headline.

Once the photographers had finished, Caitlin was asked if she'd like to show her guests around the rest of the park.

'I just need to speak to Aileen and Mrs Johnstone, Caitlin,' said Mr Miller. 'Stefan you can come with me as well. You OK with that, Caitlin?'

'No problem,' and she led the others towards the much

larger polar bear enclosure.

'Are you OK with Archie being in a place like this?' asked Ryan as they walked.

'How do you mean?' replied Caitlin.

'Well, don't you think they're better off being free? Being able to wander around where they should really live?'

'Like I said when your school visited, here they're well looked after and people get to know about them,' said Caitlin. 'And by getting to know them, and seeing them so close up, they can see how beautiful they are and that they need protecting. Then maybe they'll be helped. Bears in the wild that is.'

'We saw that on your presentation,' said Grace. 'Global warming and all that.'

'Exactly,' said Caitlin.

'So you're OK with them being trapped in here?' said Ryan.

'Trapped?' said Caitlin and she pulled a face. 'If by

being "trapped," helps them, aye.'

'Yeah,' said Grace, 'but do you think they might feel happier if they were out in the wild?'

'Well, none of the polar bears here are actually from the wild. They were all born in zoos.'

'So, they'll never know what it's like to be free?' observed Sophie.

'Well, that might be…' Caitlin tried to respond.

'Hang about Caitlin McGill,' said Ryan, 'you're the one that talks to polar bears, so why don't you ask them? See if they're happy being in here or if they like to have dreams of being back with their pals in Poland.'

'Poland? They don't have polar bears, you doughnut.'

'Whatever.'

'I guess they're safe here though, eh?' said Grace, who was looking at Jonah and Sandy who were not far from the perimeter fencing.

'Aye, safe. And educating folk,' said Caitlin, directing

her reply at Ryan.

'Well, that's maybe so,' he replied, 'but being cooped up in this pen with everyone staring at you or being free to roam wherever you want, I know what I'd choose.'

'Aye, but no one wants to come to see a turnip,' Grace chipped in.

'Aye, right then,' said Ryan.

Caitlin didn't want to continue the argument and she looked at the bears, so big and perfect. And yes, this was Scotland, not the wild expanses of the Arctic Circle.

'Why don't they just let them back into the wild and let folk see what happens to them?' said Ryan, still unconvinced.

'Well there are ones you can watch on a tracking thing, via a satellite, on the Internet,' answered Caitlin.

'Really?' said Sophie.

'Well there you go,' said Ryan. 'Better than being behind a wire fence.'

'Look how close we can get to them though. And if the polar bears weren't here, who would bother about them?' said Caitlin, offering the question up to her friends.

Jonah and Sandy were only a few feet back from the fence now.

'Wow!' said Sophie, 'look at the size of them,' and she and Grace got their phones out.

Later, Stefan met up with the small party and showed them how to prepare food for some of the park's attractions. They all loved how the animals seemed to anticipate the food coming. It was as if they knew it was time to eat as they all moved restlessly in their enclosures. The snow leopards hugged close to the fence as their food was thrown into them. And the four friends laughed and pointed at the macaque monkeys whose shy, adorable babies held their attention.

At one point, Caitlin did her talk to some visitors as they re-visited the polar bears, who were due their second feed.

Yet in no time at all, it seemed the group were heading the short distance to the Miller's house.

Inside they all made their way to the kitchen.

'Well hello to you Caitlin, and hello to you all,' and a beaming Mrs Miller, small and with a happy, rosy face came and shook Caitlin's hand.

Caitlin ignored it and instead she gave her a small hug.

'Hi, I'm Caitlin. Thanks for letting me stay,' she said, still with her hands around the adult.

'Och, I know who you are, lady, and what's more, it's absolutely lovely to meet you. Alistair and Stefan have told me so much about you.'

'Aye, that you're a loon,' said Stefan.

The small group laughed.

'Alastair,' said Mrs Miller, 'can you show these folks into the dining room, but not this one,' and she placed her hands on Caitlin's shoulders.

'Right you are, Mary,' and everyone filed out of the door.

'OK birthday girl, we've got a wee surprise for you,'

and Mrs Miller winked.

'Nice,' smiled Caitlin who wondered if the surprise was chocolate flavoured.

Mrs Miller grabbed a tea towel. 'Blindfold?'

'OK,' and Mrs Miller wrapped it around her head.

Holding her hand, she guided the eleven-year-old into the dining room, where she was greeted with the singing of, 'Happy Birthday.'

Caitlin grabbed the towel away from her eyes and there, right next to a tall, white cake, sat her best friend.

-52-

Caitlin burst into tears and just about screamed the room down in delight. 'Forth!'

And there he was, whole and complete, with a slight scar of stitches across his tummy.

The others looked on, Sophie smiling, Ryan shaking his head, Grace so excited for her friend and Billy barking in amongst all the mayhem.

'Forth!' repeated Caitlin, and she squeezed him for her all her might.

'You've Mary to thank for this,' said Mr Miller.

Caitlin tried to say thank you, but she was still shedding tears of happiness.

'Well maybe thank my mum. She was a seamstress. Taught me all I know with a needle and thread. Oh, and I gave him a wee bath.'

'Listen, Miss McGill, this is your birthday,' said Mr Miller, 'less of your tears, and more eating your cake, then opening your cards and parcels.'

Caitlin dried her eyes and blew out the candles.

'Not a bad birthday for you then?' said Aileen.

Caitlin nodded. *What a day,* she thought, *what a day.*

*

Later that night having said goodbye to her friends, Mrs Miller showed Caitlin to her room. Inside was all very tidy with a small bed, wardrobe and from wall to wall, polar bears. They were on the duvet cover as well as posters detailing facts and figures of the creatures. They were the ornaments and the soft toys adorning shelves and a windowsill. There was even a clock in the shape of a white bear whose front legs indicated the time.

'Some of these things were Stefan's but we thought you

might like them.'

'I love it,' and Caitlin landed on her back on the bed, Forth held aloft in her hands. 'We both do.'

'Good, right, the bathroom's just next door. If you need anything, let me know. I think Alastair is wanting to get an early start tomorrow. You'll be OK with that though?'

'Yes. Sure. Thank you, Mary.'

'Sleep well, Cat.' And she shut the door behind her.

With Forth tucked under the covers alongside her, Caitlin gazed at her friend.

'I missed you, pal,' said the girl.

'I wondered where you were,' said the young bear.

'Where I was?'

'Yes. I remember being sniffed at by one of the polar bears. Then it went dark. And then I woke up, here. And I've been just here a while now. No one said where you were or where here actually was.'

'They didn't tell you?'

'No.'

'What did they say then?'

'Nothing.'

'Nothing?'

'Yes. No one spoke to me. Well, only once. Mrs Miller held me one day and said, "there you are now," but that was all.'

'Right. You had a nasty accident.'

'I did?'

'Yip.'

'I'm alright now though?'

'Well, you look OK. Maybe a bit sleepy. Quite a day, eh?'

'Will I see the polar bears again in the morning? From behind the fence that is?'

'Aye. Of Course. And you'll see Archie, the baby polar

bear.'

'Archie? Really? Will he be in a bed like this?'

'I don't think so, pal. I guess he'll be comfy though. He's going to be laying right next to his mum.'

'I remember that. With my mum that is. Her warmth. Her breathing.'

Caitlin grabbed Forth and pulled him up close and purposely breathed heavily against his cheeks. Then she moved her head back.

'Forth, it's nice here isn't it?'

'It is. It's like another type of home isn't it?'

'Aye, right enough, but a nice one.'

'Do you think it could be like a family home? I mean there's a dad in it and a mother. And a son?'

'Yes. That's exactly what it's like.'

'A family home but one where we don't have a mother or father.'

'That's true, we're just guests but they're treating us like…well, family. Maybe that's just their way of being friendly and that.'

'So while we're here, we can pretend it's our family?'

'Maybe. Forth, there's something else.'

'What?'

'You know I was eleven today.'

'Yes.'

'So, because I'm getting older, I…erm…well, I'm just getting older that's all, so maybe I'll do things maybe more sort of, erm…grown-up.'

'Like an adult bear?'

'Yes. That's it, like an adult bear. They're quite solitary, aren't they?'

'If that means on their own then yes. They are quite good at being solitary.'

'Exactly. So, I'm maybe getting to be an adult, as I get

older and that.'

'You getting-to-be-an-adult peoples means you get to be more solitary then?'

'Erm…in some ways but it may mean not being young and doing er…young things, you know?'

'So, what you've been doing is just for young peoples and now you're not going to do young things as much because you're learning to be an older peoples?'

Caitlin sighed. 'Sort of like that, pal. You would go out into the world by yourself when you got older, wouldn't you?'

'Maybe I'll get older right beside you so we can do growing up things together?'

Caitlin didn't answer but kissed her furry friend on his head then reached over and switched her light off. 'Night, pal,' and she closed her damp eyes.

*

In the morning when Caitlin appeared with Forth, breakfast was well underway. She went to get a pile of plates.

'Och, you're fine,' said Mrs Miller. 'Sit yourself down. Now, what would you like?'

Caitlin looked at Mrs Miller's smiling face. 'I don't always run away you know. Not from places I like.'

'We know.' It was Mr Miller.

'Still here?' said Stefan who appeared behind his dad. 'Thought you may be away on a remote island by now.'

'Don't listen to him Caitlin, he's teasing' said Mrs Miller.

'Listen, we know quite a lot about you,' said Mr Miller. 'I've been chatting to Aileen. It's quite a lot you've been through.'

'More than some adults,' added Mrs Miller.

'So, you've nothing to prove here,' her husband continued. 'Just relax and have your breakfast, OK?'

'Thanks,' is all Caitlin could think to say, and she sat

down, putting Forth onto his highchair.

'Spades are in the shed,' said Stefan smiling, 'just in case you feel you want to escape by tunnel.'

'Stefan!' snapped Mrs Miller but Caitlin was laughing.

It was a busy morning in the park: feeding the animals, cleaning out the snow monkey's cages and then helping in the shop. And Forth got to meet Archie. Yet with Stefan in close attendance, and the new baby bear only having eyes for his mother, Forth just looked on, silently.

Soon the two friends were being whisked away back to South Queensferry. Yet as soon Caitlin headed home, all she could think about was the next time she would be back.

-53-

The weeks rolled by as spring soon became summer. There were still fortnightly trips to see Archie and the rest of the other animals. Caitlin didn't mind that these were now just day trips. That she was working with the animals in a place where she felt welcomed and wanted was enough.

The young girl felt a change. She wasn't sure what the change was, but she felt it happening. Was she getting older? Was it because after all the moving about, the running away, the meeting her mother, all that worry and agitation was now flattening out into this different, peaceful life she was enjoying? New. Fresh. And settled.

She still saw Gran. And she was able to tell all her news to her one, close relative. And there were times when Caitlin felt that her grandmother may not be in the home much longer. That she was just the gran she'd always knew. That maybe she could come home, there and then, come back and be with her, "wee angel". Then there were the days when her grandmother seemed so distant and different that any chance of them being back together in the flat, seemed remote.

Change would also be taking place at school. It was the last day in Miss Bell's class and the children were excitedly saying their goodbyes as they left at home time.

Grace asked Caitlin what she was doing over the holidays.

'I'm up at the park, but for a full week this time,' said Caitlin.

'Wow! Well, say hello to Archie for me.'

'Will do.'

'I bet Forth can't wait.'

Caitlin gave a brief smile but didn't say anything.

*

With her case packed, Caitlin stroked Forth on his head. She stared into his eyes, sighed then placed him on the windowsill and slowly closed the bedroom door behind her.

There was that slight feeling of guilt as if Forth was missing out on her latest adventure. She consoled herself as this was what being eleven was all about. It was about growing up and not needing to have a soft-toy by her side all the time. Especially not a toy she spoke to. And this feeling she had, one tinged with some regret, would get better day after day.

It was Stefan who asked where he was.

'Back at Mrs Johnstone's,' Caitlin replied.

'Oh, OK. You'll be missing him though?'

'Not really. And are there no' real polar bears here, by the way?'

Stefan shrugged and passed her some more fruit to chop.

Caitlin was kept busy for her stay. Not that she minded. Preparing food, cleaning and mucking pens out, all of the jobs she was now used to. She loved it.

'You're quite a star, lady' said Mr Miller at one of her tea breaks.

'Right, Caitlin' said Stefan, 'this is where you need to ask if your pay is going up.'

She smiled.

'Aye, we'll have to get you on some long-term contract,' said Mr Miller.

'Really? Like a load more visits?' replied Caitlin.

'Well, just watch this space,' Mr Miller winked at Stefan and the young girl felt a wave of excitement wash over her.

The only bad part of being busy wasn't the tiredness from being rushed off her feet. It was the fact that her seven days flew by.

And so, before she knew it, Mr Miller was putting her suitcase into the back of his car.

Caitlin looked puzzled.

'What's up?' asked Stefan as he opened the car door.

'You don't normally come back with me? Neither does your mum,' noted Caitlin.

'Well maybe it's to do with your long-term contract?' said Stefan.

'Oh, right. And you all have to come back with me for that?' said Caitlin, still curious.

'Mmm...well, yeah.'

She was even more puzzled when they eventually parked up at South Queensferry.

'Aren't we going to Mrs Johnstone's?' asked the eleven-year-old.

'Not just yet,' answered Mr Miller and he nodded towards Aileen who was walking towards them.

'Has something happened to Gran?' Caitlin asked as she stepped out of the car.

'No, no,' said Aileen. 'It's fine. We just need to have a nice wee chat.'

Caitlin sighed. *It's my mum. She's wanting me in*

Manchester again. Or is she moving back to Scotland? Then what's going to happen?

Inside a nearby café, Caitlin remained quiet until her impatience couldn't be silenced any longer.

'What's wrong then?'

'Nothing's wrong, Caitlin,' said Aileen. 'Quite the opposite. Alastair, would you like to say a few words?'

'Right you are. Erm, Cat... Caitlin...I know you've been liking it at the park and that, well we've liked having you and staying at our bit. So, erm... how about a long-term contract?'

'Sure,' and she let out a sigh of relief. She'd be working at the park for months to come. 'And I'll get paid?'

'Well, er...yes. And no.'

Caitlin frowned. 'Oh. OK.'

Mr Miller glanced at the others and then sat upright. 'Caitlin, how would you feel if you were to stay at our bit? For quite some time, that is? I mean, erm...'

Mrs Miller helped her husband out. 'What he's trying to say, Caitlin, is how would you like it if we were your long-term foster parents?'

Caitlin sat silently. She looked at Aileen then she looked back at Mr Miller. Everyone was waiting on the eleven-year-old's response.

'Well?' prompted Aileen.

'Really? I mean, forever'

They all nodded.

'And Gran?'

'We'll put a transfer in for her,' said Aileen.

'Your gran is part of this,' added Mr Miller. 'There's a home just on the outside...,' but he was interrupted as Caitlin grabbed hold of him.

'Yes,' she said, happiness in the form of tears, on her face. Then she hugged a tearful Mrs Miller and then she approached Stefan.

'Not tears again! Jeez! You can say no, you know,' he

said smiling.

Caitlin laughed and gave him a small punch on his shoulder.

'After chatting to Mr and Mrs Miller,' said Aileen, 'we feel the environment is ideal for you Caitlin. Although yes, it's some distance away from home. And there will be a new school, new friends. It's a lot of change.'

Caitlin couldn't quite take it all in. Her mind was rushing with emotions and images. They were about the first day in a new school, waking up in her new home and saying all her goodbyes to Grace, Ryan, her class and her sailing club.

'Midge?' she asked.

'We'll get you involved with the sailing club at Loch Insh,' said Mr Miller.

'What about my mum?' Caitlin asked Aileen.

'Well, contact with your mum will remain in place, so communication between the two of you can continue. That's written or phone conversations but that's all.'

'Does she know about all this?' asked Caitlin.

'Yes, and as a matter of fact, here,' and Aileen passed her an envelope. 'From your mum.'

Caitlin thought to open it, but Mrs Miller began to say something.

'Stefan…go on, I think you might want to say your bit?'

Stefan hesitated. 'Erm…do I have to?'

'It may help,' replied his mother.

Caitlin frowned. 'What is it?'

'I'm adopted,' Stefan sheepishly replied.

'Oh.' said Caitlin.

'Aye. When I was two.'

'That Stefan had been adopted helped the process,' added Aileen.

'Right,' said Caitlin, holding her gaze on Stefan.

'So, I know a wee bit about…you know…all this,' he

415

said.

Caitlin wanted to press a pause button to give her a chance to take all of what was being said to her.

'There is a ton of paperwork to do, Caitlin McGill,' said Aileen. 'Not just yours but your gran's as well. A place must become available up at the new home. And that's if someone local doesn't get it first. Also, we feel it's best that you both move up together or if not, at a very similar time.'

'Are you OK with all this, Cat?' Mrs Miller asked.

'Yes. It's just…'

'A fair bit to take on board, eh?' suggested Mrs Miller.

'Aye. So, when do I go home with you?'

'It may be a few months,' said Aileen. 'So, you'll just have to be patient.'

'Mind, it won't be all about being in the park, young lady,' said Mr Miller.

'I know. It'll be about family as well.'

'Exactly,' smiled Mr Miller.

'Cat, it will be a pleasure to have you as part of our family,' said Mrs Miller.

And Caitlin McGill sat and laughed and smiled and blinked back the tears.

-54-

Hi Cat. U back yet?

Hi Grace. Yip. How was ur hols?

OK. Sorry. No signal. In Sth France.

U?

Got a family! lol!

Really? WOW! 😳😳😳

Who? Where? When?

The Millers! Highland Park People?

!!!!WOW! WOW!

!!!! U R going!!!!

!!!! !!!!

I no...

Sad & happy

Come 4 holiday?

You bet!!!!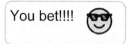

BFF?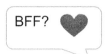

BFF!

Told ur Gran?

Not yet. Not sure she'd understand?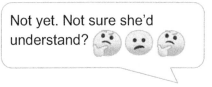

Forth?

Do I tell a toy?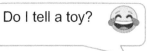

??

He was ur best friend!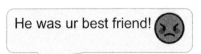

OK.

Good

Schl Tues

I no...

BTW does ur mum no about ur new family?

Yip. She sent a card.

-55-

Caitlin put her phone down, snuggled down under her quilt and read again the words inside a heart covered card.

Hi Caitlin,

Heard your news. You have a new family that's going to look after you.

That made me happy but it also made me a wee bit sad.

Whatever happens, I will always be your mum. Please remember that.

Maybe I'll see you in Manchester again someday? I would love that.

I just want you to be happy.

All my love

Mum xx

Was there a bit inside the young girl that wanted to hear her mum fight for her? To demand she doesn't go to live with the Miller's, that she was moving up from Manchester to be back in the flat and be a mum who stays. Forever.

That was just a daydream. Caitlin knew that the reality was of eventually living in a place up north, away from her past. That felt right. And meant such a lot. Being wanted by a family, as friendly and caring as the Millers, a family that looked after polar bears; could she have wished for anything better?

She glanced at Forth. Her friend, through all this time of change, was still facing out of the now curtained window. Was he looking out for what was coming next in his life? That the time had come for the cub to leave his guardian's side and stride out on his own journey, to follow new paths?

'Night, pal,' said Caitlin as she turned off the bedside light. There was no reply.

*

Back at school with her new teacher, Miss Collins, there was the routine writing of what you did in the holidays. Hands shot up to read about time spent on sandy beaches or having sleepovers with friends or just being sat with their computer console.

So, when it came to Caitlin's turn and she read out aloud, "In the holidays I got a new family," the audience either laughed or pulled puzzled faces.

'Is this you going to be fostered, Caitlin?' asked Miss Collins. She nodded and went and sat back down.

'Mrs Reid did tip me off, actually,' continued Miss Collins. 'What lovely news, maybe you can tell us some more later? OK, maths jotters out please.'

At break, both Sophie and Grace questioned their friend about keeping in touch and what it might be like to live away from any big towns.

'I have a Highland Park to stroll around in. That has to be good?'

'That's cool,' agreed Sophie, 'but shops for shoes and t-shirts? There won't be many of those?'

Caitlin just laughed.

'Forth is excited too, I take it?' asked Grace.

'Erm…I guess.'

'He doesn't come with you to school now,' said Sophie.

'Aye, true.'

'That's a shame,' said Grace.

'Seriously? Do you think I'm the numpty that's going to go to a new school with a cuddly toy under my arm?'

'Well, it wasn't long ago you brought him here, Caitlin McGill,' said Grace.

'That was when I was ten years old.'

'He was your pal, Caitlin. You were so close,' said Sophie. 'We even made you a special place in the class for him.'

'I know, but that was back then. I mean, when do I stop having cuddly toys as a pal? Fourteen? Eighteen? My twenties? Sakes!' She felt agitated.

'You've been through a lot with him. You're the "polar bear girl." No one would mind seeing you with the wee man. Only you by the sounds of it,' said Grace and she walked back towards the school.

*

September brought with it colder days. And almost daily, Caitlin would ask Mrs Johnstone if she'd heard any news about a moving date. She hadn't.

Meanwhile, things still seemed exactly like before. She still visited her gran. And every second weekend there were the trips to the Highland Safari Park. These days they were always sleepovers, from straight after school on a Friday through to Sunday afternoon. And Forth would stay at Mrs Johnstone's, remaining on the windowsill, waiting on his friend's return.

October held a half-term holiday. And on the day she broke up, all the Millers were sat waiting at Mrs Johnstone's.

Caitlin didn't say anything but put on a curious, smiling face.

'A wee surprise, Caitlin,' said Mrs Miller, 'get a bag packed as we're going to a wee cottage on Arran for a week.

'Really? Now?'

'Yes, really and aye, the now,' said Mr Miller, smiling.

'Dad, is she going to be wanting to do shops all the time and buy make-up and all that other girly stuff?' said Stefan but Caitlin knew he was joking and she ran upstairs to pack.

When she finished, she zipped up her bag and was about to go downstairs when she turned to speak to Forth.

'See you later, pal. You look after Mrs Johnstone and Billy, OK?'

Without waiting for a reply, she closed the door behind her.

At Ardrossan harbour, with their ferry coming into view, Caitlin turned to her side and looked at the three people stood by the car. So this was happening: being with a family, on a family holiday, the four of them.

And on the island, they caught buses together. They ate in cafés and restaurants together. They shopped together. And Caitlin was bought things like credit for her phone, something to take back for Mrs Johnstone or just some chocolate for herself. And this was family. And this is, she told herself, what her life was going to be like from now on. She had to pinch herself to make sure that this wasn't people just being nice to her, that these three people were willing to share their lives with wee Caitlin McGill. And every day of her holiday she woke up excited, happy and without worry. She did miss someone though, in this new chapter of her life.

One evening, Caitlin was writing out a postcard for her gran. She stopped halfway through a sentence and wiped a tear from her eye.

'Wishing she was here?' said Mr Miller.

She nodded.

'Gran's in the best place for her right now. You know this don't you?'

Caitlin nodded again. 'Gran would have loved this though,' she blurted out.

'Och, don't upset yourself,' said Mrs Miller and she went and put an arm around the young girl's shoulders. 'Listen, when she moves north, we'll be able to take your gran out, show her around her new bit. How about that?'

Caitlin gave a quick smile, sighed and stuck on a stamp.

Later, she knocked on Stefan's door.

'Yeah?'

Inside, Caitlin found him lying on his bed reading.

'What's up?' he asked.

'I can't get any signal. Have you any in here?'

'Nope,' and he leaned over to pull out his suitcase and grabbed another book from inside it. Caitlin spotted something.

'What's that?' she asked and pointed at what looked like a brownish rag.

'Poops.'

'Poops?' laughed Caitlin.

'Aye, Poops.'

'What is *Poops?*' said Caitlin still laughing.

'This is Poops,' and Stefan picked up the piece of cloth that had the eyes, a small nose and the paws of a very worn-out teddy bear. 'I've had him from the day I was born.'

'So, do you take your teddy bear with you all the time?'

'Aye. I know he's just in the suitcase but he's always close by. He comes with me whenever I'm away. He reminds me of who I was and where I am now.'

Caitlin was quiet.

'Which reminds me, I've not seen Forth for a wee while now?'

'I'm eleven. I just think I'm too old for a cuddly toy.'

'Too old? Nonsense. Poops is a part of me, a part of my life.'

'I have a new life now.'

'Aye, but it's still just one life; your life.'

Caitlin didn't know how best to answer that, and she went back to her room.

The rest of the week it rained. And it rained. And it rained. Not that the weather took any shine off Caitlin's face. And it was hard to see that the weather put any of the Miller's off from enjoying the time they were having together.

And then there was the driving back to Mrs Johnstone's and the young girl noticing Forth, faithfully watching from the window.

After saying her goodbyes, Caitlin rushed upstairs and hugged the cub.

'Sorry, pal. It's just...you know...things are maybe different now? It's hard to explain. We're still friends and that but...anyway, it rained. A lot. And...sheesh, what am I doing!' and she went back downstairs.

*

When November arrived, Caitlin went to school in the dark and came home to the streetlights flickering on. And on one of those days, she didn't expect Mrs Johnstone to be waiting at the door to welcome her in out of the wet.

'A letter for you, Miss McGill,' said Mrs Johnstone, and she handed it to Caitlin who immediately ripped it open.

'December the twentieth! Gran is to move on the twentieth of December! So that means I can get to the Millers then?'

'Yes. Well, you're only three days from breaking up for Christmas. So for the sake of a couple more days, you can finish off your term.'

Caitlin didn't reply but went up to her room and marked her calendar. A circle was already penned in around the twenty-third with, *SCHOOL FINISHES* wrote on it. She crossed that out and changed it to *JOIN MY NEW FAMILY.*

'Well, what do you think to that, pal?' she said. There

was no reply. The cub still had his eyes fixed on the skyline of Edinburgh.

*

December rushed to get in. And it came as busy as any other. There was the school's annual Christmas show to rehearse, which seemed to happen daily. Caitlin and Grace were to be the star attraction: the donkey, with Caitlin the head and Grace at the rear. Caitlin suggested that they could be a polar bear. Miss Collins wasn't too keen on the idea although it did make the class laugh.

Then there was a Christmas Fayre with Caitlin's class organising the posters and tickets and just about everything else to do it with it. Caitlin's suggestion of using the money to go towards helping polar bears was, this time, well received by Miss Collins as well as the rest of her classmates.

And Christmas was happening at Gran's home as well. Aileen had dropped off the Christmas decorations from the flat

433

which Caitlin now used to decorate her grandparent's room.

Matthew popped his head around the door. 'Maybe the times right to tell your gran about her moving? I think it would be nice to come from you,' he whispered.

Caitlin smiled and she went and lay alongside her grandmother who smiled into the face of her granddaughter.

'Gran, how about we move to a new hotel?'

'Why? What's wrong with this one?'

'Erm…nothing but the new one is out in the country, up north, near the hills and Bens all covered in purple heather. Sure, you can see the snow on their tops from your bedroom, so you can.'

'Really? And do they have nice firm beds? Mind, this one is too soft.'

'Aye. And someone to make your tea. And it's quite a lot smaller than here so it'll be nice and cosy and quiet.'

'Och, that'll be nice. Decent breakfasts?'

'Oh aye! Nice crispy bacon, just as you like it.'

'Well, that's all right then. Still,' and the old lady hesitated then began to cry, 'I'll miss you though, my wee angel.'

Caitlin hugged her. 'No, you dafty. I'm coming too! I'm no' letting them take you up by yourself. I'll still be coming over and pestering you.'

'Oh, that's good, that's really good,' sniffed Gran.

'What are you like, eh?'

'I know. I'm awfully daft nowadays, so I am,' and she dabbed her nose with a tissue. 'Davy, he'll pop up and see me? It's been a while since I've seen him. He's maybe busy, eh?'

Caitlin smiled. 'Aye, he's been busy Gran what with Christmas and that, but he'll be up to see you so he will.'

'Oh, good. Will I pack now?'

'No, not just yet Gran. A few more days then the folk here will help you pack, OK?

'Right you are, darling. Oh, and where's your wee dug by the way?'

Caitlin didn't reply but gave her gran another hug.

*

And then came her last day in her Queensferry school. And it was like Christmas Day had come early with the gifts and cards she received.

At the school's main entrance, Grace had a few tears as well as some big hugs for her friend.

'Listen,' said Caitlin grabbing her pal by her shoulders, 'it won't be long till you can come up and visit. OK?'

'I know but it won't be the same,' answered Grace, tearfully.

'I know. It'll be better,' and Caitlin gave her pal another hug.

'Bye,' said Grace.

'Bye, pal. For now.'

'Take care,' said Sophie and she left by way of a small hug as well.

'Thanks. And you.'

The headteacher came out of her office and shook Caitlin by the hand.

'Well, Caitlin McGill, a new school, a new home and a new family. Ready for the next part of your life?'

'Yes, Mrs Reid, I can't wait.'

'Good. Right, here's your taxi. We've loved having you here Caitlin. And I'm sure you'll be as popular at your new school. You take care and maybe let us know how you're settling in, OK?'

'I will,' said Caitlin and she smiled then got into her taxi. As she left the car park, she gave her school one final glance.

*

The following day, Mr Miller arrived not long after Caitlin had packed the last of her things.

At the door, she knelt to stroke Billy, who was excitedly running in circles.

Mr Miller took her case to the car, leaving Caitlin with Mrs Johnstone to say their goodbyes.

'Right, one last smile please, for the album.' Using her phone, Mrs Johnstone clicked a smiling Caitlin with Forth pressed against her cheek.

'And here's a wee photo for you,' and Mrs Johnstone passed her a framed picture of Billy, sitting alert on the sofa.

'Thanks. And thank you. For everything,' and Caitlin grabbed hold of Mrs Johnstone and squeezed as hard as she could with Forth squashed between them both.

'Och. Don't. I'm not one for goodbyes, Caitlin. So, listen. You get in that car and you have a lovely life.' Her voice cracked a little at the end of her sentence and she raised her arm and gave a small wave of her hand before she caught hold of Billy.

'Bye. And I won't forget you,' but Mrs Johnstone couldn't answer, and she made to close the door.

In the car, Mr Miller informed Caitlin that he was to meet Aileen at the flat. There he would collect the last of her belongings that had been packed into boxes.

'There's not much so it shouldn't take too long.'

'Erm…OK.'

'Are you alright about going back to the flat?' said Mr Miller noting Caitlin's pained expression.

'Erm…would it be alright if me and Forth have a look round Queensferry just one last time?'

'Sure. I get it. Maybe you don't want to go back to old memories? I'll meet you back on the high street, after an hour, yes?'

Caitlin agreed. 'I just want time on my own with Forth.'

'Not a problem. Nice to see the wee man again. How's he doing?'

'Fine. We're…erm, just going to say goodbye.'

'No problem. Yes, there won't be many times you'll need to be back at South Queensferry, I shouldn't imagine.'

'No,' said Caitlin, but it wasn't just the town she had in mind to say goodbye to.

-56-

On the footbridge, Caitlin, her eyes already teary, placed Forth up onto the railings. The burn's brown water rushed past, inches beneath her feet.

'Forth, listen I…,' started Caitlin. 'I…erm…I'm older and…' She paused. 'And you're a toy bear…no, you are a polar bear…but not really…I mean…sheesh! What am I doing!' She shook her head. 'It was all a game, pal.'

'A game? What was?' asked Forth.

'This.'

'This?'

'Us.'

'Us?'

'Yes. All a game. A game of *let's pretend*. A game of make-belief. It wasn't real. This isn't real.'

Forth was quiet. He stared back at his friend.

'Listen, pal, I thought we'd always be together. I never wanted you to go, remember? But I... I... erm... just got older that's all. And I know this sounds...crazy, but you've got to know that I'm doing this because I care for you. You do see that don't you?'

'Doing what for me?'

'Letting you go. Freeing you.'

'You letting me go is you caring for me?'

'Aye.'

'OK, but I might not like the bit that could happen when I have to go.'

'What bit?

'The bit that means I won't see you again.'

Caitlin sunk her face into the top of Forth's head. 'I'm so sorry pal. This is so...'

'There will be warm water and tuna though?' asked the

cub. His best friend raised her head and forced a smile, despite her wet face. 'And I'll still be cute?'

'What am I doing, talking to a...,' Caitlin shook her head then sighed. 'Of course, Forth. Always.'

'Good. I like cute.'

'You're not scared are you pal?'

'Me? Not really. I'll growl, and I'll roar like this...GRRRARARARARARRRRR!'

'There you go,' said Caitlin, trying to put on a happy face. 'You'll definitely be left alone by any bad folk with that noise.'

Caitlin looked at her white, furry friend. 'Are you ready, pal?'

'I think so, but can I ask you something?'

'Jeez, this is nonsense...,' said Caitlin, as she blew out her cheeks. 'Aye, of course, pal. What is it?'

'So, my paws, they're not real then?'

'No, pal. Just material, cloth.'

'So how come I can feel you when you hold me?'

Caitlin shook her head, tears streaming.

'My eyes though, are they real?' asked the young bear.

'No Forth,' Caitlin sniffed. 'They're... they're just beads.'

'So how come I can see pictures behind them when we're asleep?'

'Pictures?'

'Yes. Of me with you. Like when we go into town. Or when we're at your school. Or just lying with you on your bed.'

'Forth, pal...don't...it's...' Caitlin looked up at the sky and blinked to clear her eyes.

'And there's a pain inside me,' said the polar bear. 'Above my tummy.'

The eleven-year-old girl silently let the tears run as she looked at the cub.

'That's not right is it?' asked Forth. 'Is there something broken?'

Caitlin lay her face on the his furry tummy. She cried so hard she could hardly catch her breath.

After a moment, the girl took a deep breath, stood back from her pal and wiped her face on her sleeve. She looked into the small bear's dark eyes. Could she do this?

'You know,' she said, 'that I wanted to get you to a family, to be with another wee person, so they can get to have adventures with you as well.'

'Am I not getting a family then?'

'Yes. I hope so. And this is the only way I think I can do this. It's something I want to give to you because that's how much I care. Can you imagine that? Don't you see?'

'Even though we've got to be apart?'

Caitlin nodded. 'I know. It sounds stupid doesn't it?'

'I suppose my mother would have to say goodbye when I'm two.'

'Exactly. That's what I'm doing. Being just like a mother polar bear,' she sniffed.

'So, then I'll be free, and I'll meet other human peoples?'

'Yes, pal.'

'I'll still miss you though.'

Caitlin, her face still damp, nodded. 'I know. And me too. But those pictures behind your eyes, they will still be there. And then they'll be other pictures. Pictures of you with another pal, another somebody.'

Forth didn't say anything.

Knowing it would be her last, Caitlin hugged Forth as tight as she dared, taking in his fleecy, soft feel, and his familiar soft-bear smell. Then, with arms outstretched she gazed at her best friend that she was now saying a final farewell to, but could she do this?

Caitlin again looked up to the sky. This was just so stupid. Yet it felt so real. Forth was more than just a toy. More than just a white lump of fur. More like a companion, a true friend, always by her side during all she'd been through.

'So pal, this burn will take you back to the Firth of Forth and then out to the North Sea. Then after that, the whole world. All for you to go and explore and hunt and build dens in. You'll have so many adventures, not just sat in my bedroom all day.'

Caitlin looked at the water. She looked back at Forth. She remembered him being by her side when she ran away, the days in school, being on Midge or just being curled up with him. So, could she do this?

'Forth?' said Caitlin.

'Yes?'

'Oh, nothing. I mean... erm. Sheesh! This is just so, so...stupid. I...erm...'

'What is it?'

'I...,' she had a big lump in her throat. The words were hard to say, hard to get out. 'I... I love you...and I...I always will... you remember that, OK?'

'Love? What is a love?' asked Forth.

Caitlin just shook her head. 'It's complicated pal, but it comes from your heart,' and she pointed to her chest.

'Where I have that pain?'

Caitlin, a head full of tears and sadness, nodded.

Could she really do this? *Pick him up, take him home and lie with him, back on the bed. Hang on, you're eleven Caitlin McGill and one day a certain teddy bear will just be on a shelf or in a box with all the other childish things. He'll just become history, and then forgotten, just disappear, this...this children's toy.*

This was a good thing, wasn't it? To offer a polar bear cub to someone else who would want to go on adventures with a loyal and loving companion such as Forth. That felt good, however painful the reality was. Not discarding him to the bottom of a box destined for a charity shop felt like she was letting this polar bear cub go free, back to the wild. Back to where their journey started, back into the Firth of Forth.

'Goodbye, Forth.'

'Bye, Caitlin. I'll miss you,' the polar bear cub said, its

voice cracking.

'I'll miss you too, Forth, such a lot.'

She hesitated and took one last look at him. *Don't do this.*

She let go.

And as soon as she did, she wanted him back, wanted to put him right back into the rucksack.

Too late. Forth was in the water. Falling back first with a small slap, he sped quickly under Caitlin's feet. She watched quietly until the last speck of white disappeared around a bend.

What awaited her friend? What lay ahead for the young bear? Would he get a new family, or would he drift off to the other side of the world?

Then again, I ask you, who is free?

Caitlin sighed. Her eyes were watery, glazed from the crying. She looked into the ceaseless movement under her feet.

-57-

Simzar untied Forth and lifted out from under a tarpaulin in the back of the van. He carried the bear onto a narrow, wooden bridge that went over a sliver of sprinting water. In the early morning dim, through trees and a ramshackle fence, Simzar could just make out the wide Firth of Forth which lay waiting for the burn to join it.

'So, this is your journey's end and its beginning, young one. The big river will take you to other countries. Perhaps you'll survive and make it. Perhaps you'll be captured and be treated well and not as a gift. Either way, your destiny is out of your hands. Let fate and your future guide you.'

With that, he took the rope off Forth's neck.

The young bear sat still for a moment, not sure what to do. He looked at Simzar, sniffed down at the stream then back at the two-legged creature.

Simzar picked up the cub and gently placed him into moving water.

It felt cool on Forth's fur. He raised his head, shook it, and without objection, let the burn's swift tow take him towards the wide and dark, Firth of Forth.

'Freedom my friend. Freedom'

Simzar kissed a necklace he was wearing, looked at the sky and, in his language, said a small prayer and walked away. With the hired van's keys and the three canisters of diesel, he too could make good his escape.

The darker water of the wide river felt heavy on Forth. It pushed him along as if he was nothing but discarded litter; unwanted and ignored. Yet this was no concern for the bear. Without question or resistance, he let the water's strength take him.

Drifting in the wide river, it seemed too busy for Forth to be safe. It seemed like there were boats of all different *sizes crossing the river or going up and downstream. Where could he get to that was safe, that was away from these strange and noisy creatures?*

Back-eddies caught hold of the cub and he drifted towards the shore and the safety of the shallows.

-58-

From nearby, someone whistled for their dog and the world came back into focus. And with it, the realisation that Caitlin had been chatting away to a stuffed toy, one that she had just let drop into the dirty water of a burn.

She dried her eyes as best she could and walked away from the bridge, hands in pockets, shaking her head.

*

Forth stared at the branches of trees. Stared at clouds that were moving in the opposite direction. The young, white bear passed grassy banks, a pebble shore then a play-park, busy with children in hats and scarves, all with their families. An old woman, with a shopping trolley full of loaves, was feeding a large group of ducks. No one noticed the cub.

He was now only a few feet away from a reed bed that met a sloping grassy bank. The vegetation stopped him but only momentarily and he circled, quite gracefully, to the next clump of reeds. Here he headed ever closer to the shore, still staring up at the sky.

The bear looked as if he was unconcerned about his fate. It was as if he accepted it, without struggle or argument. As if this was yet just another part of his brief life. As if this was the life of a small, cuddly polar bear toy. As if...

-59-

At the sailing club, Caitlin turned back to look at the three bridges.

There was that funny feeling inside her of leaving something familiar and known. All she'd ever known was South Queensferry; it's every little street and shaded alleyway. And now leaving it to go somewhere unknown and new felt, sad? Strange? Scary? It was hard to tell.

On the rail bridge, a train was pulling away and passing over Inchgarvie. She gave an ironic laugh to herself: that wee island where she'd hoped to live out her days. Beyond it the old road bridge and behind that, the new Queensferry Crossing where she'd found her gran; cold, wet and quite alone in her own world.

And there in the club's yard, was Midge. She'd make a good boat for next season's new members.

These things, the bridges, her boat; they would still be

here when she left. Still be here for her to visit, to visit with her new family. And her memories? Well, she'd take them with her wherever she went.

The Firth of Forth was running hard. The tide and the river's heavy state saw it pushing insistently around a solitary boat, moored up close by.

Caitlin realised, that if she waited long enough, a furry white object may come floating along. How would that make her feel? She tried not to look too closely into the water. To see a close friend floating helplessly downstream was more than she could take right now. Hopefully, he'd already been spotted, picked up and being taken to the warmth of a new house and a new family.

She gave the wide river one more glance.

'Bye, pal.'

*

Walking back towards the town, Caitlin saw Mr Miller already parked up by the road and shutting the boot of his car. Behind him, she thought she could make out a familiar friend, cycling away and out of sight.

'That was your pal, Ryan,' confirmed Mr Miller as they got into the car.

'Oh? What did he want?'

'He was asking after you and we'd got talking about polar bears.'

'Right.'

'Yeah, polar bears. You wonder if the wee ones are sad when they leave their mother, you know, when they're all grown up and that?'

'I don't know. Maybe,' said Caitlin.

'Yeah, you wonder if they miss the safety of their parent. And then you wonder if their mothers miss them, you know, not just for a few days but perhaps always?'

'I don't really know,' said Caitlin. She was curious as

to why Mr Miller, with all his knowledge of polar bears, was asking her such questions. Then it dawned on her.

'Just so you know, I've let Forth go free.'

'Right. Your best pal. You just, what? Left him somewhere to fend for himself?'

'Aye.'

'Got to say, I'm surprised, Caitlin. He was your best pal. You've been through a fair few adventures with the wee man. So why get rid of him?'

'Because I'm eleven and because he's just a toy. And besides, I thought it would be great for a new family to find him and look after him.' Caitlin defended herself as if she had done something wrong.

'So, you're not going to miss him?'

'Aye.'

'And you wouldn't want to keep him to remind you of all your times here?'

Caitlin shrugged.

'Stefan has a teddy. You know that don't you? And he has him because he's part of him growing up. In fact, he has him *because* he is older.'

'Maybe I did it to let him be free?'

'Free? From what, Caitlin?'

'I'm not sure.' She paused. 'Then again, I ask you, who is free?'

Mr Miller looked puzzled. He shook his head and started the car. 'OK, your choice, lady. Anyway, let's get you to your new home, eh?'

Caitlin nodded and sat quietly for the whole of the journey.

-60-

Christmas Eve was a day of getting everything ready and not just at Caitlin's new home. There were still the jobs to do at the Safari Park. The shop still needed restocking. Animal pens still needed cleaning out. And a polar bear mother and her cub still needed to be fed. Caitlin noticed that Archie was already bigger.

Stefan was with her as they began throwing the young bear and his mother's lunch over the fence.

'Archie and Forth would have got on, wouldn't they?' said Stefan.

'What a real polar bear and a toy one? I don't think so.'

'It's not that long ago you were bringing Forth to see Archie.'

'Well, yes. I did. That was then though.'

'Aye. You're right. So now you're all grown up, I guess

460

that can't happen. Shame.'

Caitlin didn't say anything.

'And I'd hope you not having Forth anymore was because of what you think is the right thing to do, and you're not doing it because you're worried about what others may say.'

Caitlin was still silent as she gazed at the young bear as he tucked into a melon.

Once home, Caitlin helped Mrs Miller to get the Christmas Day food ready. Mrs Miller also got her to help dress the Christmas tree that they saved putting up for her arrival. She even helped her wrap Mr Miller's parcel: a brand-new set of overalls.

And in the evening, when they were all sat with their hot drinks, Caitlin had to tell herself that this was it. There was no going back down the road to Queensferry, that this was now her home.

'You OK, Cat?' asked Mr Miller.

'Aye, of course.'

'It'll get some getting used to,' said Mrs Miller. 'For you and for us.'

Caitlin nodded.

'You can always run away to, erm... I don't know... Outer Mongolia?'

'Stefan!' said Mrs Miller.

'No, you're fine. Think I'll stay here and wind you up. I'd like a big brother to come with me to do some girl-shopping.'

Stefan looked dismayed.

'Ha. Yes, I think that's a great idea,' laughed Mrs Miller.

'Nae chance!' replied Stefan.

'I'll get to see Gran tomorrow?' asked Caitlin. I've never woken up on Christmas Day without her.'

'Of course. That was always going to be part of the day,' said Mr Miller. 'We'll go first thing, OK? We'll get a cup of tea there and see her open her parcels,'

'Great,' said Caitlin.

So on Christmas Day morning, Caitlin woke, dressed and had her jacket on as she made her way downstairs.

Mr and Mrs Miller were already up and were stood next to a sofa covered in parcels.

'Merry Christmas,' said Mr Miller and he shook Caitlin's hand.

'Merry Christmas,' replied Caitlin.

'Aye, Merry Christmas,' said Mrs Miller and she hugged the eleven-year-old. 'You're the best parcel, you know that don't you?'

'Thanks. And all of you, all of this, is mine too.'

'As soon as sleepyhead gets up were away, in fact, I'll go up and give him a shout.'

There was no need as Stefan groggily appeared at the top of the stairs.

'Jeez oh! Merry Christmas! Is it Stefan?' said Mr Miller and his wife and Caitlin laughed.

At the home, Caitlin rushed into her gran's room to find her sat up in bed singing along to a Christmas carol playing on the television. The Millers followed her in.

'Happy Christmas, Gran,' said Caitlin and she hopped onto the bed and kissed her grandparent on her cheek.

'Oh, thank you, my wee angel.'

'Gran, I'd like you to meet my new...erm, pals.'

'Hi, Mrs McGill,' said Mr Miller and he, Mrs Miller and Stefan took turns to shake her hand.

'Oh, quite a crowd. Are they your teachers?'

'No Gran, they're looking after me. Just while you're here,' said Caitlin, careful not to confuse her.

'Oh, well she's a wee angel so she is,' said Gran.

'Aye, she is,' said Mrs Miller.

'She's nae bother,' continued Gran, 'And she does so much for me, so she does. She'll make a great daughter so she will.'

Caitlin pulled a face. Did Gran know? Yet how could she?

'Och, we already know, Mrs McGill,' said Mrs Miller.

'And who's this Mrs McGill. You can call me Gran. All of you that is. Or Grandma. I don't mind.'

Caitlin silently shook her head. Did this old lady know more than she let on?

After opening parcels, Gran and the Millers were invited into the home's open area where the other residents were given a special Christmas breakfast. They all opened their parcels, as a man played the piano, and a local choir came in to sing some carols. Caitlin and the Millers joined in and when they returned to Gran's room, she lay on her bed and started to close her eyes.

'Bye Gran,' said Caitlin, but she was already asleep.

Back at the Miller's house, Caitlin was shown all her presents.

'Wow! All of these?'

'Yes,' said Mr Miller, 'but first, this one,' and he passed Caitlin a parcel that was sat under the tree. It was covered in white frosted paper with a label that said, "A friend is for life – not just for Christmas."

Caitlin didn't understand but started to rip open the paper.

She dropped him. She couldn't believe it.

'Forth!' And there, still wrapped in some of the paper was her furry best friend.

'It's Forth!' she exclaimed as if the rest of the house didn't know. 'But...how? You're here? Oh, pal, I'm so, so sorry,' and she grabbed hold of her friend and hugged him as she swung around and landed on an armchair.

Mrs Miller had to wipe a tear away.

'How?' asked Caitlin.

'Ryan,' said Mr Miller.

'Ryan?'

'Aye. He saw you down at the burn. Saw you drop the

polar bear and walk off. Lucky for you he watched him all the way down the Firth of Forth. He couldn't understand why you'd just get rid of your pal like that. I had to agree with him, as neither could I.'

'Think you need to put Ryan in amongst your thank you cards, eh?' said Mrs Miller.

Caitlin was silent as she looked at her white friend.

'I've given him a wash and a wee cycle in the tumble drier,' said Mrs Miller. 'I hope he's OK?'

'Aye, he's fine,' said Caitlin. 'Perfect in fact.'

'So is this where I'll stay now?' said the polar bear cub.

Caitlin laughed and cried at the same time.

'Of course, pal. You've to stay here. Forever,' and she grabbed him again as she lay out on the sofa.

'Oh, good,' said Forth, 'I think I like here.'

Epilogue

In time, Caitlin grew up and got to be in her twenties. She qualified as a zoologist where she specialised in arctic animals and so was paid for doing something she loved.

And from time to time, she'd come home, and Mr and Mrs Miller would welcome her with kisses and the odd time Stefan would be there as well. Caitlin would give him, and his pregnant wife, a hug. Then she'd hang up her coat, kick off her boots and go up to her bedroom. And next to a picture of her late gran surrounded by the Miller's and herself, there would be Forth, waiting for her, waiting for her to lift him and hold him to her cheek and be gently squeezed. She'd tell him all her news about her work and how the planet was doing and then she'd bring him through to the living room where, in another time, Stefan's children and her children would smile and laugh, with Forth seated at his highchair, next to Caitlin. And everyone around the table was family.

And on one of the coldest nights known in Edinburgh

for some time, sheltered in the graveyard of the Canongate Kirk, Michael James Patrick Kelly unfolds a well-worn party invite. Addressed to Michael Vagabond, Princes Street Gardens, he smiles as he remembers when a postman tapped him on the shoulder to say, 'I think this is for you.' And he remembers the sender: a young girl with her friend, a polar bear cub. He remembers being sat with them, on a bench one January day. And he smiles when he remembers their words, their chat and more than that: their acceptance of him. With stiff fingers, he folds it back up, returns it to his inside pocket, the smile still clinging to his face, to sleep the longest of sleeps, with a dream of a polar bear cub that talked.

About the Author

A P Pullan has taught for over twenty years in schools in England and Scotland. He now lives in Ayrshire with his wife and a selection of cuddly toys, including Findlay the polar bear, who lives in a cup. He enjoys sailing, eating scones and collecting driftwood.

A P Pullan can be contacted at:

https://theweepencil.wordpress.com/

Printed in Great Britain
by Amazon

61405346R00271